Othello

（中英文双语对照）

奥赛罗

【英】威廉·莎士比亚 著

孙大雨 译

上海三联书店

OTHELLO

DRAMATIS PERSONAE

Duke of Venice
Brabantio, a Senator
Other Senators
Gratiano, Brother to Brabantio
Lodovico, Kinsman to Brabantio
Othello, a noble Moor, in the service of Venice
Cassio, his Lieutenant
Iago, his Ancient
Roderigo, a Venetian Gentleman
Montano, Othello's predecessor in the government of
    Cyprus
Clown, Servant to Othello

Desdemona, Daughter to Brabantio and Wife to
    Othello
Emilia, Wife to Iago
Bianca, Mistress to Cassio

Messenger, Herald, Officers, Musicians and Attend-
    ants. &c.

SCENE: The First Act in Venice; Second to Fifth Act at a
    Seaport in Cyprus

剧 中 人 物

威尼斯公爵

孛拉朋丘，一知政事大夫

其他知政事大夫数人

格拉休阿诺，孛拉朋丘的兄弟

罗铎维哥，孛拉朋丘的亲戚

奥赛罗，一摩尔族贵胄，威尼斯城邦的将军

凯昔欧，奥赛罗的副将

伊耶戈，奥赛罗的旗手

洛窦列谷，一威尼斯士子

蒙塔诺，奥赛罗的前任塞浦路斯岛军事首脑

小丑，奥赛罗的家僮

玳思狄莫娜，奥赛罗的妻子，孛拉朋丘的女儿

爱米丽亚，伊耶戈之妻

碧盎佳，神女，与凯昔欧相好

信使、传令官、军官多人，乐人多人，侍从多人

剧景：第一幕，在威尼斯；第二至第五幕，在塞浦路斯岛上
　　一海港

ACT I.

SCENE I. Venice. *A street*.

[*Enter* Roderigo *and* Iago.]

Roderigo   Tush, never tell me; I take it much unkindly
That thou, Iago, who hast had my purse,
As if the strings were thine, shouldst know of this.

Iago   'Sblood, but you will not hear me: —
If ever I did dream of such a matter,
Abhor me.

Roderigo   Thou told'st me thou didst hold him in thy
hate.

Iago   Despise me, if I do not. Three great ones of the city,
In personal suit to make me his lieutenant,
Off-capp'd to him: — and, by the faith of man,
I know my price, I am worth no worse a place: —
But he, as loving his own pride and purposes,
Evades them, with a bumbast circumstance,
Horribly stuff'd with epithets of war:
And, in conclusion, nonsuits
My mediators: for, *Certes*, says he,
I have already chose my officer.

第 一 幕

第 一 景

[威尼斯。一街道。]
[洛窦列谷与伊耶戈上。]

洛窦列谷　嘘！
切莫跟我来这一套，我很不乐意，
伊耶戈，你拿了我的钱包，像是你
自己的一般，却竟然知道这件事。

伊　耶　戈　他奶奶，可是您不听我分说：
假使我能梦想到这样的事儿，
把我当狗矢。

洛窦列谷　你跟我说过，你一向对他有仇恨。

伊　耶　戈　鄙弃我，若是我不那么。城里三位
大老，脱着帽，都将我向他推毂过，
当他的副将；而且，凭人的真诚
说话，我知道自己值多少，我十足
配得上那样的位置；可是他爱的是
他自己的骄傲和一意孤行，闪避了
他们，使一派浮夸、曲折的废话，
那中间满都是一些战阵的言辞；
总之，他拒绝我的居间人；因为，
"肯定，"他说，"我已经选好了副将。"

And what was he?

Forsooth, a great arithmetician,

One Michael Cassio, a Florentine,

A fellow almost damn'd in a fair wife;

That never set a squadron in the field,

Nor the division of a battle knows

More than a spinster; unless the bookish theoric,

Wherein the toged consuls can propose

As masterly as he; mere prattle, without practice,

Is all his soldiership. But he, sir, had the election;

And I, — of whom his eyes had seen the proof

At Rhodes, at Cyprus, and on other grounds,

Christian and heathen, — must be *belee'd and calm'd*

By debitor and creditor, this counter-caster,

He, in good time, must his lieutenant be,

And I — God bless the mark! his Moorship's ancient.

Roderigo   By heaven, I rather would have been his hang-
man.

Iago   Why, there's no remedy; 'tis the curse of service,

Preferment goes by letter and affection,

And not by old gradation, where each second

Stood heir to the first. Now, sir, be judge yourself

Whether I in any just term am affin'd

To love the Moor.

Roderigo   I would not follow him, then.

Iago   O, sir, content you;

I follow him to serve my turn upon him;

We cannot all be masters, nor all masters

Cannot be truly follow'd. You shall mark

Many a duteous and knee-crooking knave,

那是个怎样的人呢？
您说当真嘛，是个算术大家，
名叫玛格尔·凯昔欧，莆洛伦斯人，
有个漂亮老婆差不多注定了
叫他受罪的霉家伙；他从未在战场
上面调遣过队伍，战阵的性质
他懂得不比一个纺织女娘
来得多；除非把书本理论来充数，
那上头，那些峨冠博鳌的知政事
也能跟他一个样，舌灿着莲花：
光纸上谈兵，眇无实际，原来是
他全部的韬略。但是他，先生，却中选
膺命；而我——他亲眼见到过确证，
在罗德斯、塞浦路斯、其他的基督徒、
邪教徒战场上——倒被这"借方和贷方"
把风收了去，使篷帆跌落；这笔账，
只有天知道，一定得当他的副将，
而我——请原谅！——他摩尔大人的旗手。

洛窦列谷 凭老天，我却愿意做他的吊绞手。

伊　耶　戈 啊也，没办法可想：这军差戎伍中，
糟就糟在升迁需要仗介绍信
和喜爱，不凭下手顶上手的晋级
年资，按着陈年惯例一步步
往上升。现在，先生，您自己去判断，
我同他的关系是否说得上什么
敬爱这摩尔人。

洛窦列谷 　　　　　　若是我，就不去跟他。

伊　耶　戈 啊！先生，把心情放舒泰；
我追随着他，聊不过奔走一遭儿；
我们不能全都作长官，长官
也不能全得到忠诚的伺候。您可以
看到好些恭顺、屈膝的随从者，

That, doting on his own obsequious bondage,
Wears out his time, much like his master's ass,
For nought but provender; and when he's old, cashier'd:
Whip me such honest knaves. Others there are
Who, trimm'd in forms and visages of duty,
Keep yet their hearts attending on themselves;
And, throwing but shows of service on their lords,
Do well thrive by them, and when they have lin'd their
    coats,
Do themselves homage: these fellows have some soul;
And such a one do I profess myself. For, sir,
It is as sure as you are Roderigo,
Were I the Moor, I would not be Iago:
In following him, I follow but myself;
Heaven is my judge, not I for love and duty,
But seeming so for my peculiar end:
For when my outward action doth demonstrate
The native act and figure of my heart
In complement extern, 'tis not long after
But I will wear my heart upon my sleeve
For daws to peck at: I am not what I am.
Roderigo What a full fortune does the thick lips owe,
If he can carry't thus!

Iago   Call up her father,
Rouse him: —make after him, poison his delight,
Proclaim him in the streets; incense her kinsmen,
And, though he in a fertile climate dwell,
Plague him with flies: though that his joy be joy,
Yet throw such changes of vexation on't,
As it may lose some color.
Roderigo Here is her father's house; I'll call aloud.
Iago Do; with like timorous accent and dire yell

对自己那过于殷勤的奴役有偏爱，
挨了一辈子，像他主人的驴儿般，
只是为草料，等他人一老就给
抛弃掉；这样忠厚的仆从，请为我
给他顿鞭子吃。另外有些人，他们
修饰得在外表和形态方面很尽责，
却将内心保留着替自己去操劳，
他们对上头只使出殷勤的表现，
自己却获益匪轻，他们把口袋
装满时，将自己当作主人翁；这些人
有灵魂：我声言我便是这样的人物。
正好比，先生，您确是洛窦列谷，
假使我是那摩尔人，我不愿自己是
伊耶戈：我追随着他，无非为自己
奔走；让上天来替我裁决，我对他
说不上敬爱与情谊，不过好像是
如此罢了，为的是我特殊的目的：
因为，当我外面的行动显示出
我衷忱运用和内心形态的表象时，
过不久我将把我的心佩在衣袖上，
给穴鸟去剥啄：我不是我这般模样。

洛窦列谷 假使厚嘴唇能在这上头也这般
取胜，他将有多么大一份财富！

伊　耶　戈 叫起她父亲，叫醒他；追赶他，毒化
他那阵欢乐，公开在街头揭发他；
鼓捣起她家的亲戚；虽然他好比
在丰实之乡居住，叫苍蝇去叮他，
让烦恼缠绕个不休；虽然他的欢乐
是欢乐，把困窘的事变尽往上倾泻，
使它消失掉光彩。

洛窦列谷 这里是她父亲的房子；我要来叫嚷。

伊　耶　戈 来吧；用恐惧的声调和怕人的呼喊

As when, by night and negligence, the fire
Is spied in populous cities.

Roderigo What, ho, Brabantio! Signior Brabantio, ho!

Iago Awake! what, ho, Brabantio! thieves! thieves!
thieves!

Look to your house, your daughter, and your bags!
Thieves! thieves!

[Brabantio *appears above at a window.*]

Brabantio What is the reason of this terrible summons?
What is the matter there?

Roderigo Signior, is all your family within?

Iago Are your doors locked?

Brabantio   Why, wherefore ask you this?

Iago Zounds, sir, you're robb'd; for shame, put on your
gown;

Your heart is burst, you have lost half your soul;
Even now, now, very now, an old black ram
Is tupping your white ewe. Arise, arise;
Awake the snorting citizens with the bell,
Or else the devil will make a grandsire of you:
Arise, I say.

Brabantio   What, have you lost your wits?

Roderigo Most reverend signior, do you know my voice?

Brabantio Not I; what are you?

Roderigo My name is Roderigo.

Brabantio   The worser welcome:
I have charged thee not to haunt about my doors;
In honest plainness thou hast heard me say
My daughter is not for thee; and now, in madness,
Being full of supper and distempering draughts,
Upon malicious bravery dost thou come

来报警,如同夜间悄无人注意,
瞥见居民密集的城市里火起。

洛窦列谷　喂喂! 孛拉朋丘! 孛拉朋丘大夫,喂喂!

伊 耶 戈　醒来! 喂喂! 孛拉朋丘! 捉贼!
捉贼! 捉贼! 瞧您的房子、女儿
和钱袋! 捉贼! 捉贼!

　　　　　　　　　　[孛拉朋丘出现于高处窗头。

孛 拉 朋 丘　是什么道理叫喊得这样吓人?
是怎么一回事?

洛 窦 列 谷　大夫,您家人都在里边吗?

伊 耶 戈　　　　　　　您门户
都锁了?

孛 拉 朋 丘　　　为什么? 你们为什么问这个?

伊 耶 戈　他奶奶! 大人,您给强盗打劫了;
请顾全身份,披上了长褂;您的心
碎了,您掉了半个灵魂;就是
现在,正好是现在,有只黑的
老公羊爬在您那白的小母羊身上。
起来,起来! 摇铃把打鼾的公民们
唤醒,不然那魔鬼要使您变成个
爷爷。起身哟,我说。

孛 拉 朋 丘　　　　　　什么! 你们
神经错乱了?

洛 窦 列 谷　　　　　非常尊敬的大夫,
您认得我这声音吗?

孛 拉 朋 丘　　　　　　认不得,您是谁?

洛 窦 列 谷　我名叫洛窦列谷。

孛 拉 朋 丘　　　　　　特别不欢迎:
我警告过你,莫到我门前来鬼混:
你听我非常开诚地说过,我女儿
不能嫁给你;现在,发着疯,吃饱了
晚饭,灌得酩酊,恶意来捣乱,

To start my quiet.

Roderigo Sir, sir, sir, —

Brabantio   But thou must needs be sure
My spirit and my place have in them power
To make this bitter to thee.

Roderigo   Patience, good sir.

Brabantio What tell'st thou me of robbing? this is Venice;
My house is not a grange.

Roderigo   Most grave Brabantio,
In simple and pure soul I come to you.

Iago Zounds, sir, you are one of those that will not serve
God, if the devil bid you. Because we come to do you
service, and you think we are ruffians, you'll have
your daughter covered with a Barbary horse; you'll
have your nephews neigh to you; you'll have coursers
for cousins and gennets for germans.

Brabantio What profane wretch art thou?

Iago I am one, sir, that comes to tell you your daughter
and the Moor are now making the beast with two
backs.

Brabantio Thou art a villain.

Iago   You are — a senator.

Brabantio This thou shalt answer; I know thee, Roderigo.

Roderigo Sir, I will answer anything. But, I beseech
you,
If't be your pleasure and most wise consent, —
As partly I find it is, — that your fair daughter,
At this odd-even and dull watch o' the night,
Transported with no worse nor better guard
But with a knave of common hire, a gondolier,
To the gross clasps of a lascivious Moor, —
If this be known to you, and your allowance,
We then have done you bold and saucy wrongs;

你来搅扰我的安宁。

洛窦列谷　大人,大人,大人!

莩拉朋丘　　　　　　　　但你得弄清楚,
我的生性和地位有力量叫你
为这事吃苦。

洛窦列谷　　　　　　　　镇静些,请您老人家。

莩拉朋丘　你跟我说什么打劫? 这是威尼斯:
我这房子不是所荒僻的田庄。

洛窦列谷　最尊敬的莩拉朋丘,我一秉诚恳、
纯洁的精神来找您。

伊耶戈　他奶奶! 大人,您是这样一个人,假使魔鬼要您去侍
候上帝,您就偏不肯。因为我们来为您好,您便把我
们当作混混儿,原来您愿意自己的女儿给一只巴巴
利红鬃马压在身上;您愿意您的外孙对您嘶鸣;您愿
意您的外孙儿、外孙女儿们都是些龙驹快马,您的近
亲小辈是些西班牙种的小马。

莩拉朋丘　你是什么脏嘴巴的贱东西?

伊耶戈　我是这么一个人,大人,来告诉您,您女儿跟那摩尔
人现在正在两张背皮朝外,干那畜生的勾当。

莩拉朋丘　你是个坏蛋。

伊耶戈　　　　　　您是个——知政事大夫。

莩拉朋丘　这你得负责;我认得你,洛窦列谷。

洛窦列谷　大人,什么事我都得负责。但是,
我请您,假使您高兴而且考虑后
还同意,——我见到,事情确有点这样,——
让您那标致的姑娘,在午夜才过,
当这昏沉的宵静时刻,给一个
不好不歹的保护人、雇来的众家奴,
一名鹅舺船夫,载送给一个
淫乱的摩尔人,投进他粗鄙的搂抱,——
假使这件事您知道而允许,那我们
便对您犯下了粗鲁、莽撞的大不敬;

But if you know not this, my manners tell me
We have your wrong rebuke. Do not believe
That, from the sense of all civility,
I thus would play and trifle with your reverence:
Your daughter, — if you have not given her leave, —
I say again, hath made a gross revolt;
Tying her duty, beauty, wit, and fortunes
In an extravagant and wheeling stranger
Of here and everywhere. Straight satisfy yourself:
If she be in her chamber or your house,
Let loose on me the justice of the state
For thus deluding you.

Brabantio   Strike on the tinder, ho!
Give me a taper! — Call up all my people! —
This accident is not unlike my dream:
Belief of it oppresses me already. —
Light, I say! light!

[Exit from above.]

Iago   Farewell; for I must leave you:
It seems not meet nor wholesome to my place
To be produc'd, — as if I stay I shall, —
Against the Moor: for I do know the state, —
However this may gall him with some check, —
Cannot with safety cast him; for he's embark'd
With such loud reason to the Cyprus wars, —
Which even now stand in act, — that, for their souls,
Another of his fathom they have none,
To lead their business: in which regard,
Though I do hate him as I do hell pains,
Yet, for necessity of present life,
I must show out a flag and sign of love,
Which is indeed but sign. That you shall surely

但您若不知这件事，我品行的常规
告诉我，我们蒙受了您不当的斥责。
莫以为，绝无一点儿礼让之感，
我会来戏谑、玩忽您老的尊严：
您女儿，如果您未曾允许她那样做，
容我再说声，干了桩荒唐的忤逆；
把她的名份、美貌、理智和幸运
攀上了一个浮游浪荡的陌生人，
他属于此间，也属于任何哪一方。
马上弄一个明白：她若在闺房中，
或在您屋里，就行使公邦的法律
来将我惩处，为了我这般欺骗您。

孛拉朋丘　喂喂，打上取灯儿！给我一支
蜡烛！把家人全都叫起来！这变故
倒不是不像我的梦，我相信了它，
已经在感到难受。点上火，我说！
点上火！　　　　　　　　　　　　［自高处退下。

伊　耶　戈　　　　再会，我一定得和您分手：
这似乎对我的地位不适当，没好处，
如果由我来作控告那摩尔人的见证，
因为，我若待下去，就得去作证；
我知道公政院，为了邦国的安全，
不能将他撤职，不管这件事
会怎样引起申斥，惹得他恼火；
因迫切的需要，他已被任命去指挥
塞浦路斯的战事，——实际上这已在
进行中，——而且，即令为拯救灵魂，
他们也找不到他那样能干的统帅；
关于那，虽然我恨他甚于憎恶
地狱的惨刑酷虐，我还得为目今
过日子的需要，打着敬爱的旗号，
不过那只是标志而已。为了您

find him,

Lead to the Sagittary the raised search;

And there will I be with him. So, farewell.

[*Exit.*]

[*Enter, below,* Brabantio, *and* Servants *with torches.*]

Brabantio It is too true an evil: gone she is;

And what's to come of my despised time

Is naught but bitterness. —Now, Roderigo,

Where didst thou see her? —O unhappy girl! —

With the Moor, say'st thou? —Who would be a father!

How didst thou know 'twas she? —O, she deceives me

Past thought. —What said she to you? —Get more tapers;

Raise all my kindred! Are they married, think you?

Roderigo Truly, I think they are.

Brabantio O heaven! —How got she out? —O treason of
the blood! —

Fathers, from hence trust not your daughters' minds

By what you see them act. —Are there not charms

By which the property of youth and maidhood

May be abused? Have you not read, Roderigo,

Of some such thing?

Roderigo   Yes, sir, I have indeed.

Brabantio Call up my brother. —O, would you had had
her! —

Some one way, some another. —Do you know

Where we may apprehend her and the Moor?

Roderigo I think I can discover him, if you please

To get good guard, and go along with me.

Brabantio Pray you, lead on. At every house I'll call;

I may command at most. —Get weapons, ho!

准能找到他,把已经轰起来的搜寻
人众领往"人马骁"馆驿;我将在
那边,跟他在一起。就这样,再会。　　　　　[下。
　　　　　[孛拉朋丘与执火炬之仆从数人上。

孛 拉 朋 丘　这是太真确的一件坏事:她去了,
　　　　　我这被鄙视的余生再没有别的,
　　　　　只剩下痛苦。现在,洛窦列谷,
　　　　　你哪里看到她? 啊,苦恼的女儿!
　　　　　跟那个摩尔人在一起? 你说? 谁愿意
　　　　　做父亲! 你怎么知道那是她? 啊唷,
　　　　　她将我欺骗得难于设想。她对您
　　　　　说什么? 多来些火把! 把亲属人众
　　　　　全都叫起来! 他们结了婚吗,您想?

洛 窦 列 谷　果真,我想他们已结了。

孛 拉 朋 丘　啊,我的天! 她怎样出去的? 啊,
　　　　　我亲生骨肉的不忠诚:父亲们,你们
　　　　　从此莫再看了女儿们的行动,
　　　　　便相信她们的心。是否有魔法
　　　　　能叫年轻的处女中了魔,给糟蹋?
　　　　　洛窦列谷,您可在书本上念到过
　　　　　有这样的事?

洛 窦 列 谷　　　　　　　不错,大人,念到过。

孛 拉 朋 丘　叫起我的兄弟来。啊! 但愿您娶了她。
　　　　　有人这条路上走,有人走那条!
　　　　　您知道,我们在哪里能将那摩尔人
　　　　　同她抓到?

洛 窦 列 谷　　　　　　我想我能找到他,
　　　　　您若能带同充分的护卫,跟我
　　　　　一起来。

孛 拉 朋 丘　　　　　请您领先。我在每一所
　　　　　房廊前要叫人;好召唤尽多的人手。
　　　　　带着武器,喂喂! 叫起几个

And raise some special officers of night.

On, good Roderigo: — I'll deserve your pains.

[Exeunt.]

SCENE II. Another street.

[Enter Othello, Iago, and Attendants with torches.]

Iago   Though in the trade of war I have slain men,

Yet do I hold it very stuff o' the conscience

To do no contriv'd murder: I lack iniquity

Sometimes to do me service: nine or ten times

I had thought to have yerk'd him here under the ribs.

Othello   'Tis better as it is.

Iago   Nay, but he prated,

And spoke such scurvy and provoking terms

Against your honor,

That, with the little godliness I have,

I did full hard forbear him. But, I pray you, sir,

Are you fast married? Be assured of this,

That the magnifico is much beloved,

And hath, in his effect, a voice potential

As double as the duke's: he will divorce you;

Or put upon you what restraint and grievance

The law, — with all his might to enforce it on, —

Will give him cable.

Othello   Let him do his spite:

My services which I have done the signiory

Shall out-tongue his complaints. 'Tis yet to know, —

Which, when I know that boasting is an honor,

I shall promulgate, — I fetch my life and being

From men of royal siege; and my demerits

专司守夜的官长。亲爱的洛窦列谷,
往前走;我将不辜负您麻烦这一场。

[同下。

第 二 景

[另一街道]
[奥赛罗、伊耶戈与手执火炬之侍从数人上。

伊 耶 戈 虽然在战争行业中我也杀过人,
可是我认为良心的本质不能
让我干预谋的凶杀:我缺少邪恶,
有时候去为我干事。九次或十次,
我想要在他肋胁下戳这么一刀。

奥 赛 罗 还是现在这样好。

伊 耶 戈 　　　　　不然,他胡言
乱语,用那样卑鄙怄人的辞句
攻击您钧座,
以我那一点点敬畏上帝的虔诚,
委实难对他饶让。但请问,将军,
您可曾固定不移地结过婚? 要把稳
这件事,因为上大夫人缘奇好,
他的话,论实际效果,影响比公爵
还隆重得多;他将会分离开你们,
或者把法律能允许的任何控制
和磨难——他将会全力以赴去贯彻——
加在您身上。

奥 赛 罗 　　　　　尽他去对我施恨毒:
我对城邦公政院所尽的劳绩,
会讲赢他对我的控诉。我们还得要
知道,夸口是件光荣事:这个,
我知道以后,将会公开宣布。
我此身的生命与存在,系出君王

May speak unbonneted to as proud a fortune
As this that I have reach'd: for know, Iago,
But that I love the gentle Desdemona,
I would not my unhoused free condition
Put into circumscription and confine
For the sea's worth. But, look! what lights come yond?

Iago Those are the raised father and his friends:
You were best go in.

Othello   Not I; I must be found;
My parts, my title, and my perfect soul
Shall manifest me rightly. Is it they?

Iago By Janus, I think no.

     [*Enter* Cassio *and certain* Officers *with torches.*]

Othello The servants of the duke and my lieutenant. —
The goodness of the night upon you, friends!
What is the news?

Cassio   The duke does greet you, general;
And he requires your haste-post-haste appearance
Even on the instant.

Othello   What is the matter, think you?

Cassio Something from Cyprus, as I may divine:
It is a business of some heat: the galleys
Have sent a dozen sequent messengers
This very night at one another's heels;
And many of the consuls, rais'd and met,
Are at the duke's already: you have been hotly call'd for;
When, being not at your lodging to be found,
The senate hath sent about three several quests
To search you out.

Othello   'Tis well I am found by you.
I will but spend a word here in the house,

品位。以我的优长，用不到去冠，
我能对跟我获致的高位齐阶
并比的任何人说话。要知道，伊耶戈，
若不是我对温婉的苡思狄莫娜
情深如海，我不会使自己无家室
之累的自由，受任何规范与制限，
即令能奄有大海的金珠珍贝。
可是，你看，那边有什么灯火来？

伊 耶 戈 这是那轰动起来的父亲和亲属：
您最好还是进去。

奥 赛 罗 　　　　我不；我一定
得给他们找到：我一身的优长、
我光荣的称号、我有备无患的心神，
会将我正当地显示。这是他们吗？

伊 耶 戈 凭始初的两面神，我想不是。

　　　　　　　[凯昔欧带同手执火炬军官数人上。

奥 赛 罗 公爵的亲随人众，和我的副将。
朋友们，夜晚的良时临照诸君！
有什么消息？

凯 昔 欧 　　　　公爵向您致意，
将军，他要您十万火急去见他，
顿时立刻。

奥 赛 罗 　　　　你以为有什么事情？

凯 昔 欧 塞浦路斯岛有事，据我猜想。
事情有一点紧急；就在今晚上，
大划船一叠连送来了一打报差，
一个个后先相继，接踵而至；
好几位知政事都被叫起来，已经
会聚在公爵府邸。您紧急被召；
不能在寓邸里找到，知政事公署
派出了三起哨探去将您搜寻。

奥 赛 罗 给你们找到了，很好。我进屋只讲

And go with you.

                                          [*Exit.*]

Cassio   Ancient, what makes he here?

Iago Faith, he to-night hath boarded a land carack:
If it prove lawful prize, he's made forever.

Cassio I do not understand.

Iago   He's married.

Cassio   To who?

               [*Re-enter* Othello.]

Iago Marry, to—Come, captain, will you go?

Othello   Have with you.

Cassio Here comes another troop to seek for you.

Iago It is Brabantio. —General, be advis'd;
He comes to bad intent.

       [*Enter* Brabantio, Roderigo, *and* Officers
           with torches and weapons.]

Othello   Holla! stand there!

Roderigo Signior, it is the Moor.

Brabantio   Down with him, thief!

         [*They draw on both sides.*]

Iago You, Roderigo! come, sir, I am for you.

Othello Keep up your bright swords, for the dew will
rust them.

Good signior, you shall more command with years
Than with your weapons.

Brabantio O thou foul thief, where hast thou stow'd my
daughter?

Damn'd as thou art, thou hast enchanted her;
For I'll refer me to all things of sense,
If she in chains of magic were not bound,
Whether a maid so tender, fair, and happy,

一句话,就来跟你们同去。 　　　　　　　　　　　[下。

凯　昔　欧　　　　　　　　　　旗手,
他到来做什么?

伊　耶　戈　　　　　　　说实话,他今夜登上了
一艘旱地大楼船;如果是合法
中彩,他这就一辈子的财富临门。

凯　昔　欧　我不懂。

伊　耶　戈　　　　　　他结了婚。

凯　昔　欧　　　　　　　　　跟谁?

伊　耶　戈　　　　　　　　　　　凭圣母,跟——
　　　　　　[奥赛罗重上。
来,都督,您去吧?

奥　赛　罗　　　　　　　　　和你们同去。

凯　昔　欧　这里又来了一支队伍来找您。

伊　耶　戈　这是孛拉朋丘。将军,请小心;
他来没好意。
　　[孛拉朋丘、洛窦列谷,带同手执火炬及兵器的军官多人上。

奥　赛　罗　　　　　　　喂喂! 在那边站住!

洛窦列谷　大夫,这是那摩尔人。

孛拉朋丘　　　　　　　打倒他,恶贼!
　　　　　　　　　　　　[双方皆拔剑出鞘]

伊　耶　戈　有您,洛窦列谷! 来,先生,我对您。

奥　赛　罗　莫拔明亮的剑刃出鞘来,露水
将会使它们生锈。亲爱的大夫,
您尽可用高年,不用刀剑来命令。

孛拉朋丘　啊,你这下流的恶贼! 我女儿,
你将她窝藏在哪里? 可恶到极点,
你行施魔法于她;我将诉之于
所有有理性的人们,她可不是被
魔法的锁链所困住,这么个娇柔、
娟美、天宠的姑娘,这般不爱

So opposite to marriage that she shunn'd
The wealthy curled darlings of our nation,
Would ever have, to incur a general mock,
Run from her guardage to the sooty bosom
Of such a thing as thou, — to fear, not to delight.
Judge me the world, if 'tis not gross in sense
That thou hast practis'd on her with foul charms;
Abus'd her delicate youth with drugs or minerals
That weaken motion: — I'll have't disputed on;
'Tis probable, and palpable to thinking.
I therefore apprehend and do attach thee
For an abuser of the world, a practiser
Of arts inhibited and out of warrant. —
Lay hold upon him: if he do resist,
Subdue him at his peril.

Othello   Hold your hands,
Both you of my inclining and the rest:
Were it my cue to fight, I should have known it
Without a prompter. — Where will you that I go
To answer this your charge?

Brabantio   To prison; till fit time
Of law and course of direct session
Call thee to answer.

Othello   What if I do obey?
How may the duke be therewith satisfied,
Whose messengers are here about my side,
Upon some present business of the state,
To bring me to him?

First Officer   'Tis true, most worthy signior;
The duke's in council, and your noble self,
I am sure, is sent for.

Brabantio   How! the duke in council!
In this time of the night! — Bring him away:
Mine's not an idle cause: the duke himself,
Or any of my brothers of the state,
Cannot but feel this wrong as 'twere their own;
For if such actions may have passage free,
Bond slaves and pagans shall our statesmen be.

[Exeunt.]

结姻亲,避免了我邦多少位富有、
鬈发的佳公子,竟然会,不怕叫人家
耻笑,离开她的保护人,投入你
这样个乌黑东西的胸怀;那是
在投奔恐惧,不是在追求愉快。
让世人来替我下判断,你对她横施
恶毒的魔法,用衰损心智的药毒
或石毒,摧残她娇嫩的青春岁华,
是否违情而悖理:我要兴论争,
评情理;这说来很可信,想来极明显。
因此上,我逮捕、捉拿你,将你作为
人间的戕贼者,一个被禁的非法
邪术的潜行人。把他抓起来:若是他
抵抗,制服他,生死都在所不计。

奥 赛 罗　你们都住手,在我这方面的人,
还有其他的:假使我应当格斗,
我自己就会知晓,毋须有提示人。
您要我到哪里去答复你这番控告?

孛 拉 朋 丘　进监狱里去;等到法律和庭审
程序命令你答辩。

奥 赛 罗　　　　　　　我听从了,将怎样?
对于我那么做,公爵将如何能满足?
他的信使们目今在这里,我身旁,
有些紧急的邦国事要带我去相见。

军　　官　不错,最尊贵的大夫;公爵在会议,
而且您尊驾,我相信,也已被邀请。

孛 拉 朋 丘　什么! 公爵在会议! 在夜里,这时候!
带他去。我这不是个无所谓的争端:
公爵本人,或是我自己的不拘哪一个
议政的同僚,不能不感到这枉屈,
如同他们自己的一个样;因为,
假令这样的行动能自由地发生,
奴隶和邪教徒都能为我们当政。

〔同下。

SCENE III. *A council chamber.*

[*The* Duke *and* Senators *sitting* at a table; Officers *attending.*]

Duke   There is no composition in these news
That gives them credit.

First Senator   Indeed, they are disproportion'd;
My letters say a hundred and seven galleys.

Duke   And mine a hundred and forty.

Second Senator   And mine two hundred:
But though they jump not on a just account, —
As in these cases, where the aim reports,
'Tis oft with difference, — yet do they all confirm
A Turkish fleet, and bearing up to Cyprus.

Duke   Nay, it is possible enough to judgement:
I do not so secure me in the error,
But the main article I do approve
In fearful sense.

Sailor   [*Within.*] What, ho! what, ho! what, ho!

First Officer   A messenger from the galleys.

[*Enter a* Sailor.]

Duke   Now, — what's the business?

Sailor   The Turkish preparation makes for Rhodes;
So was I bid report here to the state
By Signior Angelo.

Duke   How say you by this change?

First Senator   This cannot be,
By no assay of reason: 'tis a pageant
To keep us in false gaze. When we consider
The importance of Cyprus to the Turk;
And let ourselves again but understand,
That, as it more concerns the Turk than Rhodes,

第 三 景

［议事厅］

［公爵与知政事大夫数人围桌而坐。军官数人侍立。

公　　爵　这些消息里没有协调一致
　　　　　能够使它们可信。

知 政 事 甲　不错，它们彼此之间有矛盾；
　　　　　我的信说有一百零七艘大划船。

公　　爵　我的，一百四十艘。

知 政 事 乙　　　　　　　我的，两百艘：
　　　　　虽然它们在正确数目上不相符，——
　　　　　在这些情形下，猜想的说法往往
　　　　　有差异，——可是它们却一致证实
　　　　　有一支土耳其舰队，向塞浦路斯来。

公　　爵　不仅如此，事情很可以理解：
　　　　　我不因情报有舛误而疏忽大意，
　　　　　但主要的一项我相信而且忧虑。

水　　手　［在内］喂喂！喂喂！喂喂！

军　　官　大划船上的报差。

　　　　　　　　　　［水手上。

公　　爵　　　　　　　现在，有什么事？

水　　手　土耳其艨艟正在向罗德斯行驶；
　　　　　我奉安吉罗大夫之命，来对
　　　　　邦政府报告。

公　　爵　对这一异动，你们怎么说？

知 政 事 甲　　　　　　　　用理智
　　　　　来检视，这件事不可能；这是出声东
　　　　　击西的虚诈戏，叫我们向差错处望。
　　　　　当我们考虑到塞浦路斯对于
　　　　　土耳其的重要性，而且也须了解到
　　　　　它比罗德斯对他更其关紧要，

So may he with more facile question bear it,
For that it stands not in such warlike brace,
But altogether lacks the abilities
That Rhodes is dress'd in. If we make thought of this,
We must not think the Turk is so unskilful
To leave that latest which concerns him first;
Neglecting an attempt of ease and gain,
To wake and wage a danger profitless.

Duke　Nay, in all confidence, he's not for Rhodes.

First Officer　Here is more news.

　　　　　　　　　　[*Enter a* Messenger.]

Messenger　The Ottomites, reverend and gracious,
Steering with due course toward the isle of Rhodes,
Have there injointed them with an after fleet.

First Senator　Ay, so I thought. — How many, as you
　　guess?

Messenger　Of thirty sail: and now they do re-stem
Their backward course, bearing with frank appearance
Their purposes toward Cyprus. — Signior Montano,
Your trusty and most valiant servitor,
With his free duty recommends you thus,
And prays you to believe him.

Duke　'Tis certain, then, for Cyprus. —
Marcus Luccicos, is not he in town?

First Senator　He's now in Florence.

Duke　Write from us to him; post-post-haste despatch.

First Senator　Here comes Brabantio and the valiant
　　Moor.

[*Enter* Brabantio, Othello, Iago, Roderigo, *and* Officers.]

Duke　Valiant Othello, we must straight employ you
Against the general enemy Ottoman. —
　　[*To* Brabantio.] I did not see you; welcome, gentle sig-
　　nior;
We lack'd your counsel and your help to-night.

他尽可轻易逞威把它来攻克，
因为它不怎么顶盔贯甲呈森严，
完全不具备罗德斯抗侵凌的能力：
假使想到了这一层，我们就不该
以为土耳其竟至那么样无能，
会将轻重颠倒置，后先不区分，
疏忽一桩轻而且有利的策划，
去冒险挑起一场没好处的危图。

公　　爵　对，能完全保证，他不攻罗德斯。

军　　官　又有消息来了。

　　　　　　　　　　［一使者上。

信　　使　土耳其部队，尊崇、宽厚的君公，
直接驶向罗德斯，在那里添上了
另一支舰队。

知 政 事 甲　　　　　　哦，我是这么想。
有多少，据你想？

信　　使　　　　　　　三十条；现在他们
转回程，分明指向塞浦路斯岛。
蒙塔诺大夫，您亲信、勇武的从者，
向您致殷切的敬意，以此相告，
请公上相信他。

公　　爵　那就准是前往塞浦路斯去。
玛格斯·路昔高斯，他不在城里吗？

知 政 事 甲　他此刻在茀洛伦斯。

公　　爵　替我们写信给他；十万万火急报。

知 政 事 甲　孛拉朋丘跟那勇武的摩尔人到来了。

　　　　　　［孛拉朋丘、奥赛罗、凯昔欧、伊耶戈、洛窦列谷与军
　　　　　　官数人上。

公　　爵　勇武的奥赛罗，我们得马上派遣您，
去抵挡犯境的公众敌寇土耳其。
［对孛］我不曾见到您；欢迎，亲爱的大夫；
我们今晚上缺少您商量与帮助。

Brabantio So did I yours. Good your grace, pardon me;
Neither my place, nor aught I heard of business
Hath rais'd me from my bed; nor doth the general care
Take hold on me; for my particular grief
Is of so flood-gate and o'erbearing nature
That it engluts and swallows other sorrows,
And it is still itself.

Duke   Why, what's the matter?

Brabantio My daughter! O, my daughter!

Duke and Senators   Dead?

Brabantio   Ay, to me;
She is abused, stol'n from me, and corrupted
By spells and medicines bought of mountebanks;
For nature so preposterously to err,
Being not deficient, blind, or lame of sense,
Sans witchcraft could not.

Duke Whoe'er he be that, in this foul proceeding,
Hath thus beguiled your daughter of herself,
And you of her, the bloody book of law
You shall yourself read in the bitter letter
After your own sense; yea, though our proper son
Stood in your action.

Brabantio   Humbly I thank your grace.
Here is the man, this Moor; whom now, it seems,
Your special mandate for the state affairs
Hath hither brought.

Duke and Senators We are very sorry for't.

Duke [*To* Othello.] What, in your own part, can you
say to this?

Brabantio Nothing, but this is so.

Othello Most potent, grave, and reverend signiors,

孛 拉 朋 丘	我也缺少您。亲爱的君侯,请原谅; 不是我的职位,也非因听到有事故, 使我从床上起身来,也不是关心着 公众的安宁,因为我特殊的悲痛, 好像打开了水闸门,它那样其势 不可挡吞咽掉一切其他的悲伤后, 依然还是那模样。
公　　爵	唔,什么事?
孛 拉 朋 丘	我女儿! 唉也! 我女儿!
公爵与知政事们	死了?
孛 拉 朋 丘	果真, 对我是死了;她给人糟蹋,从我 身旁盗窃走,给施了魔法,以及被 江湖术士处买来的药石所败坏; 因为天性要迷误到这么样荒唐, 原来无欠缺,不昏盲,心智不残废, 倘使不行施邪术,简直不可能。
公　　爵	不论在这肮脏的行径中,这般 蛊惑您女儿以及打从您那里 骗得她出走的是什么样人,您定能 把法律的血书自己去宣读,凭您 自己的解释,读出最严厉的判词; 是啊,即令是我们自己的儿子 站在您这诉讼中。
孛 拉 朋 丘	我恭诚感谢 您钧座。这人在这里,就是这摩尔人; 看来,您钧座有关国事的特旨 正把他宣召来。
公爵与知政事们	我们觉得很可惜。
公　　爵	[对奥赛罗]您能替自己对这事怎样说法?
孛 拉 朋 丘	没有得说的,就是这样。
奥 赛 罗	位重权高、庄严可敬的公和卿,

My very noble and approv'd good masters, —
That I have ta'en away this old man's daughter,
It is most true; true, I have married her:
The very head and front of my offending
Hath this extent, no more. Rude am I in my speech,
And little bless'd with the soft phrase of peace;
For since these arms of mine had seven years' pith,
Till now some nine moons wasted, they have us'd
Their dearest action in the tented field;
And little of this great world can I speak,
More than pertains to feats of broil and battle;
And therefore little shall I grace my cause
In speaking for myself. Yet, by your gracious patience,
I will a round unvarnish'd tale deliver
Of my whole course of love; what drugs, what charms,
What conjuration, and what mighty magic, —
For such proceeding I am charged withal, —
I won his daughter.

Brabantio   A maiden never bold;
Of spirit so still and quiet that her motion
Blush'd at herself; and she, — in spite of nature,
Of years, of country, credit, everything, —
To fall in love with what she fear'd to look on!
It is judgement maim'd and most imperfect
That will confess perfection so could err
Against all rules of nature; and must be driven
To find out practices of cunning hell,
Why this should be. I therefore vouch again,
That with some mixtures powerful o'er the blood,

最尊崇、久经证明的亲爱的列公们，
若说我带走了这位老人家的闺女，
真一点不错；果真，我和她结了婚：
我冒犯的顶巅和面目只有这程度，
不再多。我出言粗鲁，不善于运用
和平生活里温驯的辞风和谈吐；
自从我这副武装赋有了七年
威力，到如今九个月已然消逝去，
它总在野外，在军篷营帐之间，
给用来从事最重要的活动；有关这
广大的世界我不能谈什么，只除了
陷阵冲锋的战阵功；因此上，为自己
说话，对我的出处没多大裨益。
可是，倘蒙众位宽容地许可，
我想讲一个朴实无华的故事，
诉说我恋爱的全程；我用什么药，
什么法术，什么灵咒，什么
大力的邪魔外道（因为我被控
有这些行动），赢得了他的女儿。

孛拉朋丘　一个闺女，从来不胆大妄为；
心灵这么样贞静端详，她自己
内在的冲动会使她对自己脸红；
可是，她违反了天性，不管年龄
太悬殊，无视他邦异国，不爱惜
名誉，不顾虑一切，竟然会对于
仅仅望见了也害怕的，堕入了情网！
那一准是个残疾支离的判断，
才能去认为无疵的完美竟致会
迷误到违反一切天性的常规，
定要把地狱的诡计阴谋去体验，
以致这事变会发生。我因而再次
要断言，用某些对血液能强制的药剂，

Or with some dram conjur'd to this effect,
He wrought upon her.

Duke   To vouch this is no proof;
Without more wider and more overt test
Than these thin habits and poor likelihoods
Of modern seeming do prefer against him.

First Senator   But, Othello, speak:
Did you by indirect and forced courses
Subdue and poison this young maid's affections?
Or came it by request, and such fair question
As soul to soul affordeth?

Othello   I do beseech you,
Send for the lady to the Sagittary,
And let her speak of me before her father.
If you do find me foul in her report,
The trust, the office I do hold of you,
Not only take away, but let your sentence
Even fall upon my life.

Duke   Fetch Desdemona hither.

Othello   Ancient, conduct them; you best know the
        place. —

                    [*Exeunt* Iago *and* Attendants.]

And, till she come, as truly as to heaven
I do confess the vices of my blood,
So justly to your grave ears I'll present
How I did thrive in this fair lady's love,
And she in mine.

Duke   Say it, Othello.

Othello   Her father lov'd me; oft invited me;
Still question'd me the story of my life,
From year to year, — the battles, sieges, fortunes,
That I have pass'd.
I ran it through, even from my boyish days
To the very moment that he bade me tell it:
Wherein I spake of most disastrous chances,

或者用魔法咒成了这效验的毒汁，
他对她遂行了奸谋。

公　　爵　　　　　　　断言这件事，
如果没有比这些轻微的外表、
平凡表象的马虎的旁证较真切、
较显见的证明，并不能成为证据。

知政事甲　可是，奥赛罗，讲吧：
您可曾用过非法、强暴的行径，
去胁迫、污损这年轻姑娘的情爱；
还是以殷切的恳请，和心灵对心灵
可提供的正当的说爱谈情所获致？

奥　赛　罗　我恳请列位，派人到"人马骁"馆驿
去找这位贤淑来，让她面对着
她父亲谈起我：你们若在她言谈中
发现我卑鄙，请不光收回这信任，
我受自诸公的这职位，还要请加以
判罪，刑及我此生。

公　　爵　　　　　　　将玳思狄莫娜宣来。

奥　赛　罗　旗手，引领他们；你熟悉那地方。

[伊耶戈与从人数人下。

然后，在她到来前，好像对上天
那样真诚地承认我血液中的过误，
我要对你们尊敬的两耳说实话，
我怎样在这位佳秀的眷爱里愉快
欣荣，她在我深情中昌隆欢悦。

公　　爵　　谈吧，奥赛罗。

奥　赛　罗　她父亲喜爱我；不时请我去；经常
问起我一生的故事，一年年我所曾
经历的战斗、围城、一切的遭遇。
我把故事来诉叙，从孩童时日
直到他要我讲述故事的时候止；
那其中我谈到奇灾苦难的大事变，

Of moving accidents by flood and field;
Of hair-breadth scapes i' the imminent deadly breach;
Of being taken by the insolent foe,
And sold to slavery; of my redemption thence,
And portance in my travels' history:
Wherein of antres vast and deserts idle,
Rough quarries, rocks, and hills whose heads touch heaven,
It was my hint to speak, — such was the process;
And of the Cannibals that each other eat,
The Anthropophagi, and men whose heads
Do grow beneath their shoulders. This to hear
Would Desdemona seriously incline:
But still the house affairs would draw her thence;
Which ever as she could with haste despatch,
She'd come again, and with a greedy ear
Devour up my discourse; which I observing,
Took once a pliant hour; and found good means
To draw from her a prayer of earnest heart
That I would all my pilgrimage dilate,
Whereof by parcels she had something heard,
But not intentively; I did consent;
And often did beguile her of her tears,
When I did speak of some distressful stroke
That my youth suffer'd. My story being done,
She gave me for my pains a world of sighs:
She swore, — in faith, 'twas strange, 'twas passing
    strange;
'Twas pitiful, 'twas wondrous pitiful:
She wish'd she had not heard it, yet she wish'd
That heaven had made her such a man: she thank'd me;
And bade me, if I had a friend that lov'd her,
I should but teach him how to tell my story,
And that would woo her. Upon this hint I spake:
She lov'd me for the dangers I had pass'd;

讲起海上、陆上的动人不幸事，
谈失之毫厘、死成瞬息的城堡破，
说到被威猛的强敌俘为囚，卖作奴，
说到赎身得脱，以及我游历史
中间的行动；有硕大无朋的洞穴
平沙漠漠草不绿，粗豪的山石矿，
顽石磐磐，峻岭的峰巅摩青天，
我都有机会来谈及，经过就这么样；
还谈起彼此人吃人的生番名叫
安塞罗扑法加，以及还有帮蛮子
在肩膀下面膈肢窝里生脑袋。
爱听谈这些，玳思狄莫娜成了癖；
不过家务事时常使她不得来；
但赶快待事情一了结，她就再会来
贪心不足地倾耳听我继续谈。
见到这情形，有一次我乘机让她
殷切作要求，把长行的全部经过
细细谈，过去她曾听我把片断讲，
且又注意不荟集：我同意那么办；
随后我屡次哄得她两眼泪涟涟，
每当她听说我年轻的岁时遭逢
惨痛的凶打击。我将故事说完后，
她报谢我那辛劳以深深的长叹息：
她郑重声言，那确乎奇怪，非常
奇怪；那煞是可怜，可怜得惊人：
她宁愿不曾听说过，可是她但愿
上苍能将她做成这样一个人；
她对我致谢，要我，假使我有个
爱慕她的朋友，我只需教他讲述
我所讲的故事，那便能得到她的眷顾。
趁着这机会我说道：她爱我为了我
所曾经历的魔障，而我也爱她，

And I lov'd her that she did pity them.
This only is the witchcraft I have us'd: —
Here comes the lady; let her witness it.

[*Enter* Desdemona, Iago, *and* Attendants.]

Duke　I think this tale would win my daughter too. —
Good Brabantio,
Take up this mangled matter at the best.
Men do their broken weapons rather use
Than their bare hands.

Brabantio　　　　　　　I pray you, hear her speak:
If she confess that she was half the wooer,
Destruction on my head, if my bad blame
Light on the man! — Come hither, gentle mistress:
Do you perceive in all this noble company
Where most you owe obedience?

Desdemona　　　　　　　My noble father,
I do perceive here a divided duty:
To you I am bound for life and education;
My life and education both do learn me
How to respect you; you are the lord of duty, —
I am hitherto your daughter: but here's my husband;
And so much duty as my mother show'd
To you, preferring you before her father,
So much I challenge that I may profess
Due to the Moor, my lord.

Brabantio　　　　　　God be with you! — I have done. —
Please it your grace, on to the state affairs:
I had rather to adopt a child than get it. —
Come hither, Moor:
I here do give thee that with all my heart
Which, but thou hast already, with all my heart
I would keep from thee. — For your sake, jewel,
I am glad at soul I have no other child;

因为她对我的遭遇表示了怜恤。
这是我所用的唯一的魔法：这位
娉婷已经到；让她自己来作证。
[玳思狄莫娜、伊耶戈与随从数人上。

公　　爵　我想这故事也会赢得我女儿。
亲爱的孛拉朋丘，
以尽好的心情，接受这弄糟的事吧；
人们宁可用残破的武器，也不愿
赤手空拳。

孛 拉 朋 丘　　　　　我请您，听她说话：
如果她自认跟他同样是求爱者，
我若是还把罪责加在他身上，
让毁灭降临我的头！走到这里来，
亲爱的小姐：在这好些位尊贵中，
你见到没有，你最该从顺的在哪里？

玳思狄莫娜　尊贵的父亲，在这里，我见到一个
分裂的本份：对您，我感恩赋与我
生命与教养；我这份生命与教养
教导我如何对您该崇敬；您是我
本份的主公，我过去是您的女儿：
但这里是我的丈夫；正如我母亲
对您显示了那么多本份，爱了您
只得离舍她父亲，同样，我声言
我该对这摩尔人我的夫君尽本份。

孛 拉 朋 丘　上帝保佑你！我的事已经完毕。
请君侯钧座，继续进行邦政事：
我但愿螟蛉了孩子，不曾亲生。
这里来，摩尔人：
我在此全心全意将她给了你，
若不是你已然得到她，我是会全心
全意不将她给你。为你的缘故，
宝贝，我衷心高兴我另外没孩儿，

For thy escape would teach me tyranny,
To hang clogs on them. — I have done, my lord.

Duke　Let me speak like yourself; and lay a sentence
Which, as a grise or step, may help these lovers
Into your favour.
When remedies are past, the griefs are ended
By seeing the worst, which late on hopes depended.
To mourn a mischief that is past and gone
Is the next way to draw new mischief on.
What cannot be preserved when fortune takes,
Patience her injury a mockery makes.
The robb'd that smiles steals something from the thief;
He robs himself that spends a bootless grief.

Brabantio　So let the Turk of Cyprus us beguile;
We lose it not so long as we can smile;
He bears the sentence well, that nothing bears
But the free comfort which from thence he hears;
But he bears both the sentence and the sorrow
That, to pay grief, must of poor patience borrow.
These sentences, to sugar or to gall,
Being strong on both sides, are equivocal:
But words are words; I never yet did hear
That the bruis'd heart was pierced through the ear. —
I humbly beseech you, proceed to the affairs of state.

Duke　The Turk with a most mighty preparation makes
for Cyprus. — Othello, the fortitude of the place is
best known to you; and though we have there a sub-
stitute of most allowed sufficiency, yet opinion, a
sovereign mistress of effects, throws a more safer
voice on you: you must therefore be content to slub-
ber the gloss of your new fortunes with this more
stubborn and boisterous expedition.

Othello　The tyrant custom, most grave senators,

因为你这下子逃跑会使我暴厉，
在他们身上加桎梏。我完了，公爷。

公　　爵　让我仿照您自己的口吻说话，——
讲一句箴言，那好比是一个级步，
也许会帮助这双有情人得到
您爱宠。
当过去寄希望的挽救显得没用时，
最坏的已见到，悲伤也就完了事。
为一桩过去的不幸伤心而痛苦，
等于去走一条新辟的不幸之路。
当命运把不能保全的东西夺走，
忍耐能使那损害变得不用愁。
遭劫者微笑时，从盗窃那里偷回了些；
无益地悲伤是在跟自己过不去。

亨拉朋丘　那么，让土耳其抢掉我们的塞浦路斯；
反正失掉了不久，我们会笑呵呵。
任何人若能毫不关心地把空论
当安慰，他便能好好接受这金箴；
可是那人儿，向可怜的忍耐借了债
付悲哀，他就得生受这箴言和伤怀。
这些箴言算得甜来也算得苦，
两面都很讲得通，真意却含糊：
但说话只能算说话；我从未听见过
医疗受了伤的心能透过耳朵。
我恭诚恳请钧座，进行邦务讨论吧。

公　　爵　土耳其派一支很大的部队开向塞浦路斯。奥赛罗，
那地方的防御力量您最清楚；虽然我们在那里有位
公认为本领十分高强的督抚，可是公论（它最能产生
实效）认为由您去守卫更加安全：因此，您只得让您
那最近所交好运的光彩，给这一桩远较粗野强烈的
行军事务弄暗淡了些吧。

奥　赛　罗　习惯这暴君，最尊敬的知政事大夫们，

Hath made the flinty and steel couch of war
My thrice-driven bed of down: I do agnize
A natural and prompt alacrity
I find in hardness; and do undertake
These present wars against the Ottomites.
Most humbly, therefore, bending to your state,
I crave fit disposition for my wife;
Due reference of place and exhibition;
With such accommodation and besort
As levels with her breeding.

Duke   If you please,
Be't at her father's.

Brabantio   I'll not have it so.

Othello   Nor I.

Desdemona   Nor I. I would not there reside,
To put my father in impatient thoughts,
By being in his eye. Most gracious duke,
To my unfolding lend your prosperous ear;
And let me find a charter in your voice
To assist my simpleness.

Duke   What would you, Desdemona?

Desdemona   That I did love the Moor to live with him,
My downright violence and storm of fortunes
May trumpet to the world: my heart's subdu'd
Even to the very quality of my lord:
I saw Othello's visage in his mind;
And to his honors and his valiant parts
Did I my soul and fortunes consecrate.
So that, dear lords, if I be left behind,
A moth of peace, and he go to the war,
The rites for which I love him are bereft me,

已经把战争的床褥,硬如燧石
冷如钢,变成精冶过三次的鸭绒床:
我承认艰难跟我的本性相契合,
我对它心甘情愿,切望而不辞,
而且决意负责对土耳其用刀兵。
故而我非常谦谨地对诸公致敬,
请求为我的妻子作适当的安排,
相应地指派给地位和津贴,
授与她跟她教养相符合的日常
舒适与相当的随侍。

公　　爵　　　　　　　　　若是您高兴,
就在她父亲家中。

孛拉朋丘　　　　　　　　我觉得不便。
奥　赛　罗　我也这么想。
玳思狄莫娜　　　　　　我也这么想;我不愿
在那里居住,罣碍父亲的视听,
引得他心烦意躁。最尊崇的公爵
对我的启奏请光赐清听;容任我
在您的话言中获得当官的准许,
以有助于我的粗疏不文。

公　　爵　你要什么,玳思狄莫娜?
玳思狄莫娜　我心爱这摩尔人,愿跟他一同生活,
以及我冒死不惧怕命运的横逆
和风暴,都能向世间公开宣告;
我的心对我夫君的情性与为人,
可说是从顺得切合无间;我从
奥赛罗的心灵思想间看到他的仪容,
我将我的灵魂与命运,对他的光荣
与勇武奉献。所以,亲爱的公卿们,
假使我被留在后方,像和平时日里
一翼飞蛾,而他去前方作战,
我同他义结姻亲的礼仪将会被

And I a heavy interim shall support
By his dear absence. Let me go with him.
Othello Let her have your voices.
Vouch with me, heaven, I therefore beg it not
To please the palate of my appetite;
Nor to comply with heat, — the young affects
In me defunct, — and proper satisfaction;
But to be free and bounteous to her mind:
And heaven defend your good souls, that you think
I will your serious and great business scant
For she is with me: no, when light-wing'd toys
Of feather'd Cupid seel with wanton dullness
My speculative and offic'd instruments,
That my disports corrupt and taint my business,
Let housewives make a skillet of my helm,
And all indign and base adversities
Make head against my estimation!
Duke Be it as you shall privately determine,
Either for her stay or going: the affair cries haste,
And speed must answer it.
First Senator You must away to-night.
Othello   With all my heart.
Duke At nine i' the morning here we'll meet again. —
Othello, leave some officer behind,
And he shall our commission bring to you;
With such things else of quality and respect
As doth import you.
Othello   So please your grace, my ancient, —
A man he is of honesty and trust, —
To his conveyance I assign my wife,
With what else needful your good grace shall think
To be sent after me.
Duke   Let it be so. —
Good night to everyone. —[*To* Brabantio.] And, noble si-
      gnior,

剥夺，而因他、人不在，我还得生受
那难堪的岁月。让我和他一同去。

奥　赛　罗　让她得到诸位的准许。请上天
替我作证，我作此请求，不是要
满足我色欲的嗜好，也非为应顺
情焰的要求，——那少年炽烈的浓情，
在我胸中已熄灭，——和敦笃琴瑟
之调，而是要同她的心声相应和；
请上天莫让你们良善的灵魂
猜测我将会忽略那千钧的重负，
因为她同我在一起。那不会；假使
飞翔的小爱神用好色的游惰使我
绝智而闭聪，不能为公邦效命，
那么，让家庭主妇们把我的头盔
作水锅，让所有可耻、鄙陋的灾祸
对我的声名一齐发动总攻击！

公　　　爵　她留下还是前去，都由您私下
去决定。事态催促得急迫，迅捷
应当去应急。

知 政 事 甲　您今夜一定得出发。

奥　赛　罗　　　　　　　　我非常愿意。

公　　　爵　明朝九点钟我们再在此会集。
奥赛罗，留下个把军官在后面，
他将把我们的委任状带交给您；
还有有关品位和尊荣的别的事。

奥　赛　罗　假如您钧座高兴，我将旗手
留下；他是个诚实可靠的得力人；
我将我妻子委派给他去护送，
敬爱的君侯尽可付托他您认为
有需要交与我的别的任何事。

公　　　爵　　　　　　　　　　　这样
就是了。大家晚安。[对孛拉朋丘]高贵的大夫，

If virtue no delighted beauty lack,

Your son-in-law is far more fair than black.

First Senator   Adieu, brave Moor; use Desdemona well.

Brabantio   Look to her, Moor, if thou hast eyes to see:

She has deceiv'd her father, and may thee.

[*Exeunt* Duke, Senators, Officers. &c.]

Othello   My life upon her faith! — Honest Iago,

My Desdemona must I leave to thee:

I pr'ythee, let thy wife attend on her;

And bring them after in the best advantage. —

Come, Desdemona, I have but an hour

Of love, of worldly matters and direction,

To spend with thee: we must obey the time.

[*Exeunt* Othello *and* Desdemona.]

Roderigo   Iago, —

Iago   What say'st thou, noble heart?

Roderigo   What will I do, thinkest thou?

Iago   Why, go to bed and sleep.

Roderigo   I will incontinently drown myself.

Iago   If thou dost, I shall never love thee after. Why, thou silly gentleman!

Roderigo   It is silliness to live when to live is torment; and then have we a prescription to die when death is our physician.

Iago   O villainous! I have looked upon the world for four times seven years, and since I could distinguish betwixt a benefit and an injury, I never found man that knew how to love himself. *Ere I would say I would drown myself for the love of a Guinea-hen*, I would change my humanity with a baboon.

假使美德包含得什么都完备，
因而也就不缺少可喜的美貌，
您这位有德的贤婿便一点也不黑，
而是异常白净。

知 政 事 甲　　　　　　勇敢的摩尔人，
再会！好好待遇玳思狄莫娜。

孛 拉 朋 丘　注意她，摩尔人，如果你有眼睛瞧：
她骗了她父亲，也可能将你来骗到。

〔与公爵、知政事数人、军官数人及其他人等同下。

奥 赛 罗　我用生命来为她的真心作保证！
我一定将我的玳思狄莫娜托给你，
诚实的伊耶戈：请让你的妻子陪随她；
趁最好的时机，护送她们跟着来。
来吧，玳思狄莫娜；我只得一小时
跟你一同过，说爱和谈情，交代
日常事，关照如何行动：我们得
服从时间的限制。　　　　　　〔两人同下。

洛 窦 列 谷　伊耶戈！

伊 耶 戈　你说什么，高贵的知己？

洛 窦 列 谷　你想，我该怎么办？

伊 耶 戈　哎也，上床去睡觉。

洛 窦 列 谷　我该去跳水自杀。

伊 耶 戈　哦，你若是去那么干，我从此将永不跟你好。唉，你
这傻瓜的士子！

洛 窦 列 谷　活着如果只能受苦，再活下去就成了发傻；当死亡做
了我们的郎中的时候，他开的药方就是去死。

伊 耶 戈　啊！坏透了；我睁眼看到这世界有四倍七个年头了，
而自从我分得清什么是优惠、什么是损害以来，我从
来没有见到过有人懂得怎样去爱惜他自己。"为了
爱一只野鸡，我要去跳水自杀"，我肯说这样一句话
以前，我宁愿跟一只狒狒易地而处，让它来做人而我
去当狒狒。

Roderigo What should I do? I confess it is my shame to be so fond, but it is not in my virtue to amend it.

Iago *Virtue*! a fig! 'Tis in ourselves that we are thus or thus. Our bodies are gardens, to the which our wills are gardeners; so that if we will plant nettles or sow lettuce, set hyssop and weed up thyme, supply it with one gender of herbs or distract it with many, either to have it sterile with idleness or manured with industry; why, the power and corrigible authority of this lies in our wills. If the balance of our lives had not one scale of reason to poise another of sensuality, the blood and baseness of our natures would conduct us to most preposterous conclusions: But we have reason to cool our raging motions, our carnal stings, our unbitted lusts; whereof I take this, that you call love, to be a sect or scion.

Roderigo It cannot be.

Iago It is merely a lust of the blood and a permission of the will. Come, be a man: drown thyself! drown cats and blind puppies. I have professed me thy friend, and I confess me knit to thy deserving with cables of perdurable toughness; I could never better stead thee than now. Put money in thy purse; follow thou the wars; defeat thy favour with an usurped beard; I say, put money in thy purse. It cannot be that Desdemona should long continue her love to the Moor, —put money in thy purse, — nor he his to her: it was a violent commencement, and thou shalt see an answerable sequestration; — put but money in thy purse. — These Moors are changeable in their wills: — fill thy purse with money: the food that to him now is as luscious as locusts shall be to him shortly as acerb as the coloquintida. She must change for youth: when she is sated with his body, she will find the error of her choice: she must have change, she must: therefore put money in thy purse. —If thou wilt needs damn thyself, do it a more delicate way than drowning. Make all the money thou canst; if sanctimony and a frailvow

洛窦列谷 我应当怎么办？我承认这样痴心很丢脸；但是我的德性没有本领去改好这个。

伊 耶 戈 德性！值几个钱！我们是生就的这么样，或那么样。我们的身体是一所花园，我们的意志是个园丁；所以，若是我们要种荨麻或是播莴苣，栽香薄荷和耘除百里香，播种一种草或分植好多种，让它荒芜闲置着还是精耕细作，哎也，那力量和究竟怎样做的权力是在我们的意志里边。假如我们生命的天平没有一只理智的秤盘去均衡情欲的另一只，我们天性里的气质和卑鄙也许会引导我们到最乖张怪诞的试验上去；但是我们有理智去镇定我们热情的冲动、我们肉欲的激发、我们放浪不羁的淫荡，而据我看来，你们便把爱情叫作是情欲那玩意儿的另外一种或一枝分蘗。

洛窦列谷 不能是那样。

伊 耶 戈 这只是性情脾气里的淫欲、意志的放纵罢了。来吧，做个男子汉。跳水自杀！把猫儿和没有睁眼的小狗去淹死。我已经声言过是你的朋友了，我现在承认我把自己用最结实不过的缆索跟你的真价值拴束在一起；我从来也不会比现在这样更能帮你的忙了。口袋里放着钱；跟踪着这场战事；用一蓬假须髯丑化着你的面貌；我说，口袋里放着钱。苔思狄莫娜不可能长久继续爱着那摩尔人，——把钱装在口袋里，——他也不可能老爱她。在她身上先来了个猛烈的开始，你将见到一个同样凶暴的破裂；把钱装在你口袋里。这些摩尔人的意志好恶无常；——把钱装满你的口袋：——这食物现在对于他香甜甘美像仙桃，不久会对于他奇苦难堪像黄连。她一定得改换年轻的：当她受用够了他的肉体的时候，她准会发现她挑错了人。她准会有变化，她准会有：所以，口袋里放着钱。假使你非叫你自己打入地狱不可，去用一个比淹死较为愉快的方法。钱弄得越多越好。

betwixt an erring barbarian and a supersubtle Venetian be not too hard for my wits and all the tribe of
hell, thou shalt enjoy her; therefore make money. A
pox of drowning thyself! it is clean out of the way:
seek thou rather to be hanged in compassing thy joy
than to be drowned and go without her.

Roderigo Wilt thou be fast to my hopes, if I depend on
the issue?

Iago Thou art sure of me: — go, make money: — I have
told thee often, and I re-tell thee again and again, I
hate the Moor: my cause is hearted; thine hath no
less reason. Let us be conjunctive in our revenge a-
gainst him: if thou canst cuckold him, thou dost thyself a pleasure, me a sport. There are many events in
the womb of time which will be delivered. Traverse;
go; provide thy money. We will have more of this to-
morrow. Adieu.

Roderigo Where shall we meet i' the morning?

Iago At my lodging.

Roderigo I'll be with thee betimes.

Iago Go to; farewell. Do you hear, Roderigo?

Roderigo What say you?

Iago No more of drowning, do you hear?

Roderigo I am changed: I'll go sell all my land.

[*Exit.*]

Iago Thus do I ever make my fool my purse;
For I mine own gain'd knowledge should profane
If I would time expend with such a snipe
But for my sport and profit. I hate the Moor;
And it is thought abroad that 'twixt my sheets
He has done my office: I know not if't be true;
But I, for mere suspicion in that kind,
Will do as if for surety. He holds me well,
The better shall my purpose work on him.
Cassio's a proper man: let me see now;

假使一个浪荡的蛮子跟一个刁钻古怪的威尼斯人之间的假装的神圣和脆弱的信誓敌不过我的灵敏机巧和地狱里的族众们，你准定会受用到她；所以，得弄钱。滚他妈的跳水自杀！那样干会整个儿出岔子：奉劝你还是为享受到了那欢乐而给绞死，可莫要淹死了而弄她不到手。

洛窦列谷 你将赶快满足我的希望吗，假使我信赖那结果？

伊耶戈 你可以拿稳我：去，去弄钱。我屡次告诉过你，而且现在又一再对你说，我仇恨这摩尔人：我的行动准则铭铸在我心里：你的也并不缺少一点儿理由。让我们联合起来对他报仇；假使你能使他戴绿头巾，你对你自己做了件快乐事，对我做了件开心事。时间肚子里会生出许多事情下来。开步走；去吧：预备好你的钱。明天我们再谈这事儿。再会。

洛窦列谷 我们明天早上将在哪里碰头？

伊耶戈 在我的住处。

洛窦列谷 我会及早来看你。

伊耶戈 得了吧；再会。你听到没有，洛窦列谷？

洛窦列谷 你说什么？

伊耶戈 不许再说跳水了，你听到吗？

洛窦列谷 我改变主意了。我要去卖掉我全部的地皮。　　〔下。

伊耶戈 这样，我总叫傻瓜当我的钱袋；
因为假使跟这样的蠢货鬼混，
简直是侮辱我财源滚滚的机巧，
除非为好玩和实利。我恨那摩尔人，
而且外边都以为他在床褥间
替我行使着职权：我不知真不真，
可是仅仅为那样的怀疑，我就得
采取行动，仿佛确有那件事。
他对我很器重；我更好对他达到
我目的。凯昔欧是个适当的人儿；
且等我来想想看：拿到他的位置；

To get his place, and to plume up my will
In double knavery, — How, how? — Let's see: —
After some time, to abuse Othello's ear
That he is too familiar with his wife: —
He hath a person, and a smooth dispose,
To be suspected; fram'd to make women false.
The Moor is of a free and open nature,
That thinks men honest that but seem to be so;
And will as tenderly be led by the nose
As asses are.
I have't; — it is engender'd: — hell and night
Must bring this monstrous birth to the world's light.

[*Exit.*]

且要用双料的毒辣手段，显见我
意志的光荣伟大；怎么样，怎么样？
咱来捉摸一下看：过了些时候，
谗妄奥赛罗的耳朵，说他跟他老婆
太亲昵：他一表人才和模样温存
容易启疑窦；生就了叫女人失身。
这家伙，这天性开诚豁达的摩尔人，
看来好像是老实人他以为真诚实，
跟驴子一般能给穿了鼻子
轻轻地牵着走。
有了；想出苗头了：地狱与黑夜
准把这骇怪的新生带到天光下。　　　　　　　〔下。

ACT II.

SCENE I. *A seaport in Cyprus.*
An open place near the quay.

[*Enter* Montano *and two* Gentlemen.]

Montano   What from the cape can you discern at sea?

First Gentleman   Nothing at all: it is a high-wrought
flood;
I cannot, 'twixt the heaven and the main,
Descry a sail.

Montano   Methinks the wind hath spoke aloud at land;
A fuller blast ne'er shook our battlements:
If it hath ruffian'd so upon the sea,
What ribs of oak, when mountains melt on them,
Can hold the mortise? What shall we hear of this?

Second Gentleman   A segregation of the Turkish fleet:
For do but stand upon the foaming shore,
The chidden billow seems to pelt the clouds;
The wind-shak'd surge, with high and monstrous main,
Seems to cast water on the burning Bear,
And quench the guards of the ever-fixed pole;

第 二 幕

第 一 景

[塞浦路斯岛—海港城市。近码头处一空场。]
[蒙塔诺与士子二人上。

蒙 塔 诺　从地角上头你们能望见海上
　　　　　什么东西？

士 子 甲　　　　　　什么也没有，白浪
　　　　　滔天；在天和海洋之间，我不能
　　　　　瞥见一片帆篷。

蒙 塔 诺　我觉得风在岸上呼啸得好凶；
　　　　　从来没有更厉害的狂飚震撼过
　　　　　我们的雉堞；若是在海上也这般
　　　　　狂暴，什么橡木的船肋能支撑着
　　　　　不脱榫头，当高山一座座打下来？
　　　　　这狂风将带给我们什么消息？

士 子 乙　土耳其舰队将给刮得东分西散；
　　　　　因为只要站在喷泡沫的岸旁，
　　　　　被怒叱的波涛便像在投掷云天；
　　　　　那巨浪，被狂风所震，簇拥着高耸、
　　　　　银白的浪花一大片，像在对熊熊
　　　　　燃烧着的大熊星泼水，仿佛要浇熄
　　　　　那永定不移的北极星的两名守卫：

I never did like molestation view
On the enchafed flood.

Montano   If that the Turkish fleet
Be not enshelter'd and embay'd, they are drown'd;
It is impossible to bear it out.

[*Enter a third* Gentleman.]

Third Gentleman   News, lads! our wars are done.
The desperate tempest hath so bang'd the Turks
That their designment halts; a noble ship of Venice
Hath seen a grievous wreck and sufferance
On most part of their fleet.

Montano   How! is this true?

Third Gentleman   The ship is here put in,
A Veronessa; Michael Cassio,
Lieutenant to the warlike Moor Othello,
Is come on shore: the Moor himself's at sea,
And is in full commission here for Cyprus.

Montano   I am glad on't; 'tis a worthy governor.

Third Gentleman   But this same Cassio, — though he
    speak of comfort
Touching the Turkish loss, — yet he looks sadly,
And prays the Moor be safe; for they were parted
With foul and violent tempest.

Montano   Pray heavens he be;
For I have serv'd him, and the man commands
Like a full soldier. Let's to the sea-side, ho!
As well to see the vessel that's come in
As to throw out our eyes for brave Othello,
Even till we make the main and the aerial blue
An indistinct regard.

Third Gentleman   Come, let's do so;
For every minute is expectancy
Of more arrivance.

我从来不曾在激怒的大海上见过
同样的骚扰。

蒙 塔 诺　　　　　　若是土耳其舰队
没有入港避风，他们是淹死了；
他们不可能顶得过这阵大风。

　　　　　　　[士子丙上。

士 子 丙　有消息，伙伴们！我们的战事结束了。
这阵险恶的风暴揍得土耳其
那么凶，他们的企图就此作罢；
一艘威尼斯开来的大船，见到
他们舰队的大部分经受了一场
惨痛的船破人亡、奇灾大祸。

蒙 塔 诺　怎么！真的吗？

士 子 丙　　　　　　这船已经进了港，
一条梵洛那快船；玛格尔·凯昔欧，
那勇武的摩尔统帅奥赛罗的副将，
已经上了岸：摩尔人自己在海上，
他受命全权执管塞浦路斯岛。

蒙 塔 诺　我很高兴；这是个出色的总督。

士 子 丙　而就是这个凯昔欧，虽然他说起
土军破灭时心神鼓舞，可是他
祝祷那摩尔人无恙，却神情悲苦；
因为他们是被那幽黯的风狂
雨暴所强拆开。

蒙 塔 诺　　　　　　祈求上天他安全；
我曾在他手下服过役，这人指挥
真像个十全的军人。让我们到海边去，
喂！去看已经进来的那条船，
也为了替我们勇武的奥赛罗望远，
望到水天一碧分不清处去。

士 子 丙　来吧，让我们前去；因为每分钟
是新来慢到的希望。

[*Enter* Cassio.]

Cassio　Thanks you, the valiant of this warlike isle,
That so approve the Moor! O, let the heavens
Give him defence against the elements,
For I have lost him on a dangerous sea.

Montano　Is he well shipp'd?

Cassio　His bark is stoutly timber'd, and his pilot
Of very expert and approv'd allowance;
Therefore my hopes, not surfeited to death,
Stand in bold cure.

[*Within.*]　　A sail, a sail, a sail!

[*Enter* a *fourth* Gentleman.]

Cassio　What noise?

Fourth Gentleman　The town is empty; on the brow o' the
　　sea
Stand ranks of people, and they cry, A sail!

Cassio　My hopes do shape him for the governor.

[*Guns heard.*]

Second Gentleman　They do discharge their shot of courte-
　　sy:
Our friends at least.

Cassio　　　　　I pray you, sir, go forth,
And give us truth who 'tis that is arriv'd.

Second Gentleman　I shall.

[*Exit.*]

Montano　But, good lieutenant, is your general wiv'd?

Cassio　Most fortunately: he hath achiev'd a maid
That paragons description and wild fame,
One that excels the quirks of blazoning pens,
And in the essential vesture of creation
Does tire the ingener. —

[*Re-enter second* Gentleman.]

How now! who has put in?

　　　　　　　　　　　［凯昔欧上。

凯　昔　欧　　多谢,你们这勇武的岛上勇士们,
　　　　　　　　这么样称许这摩尔人。啊,让上天
　　　　　　　　保护他莫受风雨的危难,因为
　　　　　　　　我在危险的海面上跟他失散。

蒙　塔　诺　　他乘的可是条好船?

凯　昔　欧　　那条船打造得坚固,当舵的艄公
　　　　　　　都认为、且证明确实本领高强;
　　　　　　　所以我对他的希望,不能说是
　　　　　　　怅惘得忧烦欲绝,而确信很有救。
　　　　　　　［幕后叫声］"一张帆! ——一张帆! ——一张帆!"

　　　　　　　　　　　［士子丁上。

凯　昔　欧　　什么訇闹声?

士　子　丁　　城里走空了;在海滨岸上站得
　　　　　　　一排排尽是人,他们叫着,"一张帆!"

凯　昔　欧　　我对他的希望把来人幻形为总督。

　　　　　　　　　　　　　　　　　　　［鸣炮声可闻］

士　子　乙　　他们在鸣炮欢迎;我们的朋友,
　　　　　　　至少。

凯　昔　欧　　　　我请您,阁下,去探听实讯,
　　　　　　　到来的是谁。

士　子　乙　　　　　　我去。　　　　　　　　　　［下。

蒙　塔　诺　　可是,亲爱的副将军,你们的将军
　　　　　　　有宝眷没有?

凯　昔　欧　　非常幸运:他娶到一位贵千金,
　　　　　　　超过了言语的形容和恣肆的称颂;
　　　　　　　她胜过宣扬的文笔的妙想奇思,
　　　　　　　在未加修饰的天然素质上有分叫
　　　　　　　创制者感到疲劳。

　　　　　　　　　　　［士子乙上。

　　　　　　　　　　　　怎么样? 是谁
　　　　　　　进了港?

Second Gentleman　'Tis one Iago, ancient to the general.

Cassio　He has had most favourable and happy speed:

Tempests themselves, high seas, and howling winds,

The gutter'd rocks, and congregated sands, —

Traitors ensteep'd to clog the guiltless keel, —

As having sense of beauty, do omit

Their mortal natures, letting go safely by

The divine Desdemona.

Montano　　　　　　What is she?

Cassio　She that I spake of, our great captain's captain,

Left in the conduct of the bold Iago;

Whose footing here anticipates our thoughts

A se'nnight's speed. — Great Jove, Othello guard,

And swell his sail with thine own powerful breath,

That he may bless this bay with his tall ship,

Make love's quick pants in Desdemona's arms,

Give renew'd fire to our extincted spirits,

And bring all Cyprus comfort! O, behold,

　　　　　　[*Enter* Desdemona, Emilia, Iago,

　　　　　　　Roderigo, *and* Attendants.]

The riches of the ship is come on shore!

Ye men of Cyprus, let her have your knees. —

Hall to thee, lady! and the grace of heaven,

Before, behind thee, and on every hand,

Enwheel thee round!

Desdemona　　　　　I thank you, valiant Cassio.

What tidings can you tell me of my lord?

Cassio　He is not yet arrived nor know I aught

But that he's well, and will be shortly here.

Desdemona　O, but I fear— How lost you company?

Cassio　The great contention of the sea and skies

Parted our fellowship: — but, hark! a sail.

士 子 乙	有个伊耶戈,将军的旗手。
凯 昔 欧	他一路有莫大的福星临照:暴风雨 本身、狂涛骇浪、呼啸的罡风、 嶙峋的礁石、沙积成的滩,——沉埋在 海底,险恶地阻挠着无辜的船舶,—— 似乎也感到什么是明艳,放弃了 它们毁灭成性的行动,给安全 通过了这天仙下凡的玳思狄莫娜。
蒙 塔 诺	她是谁?
凯 昔 欧	我这才说起的这一位,我们 大将军的将军,由勇敢的伊耶戈护送来, 她登岸比我们所意料提早了七天。 伟大的乔旷,请你护卫着奥赛罗, 以你那呼气的雄风吹涨着他的篷, 好让他把他那巨舟来祝福这港口, 到玳思狄莫娜臂腕中作深情的心跳, 赋新生的火焰与我们熄灭了的精魂, 带给整个塞浦路斯岛以勇武! 〔玳思狄莫娜、爱米丽亚、伊耶戈、洛窦列谷及侍从数 人上。 啊! 看吧,船上的随和上了岸。 塞岛居民们,请你们给她以敬意。 欢迎你,贤淑的婵娟! 上苍降福泽 在你的前边、后边和四面八方, 围绕你周遭!
玳思狄莫娜	多谢您,勇武的凯昔欧。 您能告诉我我郎君有什么消息?
凯 昔 欧	他还没有到;我也不知道什么, 只除了他平安无恙,不久就会来。
玳思狄莫娜	啊! 我害怕——你们怎样失了俦?
凯 昔 欧	大海和高天的大混战将我们分散。 可是听啊! 一张帆。

[*Within.*] A sail, a sail!

[*Guns within.*]

Second Gentleman They give their greeting to the citadel:
This likewise is a friend.

Cassio See for the news.

[*Exit* Gentleman.]

Good ancient, you are welcome: — [*To* Emilia.] Welcome, mistress: —

Let it not gall your patience, good Iago,

That I extend my manners; 'tis my breeding

That gives me this bold show of courtesy.

[*Kissing her.*]

Iago Sir, would she give you so much of her lips

As of her tongue she oft bestows on me,

You'd have enough.

Desdemona Alas, she has no speech.

Iago In faith, too much;

I find it still when I have list to sleep:

Marry, before your ladyship, I grant,

She puts her tongue a little in her heart,

And chides with thinking.

Emilia You have little cause to say so.

Iago Come on, come on; you are pictures out of doors,

Bells in your parlours, wild cats in your kitchens,

Saints in your injuries, devils being offended,

Players in your housewifery, and housewives in your beds.

Desdemona O, fie upon thee, slanderer!

Iago Nay, it is true, or else I am a Turk:

You rise to play, and go to bed to work.

Emilia You shall not write my praise.

Iago No, let me not.

Desdemona What wouldst thou write of me, if thou
shouldst praise me?

Iago O gentle lady, do not put me to't;

[幕后叫声]"一张帆！——一张帆！"

[鸣炮声可闻]

士　子　乙　他们在对城防的堡垒致敬礼：
　　　　　　这也是一个朋友。

凯　昔　欧　　　　　　　　去探听消息。　　　[士子乙下。
　　　　　　亲爱的旗手，欢迎。[对爱米丽亚]欢迎，大嫂：
　　　　　　我来显示我礼数的周全，伊耶戈，
　　　　　　盼不致扰乱你的宁静；这是我的礼貌，
　　　　　　它使我大胆表示这样的敬意。　　　[吻伊]

伊　耶　戈　阁下，假使她将她的嘴唇给您得
　　　　　　那么多，如同她时常将舌头给与我，
　　　　　　您便是有得够多了。

玳思狄莫娜　　　　　　　　唉，她不做声。

伊　耶　戈　说实话，太多了；
　　　　　　我想要睡着的时候，它还在那里：
　　　　　　凭圣母，当着您夫人，我承认，的确，
　　　　　　她也将舌头放一点在她的心里，
　　　　　　想心思的时候就骂人。

爱米丽亚　你没有缘故这样说我。

伊　耶　戈　得了，得了；你们出门去就搽脂
　　　　　　抹粉，人在客厅里是清脆的铃铛，
　　　　　　进了厨房像野猫，跟人过不去
　　　　　　像圣徒一般严厉，得罪了你们
　　　　　　凶得像魔鬼，管家务都是懒婆娘，
　　　　　　上了床什么都干。

玳思狄莫娜　呸！胡说，诽谤者。

伊　耶　戈　不诽谤，是真话，否则我是个邪教徒：
　　　　　　你们起来就玩儿，上床去工作。

爱米丽亚　你不会讲我的好话。

伊　耶　戈　　　　　　　　不会，莫让我。

玳思狄莫娜　你若要跟我讲好话，将怎样申言？

伊　耶　戈　啊，温蔼的夫人，休叫我为难，

For I am nothing if not critical.

Desdemona Come on, assay — There's one gone to the
harbor?

Iago Ay, madam.

Desdemona I am not merry; but I do beguile
The thing I am, by seeming otherwise. —
Come, how wouldst thou praise me?

Iago I am about it; but, indeed, my invention
Comes from my pate as birdlime does from frize, —
It plucks out brains and all: but my Muse labours,
And thus she is deliver'd.
If she be fair and wise, — fairness and wit,
The one's for use, the other useth it.

Desdemona Well prais'd! How if she be black and witty?

Iago If she be black, and thereto have a wit,
She'll find a white that shall her blackness fit.

Desdemona Worse and worse.

Emilia How if fair and foolish?

Iago She never yet was foolish that was fair;
For even her folly help'd her to an heir.

Desdemona These are old fond paradoxes to make fools
laugh i' the alehouse. What miserable praise hast
thou for her that's foul and foolish?

Iago There's none so foul and foolish thereunto,
But does foul pranks which fair and wise ones do.

Desdemona O heavy ignorance! — thou praisest the worst
best. But what praise couldst thou bestow on a deserving woman indeed, — one that, in the authority of
her merit, did justly put on the vouch of very malice
itself?

Iago She that was ever fair and never proud;
Had tongue at will and yet was never loud;
Never lack'd gold and yet went never gay;
Fled from her wish, and yet said, *Now I may*;

因为我若不擅长批评，就一无
所能。

玳思狄莫娜　　　　　来吧；试一下。有人去海口了。

伊　耶　戈　是的，夫人。

玳思狄莫娜　我并非在嬉笑作乐，而是要故意
显得相反，来排遣我心中的情感。
来吧，你将怎样跟我讲好话？

伊　耶　戈　我来讲吧；但我的想象，说实话，
从我脑袋里出来，好比是雀胶
离粗布；它带着脑浆一起拉出来：
我的诗思在阵痛，她这样分娩了。
假使她聪明而美丽，智慧同美貌，
一个是使唤的，那一个被差遣呼叫。

玳思狄莫娜　赞得好！假使她黑皮肤而聪明，又怎样？

伊　耶　戈　假使她肤色黝黎，又聪明智慧，
会有个白面郎，跟她的黝黎相配。

玳思狄莫娜　越说越不像样。

爱米丽亚　假使洁白而又愚蠢，又怎样？

伊　耶　戈　从来没有个漂亮的女人是傻瓜，
因为她即使很傻也会生娃娃。

玳思狄莫娜　这些是说来叫傻子们在酒店里发笑的老一套笑料。
对于那又丑又傻的女人，你可有什么鄙陋的称赞？

伊　耶　戈　女人如果是又傻又长得丑陋，
倒不像那漂亮、聪明的，施诡计阴谋。

玳思狄莫娜　啊，迟钝的无知！你把最坏的称赞得最好。但是你
能怎样称赞一个真正是可贵的女人呢，她凭她那
优点的尊严，确是在向十足的恶意挑战，看它可有什
么不利于她的证词讲得出来？

伊　耶　戈　她永远美丽，可是从来不骄傲，
能谈吐自如，但决不论阔谈高，
从不少金银，但绝不夸耀插戴，
不任性所欲，但随时能自由进退：

She that, being anger'd, her revenge being nigh,
Bade her wrong stay and her displeasure fly;
She that in wisdom never was so frail
To change the cod's head for the salmon's tail;
She that could think and ne'er disclose her mind;
See suitors following and not look behind;
She was a wight, if ever such wight were. —

Desdemona To do what?

Iago To suckle fools and chronicle small beer.

Desdemona O most lame and impotent conclusion! — Do not learn of him, Emilia, though he be thy husband. — How say you, Cassio? is he not a most profane and liberal counsellor?

Cassio He speaks home, madam: you may relish him more in the soldier than in the scholar.

Iago [*Aside.*] He takes her by the palm: ay, well said, whisper: with as little a web as this will I ensnare as great a fly as Cassio. Ay, smile upon her, do; I will gyve thee in thine own courtship. You say true; 'tis so, indeed: if such tricks as these strip you out of your lieutenantry, it had been better you had not kissed your three fingers so oft, which now again you are most apt to play the sir in. Very good; well kissed! an excellent courtesy! 'tis so, indeed. Yet again your fingers to your lips? Would they were clyster-pipes for your sake!

[*Trumpet within.*] — The Moor! I know his trumpet.

Cassio 'Tis truly so.

Desdemona Let's meet him, and receive him.

Cassio Lo, where he comes!

[*Enter* Othello *and* Attendants.]

Othello O my fair warrior!

Desdemona   My dear Othello!

Othello It gives me wonder great as my content
To see you here before me. O my soul's joy!

她受到激怒,虽然报复很方便,
但她让屈枉留下,使懊恼飞迁:
她那聪明智慧决不会那么差,
愿意将鳕鱼头去换鲑鱼尾巴:
她能动脑筋,却决不随便开腔,
见求婚者跟着,可不向背后张望:
她是个娘们,如果有这样的女娘,

玳思狄莫娜 去做什么?

伊耶戈 去喂傻子吃奶和记录家务账。

玳思狄莫娜 啊,最蹩脚、没劲头的结尾! 不要去跟他学样,爱米丽亚,虽然他是你的丈夫。凯昔欧,您怎么说? 他不是出言粗鄙、口齿龌龊的瞎说八道的人吗?

凯昔欧 他说得无拘束、没礼貌,夫人;您喜欢他这说法,作为一个文人学士还不如作为一个军人的话来得合式。

伊耶戈 〔旁白〕他握着她的手掌;不错,说得好,咬耳朵说话;用这样一口小网,我要逗凯昔欧这样一只大苍蝇进圈套。是的,对她笑,笑吧;我将叫你掉进你自己那风流潇洒的圈套。您讲得对,是这样的,的确。假使这样的小手艺儿会叫您丧失掉副将军,您最好还是不曾把您那三只指头吻得这样勤的好,可是现在您又在鼓足劲儿把它们来对她殷勤致敬。好得很;吻得好! 绝妙的弯腿! 是这样,果真。又把手指放上嘴唇了? 为您的缘故,但愿它们是打针管子! 〔号角声可闻〕那摩尔人! 我听得出他的号角声。

凯昔欧 真是这样。

玳思狄莫娜 让我们碰见他,欢迎他。

凯昔欧 看啊! 他在那里来了。

〔奥赛罗与从人数人上。

奥赛罗 啊,我娇好的战士!

玳思狄莫娜 我亲爱的奥赛罗!

奥赛罗 这使我无比惊奇,见你们在此好不快乐。啊,我发自灵魂

If after every tempest come such calms,
May the winds blow till they have waken'd death!
And let the laboring bark climb hills of seas
Olympus-high, and duck again as low
As hell's from heaven! If it were now to die,
'Twere now to be most happy; for, I fear,
My soul hath her content so absolute
That not another comfort like to this
Succeeds in unknown fate.

Desdemona   The heavens forbid
But that our loves and comforts should increase
Even as our days do grow!

Othello   Amen to that, sweet powers! —
I cannot speak enough of this content;
It stops me here; it is too much of joy:
And this, and this, the greatest discords be
                                   [*Kissing her.*]
That e'er our hearts shall make!

Iago [*Aside.*]   O, you are well tun'd now!
But I'll set down the pegs that make this music,
As honest as I am.

Othello   Come, let us to the castle. —
News, friends; our wars are done, the Turks are drown'd.
How does my old acquaintance of this isle?
Honey, you shall be well desir'd in Cyprus;
I have found great love amongst them. O my sweet,
I prattle out of fashion, and I dote
In mine own comforts. — I pry'thee, good Iago,
Go to the bay and disembark my coffers:
Bring thou the master to the citadel;
He is a good one, and his worthiness

深处的欢快！假使每一次风暴后
会有这样阵平静，让狂风暴雨
尽管去吹打，即令唤醒了死亡
也在所不惜！让辛劳的船只去爬
奥灵伯那样巍峨的海浪的山头，
又突然从天而降，降落得低到
地府阴曹！若是如今便死去，
现在就会成极乐，因为我害怕
我这颗灵魂的欢快已造极登峰，
未知的命运里不会有相似的另一阵
欢愉后继。

玳思狄莫娜　　　　　　　上苍莫叫有枝节，
我们的两情缱绻和幸福无疆
将与日而俱增。

奥　赛　罗　　　　　　　　心愿如此，亲爱的天使们！
我说也说不尽这欢乐；它使我无言；
这是太过的欢乐：而这个，这个，　　　［吻伊］
是我们两心间将有的最大的违和！

伊　耶　戈　［旁白］啊！你们此刻和合得谐融一致，
但我要把宣发这乐调的弦柱抽松，
正如我言语出口来，诚实无欺。

奥　赛　罗　去来，让我们去到堡垒里。朋友们，
消息好；我们的战事已结束，土耳其人
已淹死。岛上我们的老乡们怎么样？
亲爱的，你会在塞岛被人人所爱；
他们对我都非常心爱。啊也，
我的亲人，我胡扯乱说，有失
礼貌，而讲我的欢乐，也出言愚妄。
我请你，亲爱的伊耶戈，去到埠头上
将我的箱箧起上岸。你将船主公
领往城防堡垒去；他是个好人，
他那高贵的人品应好好受尊敬。

Does challenge much respect. —Come, Desdemona,
Once more well met at Cyprus.

　　　　　[*Exeunt* Othello, Desdemona, *and* Attendants.]

Iago　Do thou meet me presently at the harbour. Come
hither. If thou be'st valiant,—as, they say, base men
being in love have then a nobility in their natures more
than is native to them, —list me. The lieutenant to-
night watches on the court of guard: first, I must tell
thee this—Desdemona is directly in love with him.

Roderigo　With him! why, 'tis not possible.

Iago　Lay thy finger thus, and let thy soul be instructed.
Mark me with what violence she first loved the
Moor, but for bragging, and telling her fantastical
lies: and will she love him still for prating? Let not
thy discreet heart think it. Her eye must be fed; and
what delight shall she have to look on the devil?
When the blood is made dull with the act of sport,
there should be, —again to inflame it and to give sati-
ety a fresh appetite, —loveliness in favour; sympathy
in years, manners, and beauties; all which the Moor
is defective in: now, for want of these required con-
veniences, her delicate tenderness will find itself a-
bused, begin to heave the gorge, disrelish and abhor
the Moor; very nature will instruct her in it, and
compel her to some second choice. Now sir, this
granted; —as it is a most pregnant and unforced position, —who stands so eminently in the degree of this
fortune as Cassio does? a knave very voluble; no further conscionable than in putting on the mere form of
civil and humane seeming, for the better compass of
his salt and most hidden loose affection? why, none;
why, none; —a slipper and subtle knave; a finder out
of occasions; that has an eye can stamp and counterfeit advantages, though true advantage never present itself: a devilish knave! besides, the knave is handsome,

来吧,玳思狄莫娜,再一次容我说,

我在塞浦路斯见到你多高兴。

　　　〔奥赛罗与玳思狄莫娜及侍从等下。

伊　耶　戈　你准定马上去到海口那里跟我碰头。这里来。假使你有勇气,——他们说庸夫俗子发生了恋爱,性情里便会有一股原来所没有的高贵之气,——就听我说。副将军今晚上在主防厅守卫;首先,我得告诉你这个,玳思狄莫娜分明在跟他恋爱。

洛窦列谷　跟他! 哪里话来,这不可能。

伊　耶　戈　让你的手指这么掩着你的嘴,让你的心灵儿来受教。你跟我注意,她初初爱这摩尔人时爱得多么猛烈,只为了他跟她吹牛,讲些荒诞不经的谎话;而她会不会永远爱着他呢,为了他对她空口说白话? 莫让你那明智的心这样想。她的眼睛一定得有所满足;而她睃着魔鬼可有什么愉快? 当肉欲玩弄得感到迟钝时,为重新点燃起它的火焰,为使得腻烦有一股新鲜的淫兴起见,必须要有相貌方面的可喜可爱,年龄、行动和神情优美,在两人之间彼此相谐和协调;这一切这摩尔人是欠缺不够的。如今,因为没有这些必须的舒适、安乐的东西,她会发现她自己的娇柔婀娜是给糟蹋了,会开始感觉到要作呕,会嫌弃和厌恶这摩尔人;她的天性本身就会提醒她,迫使她挑选第二个汉子。现在,先生,这一层认为不错之后,——因为这是最显而易见、最自然不过的说法,谁站在这幸运的如此高的梯级上面呢,只除了凯昔欧? 一个十分反复无常的坏蛋,除了装作彬彬有礼跟和蔼可亲之外,一无正气可言,为的是能更巧妙地把他那淫乱的、最秘密的色欲弄到手? 哎,没第二个人;哎,没第二个人:一个狡猾的、诈欺的坏蛋,一个投机分子,即使真的机遇从没有到来,他却会推行和伪造有利的时机;一个无恶不作的坏蛋! 此外,这坏蛋长得俊俏、后生,在他身

young, and hath all those requisites in him that folly and green minds look after: a pestilent complete knave; and the woman hath found him already.

Roderigo I cannot believe that in her; she is full of most blessed condition.

Iago *Blest* fig's end! the wine she drinks is made of grapes: if she had been blessed, she would never have loved the Moor: blessed pudding! Didst thou not see her paddle with the palm of his hand? didst not mark that?

Roderigo Yes, that I did; but that was but courtesy.

Iago Lechery, by this hand; an index and obscure prologue to the history of lust and foul thoughts. They met so near with their lips that their breaths embraced together. Villainous thoughts, Roderigo! when these mutualities so marshal the way, hard at hand comes the master and main exercise, the incorporate conclusion: pish! — But, sir, be you ruled by me: I have brought you from Venice. Watch you to-night: for the command, I'll lay't upon you: Cassio knows you not:—I'll not be far from you: do you find some occasion to anger Cassio, either by speaking too loud, or tainting his discipline, or from what other course you please, which the time shall more favourably minister.

Roderigo Well.

Iago Sir, he is rash, and very sudden in choler, and haply with his truncheon may strike at you: provoke him, that he may; for even out of that will I cause these of Cyprus to mutiny, whose qualification shall come into no true taste again but by the displanting of Cassio. So shall you have a shorter journey to your desires by the means I shall then have to prefer them; and the impediment most profitably removed, without the which there were no expectation of our prosperity.

Roderigo I will do this, if I can bring it to any opportunity.

Iago I warrant thee. Meet me by and by at the citadel: I must fetch his necessaries ashore. Farewell.

Roderigo Adieu.   [*Exit.*]

上有那愚蠢、幼稚的傻东西们所寻求的一切所需；一个十恶不赦的恶贼！而这女人已经发现了他的好处。

洛窦列谷 我不能相信她会这样；她满都是圣洁的品性。

伊 耶 戈 圣洁的狗屁！她喝的酒是用葡萄做的；假使她是圣洁的话，她决不会爱上这摩尔人；圣洁的布丁！你不看见她揉弄他的手掌心吗？你没有见到吗？

洛窦列谷 不错，见到的；但那不过表示敬意罢了。

伊 耶 戈 表示淫意，我用这只手赌咒！为淫乱和坏念头的史剧演一折楔子，一场暧昧不明的序幕。他们两副嘴唇挨得那么近，两个人的呼吸可说是彼此搂抱起来了。下流的念头，洛窦列谷！当这些亲昵的行动这般开道领路以后，紧接着是那主要的行动，由淫欲来收场。呸！但是，先生，听从我的话：我从威尼斯将你带了来。你今晚上守夜；那命令，我会叫它落在你身上：凯昔欧不认识你。我离开你不会很远：你找个机会激怒凯昔欧，或是说话说得太响，或是蔑视他的纪律；再不然采取你高兴用的其他方法，瞧当时更有利地提供给你而定。

洛窦列谷 好的。

伊 耶 戈 先生，他给激怒之后性情火烈，非常横暴，也许会打你：惹起他来，要他发作；因为那样一来，我将轰动塞浦路斯守军兵变，然后，要把事态安抚下来，不使有什么不满，便非将凯昔欧革职不可。这样，你准会经过一个较近便的过程满足你的欲望，由我来设法促成你达到目的；而那个障碍便得以极为有利地去除掉，不那么做我们的成功是没有指望的。

洛窦列谷 我一定依你说的去做，如果我能找到什么机会。

伊 耶 戈 我保证你。待一会跟我在城防堡垒里碰头：我需得把他的行李搬上岸。回头见。

洛窦列谷 再会。　　　　　　　　　　　　　　［下。

Iago   That Cassio loves her, I do well believe it;
That she loves him, 'tis apt, and of great credit;
The Moor, — howbeit that I endure him not, —
Is of a constant, loving, noble nature;
And, I dare think, he'll prove to Desdemona
A most dear husband. Now, I do love her too;
Not out of absolute lust, — though, peradventure,
I stand accountant for as great a sin, —
But partly led to diet my revenge,
For that I do suspect the lusty Moor
Hath leap'd into my seat; the thought whereof
Doth, like a poisonous mineral, gnaw my inwards;
And nothing can or shall content my soul
Till I am even'd with him, wife for wife;
Or, failing so, yet that I put the Moor
At least into a jealousy so strong
That judgement cannot cure. Which thing to do, —
If this poor trash of Venice, whom I trash
For his quick hunting, stand the putting on,
I'll have our Michael Cassio on the hip;
Abuse him to the Moor in the rank garb, —
For I fear Cassio with my night-cap too; —
Make the Moor thank me, love me, and reward me
For making him egregiously an ass
And practicing upon his peace and quiet
Even to madness. 'Tis here, but yet confus'd;
Knavery's plain face is never seen till us'd.

                                                    [*Exit.*]

伊 耶 戈　凯昔欧爱上了她,我很相信;
她爱上了他,自然而非常可信:
这摩尔人,虽然我对他深恶痛绝,
却有着忠诚、和蔼、高尚的性情;
我敢信他对玳思狄莫娜将是个
最亲爱的丈夫。却说,我也爱好她;
不完全为淫欲,——虽然我也许
犯上了同样重大的一桩罪辜,——
但部分是要满足我的报仇雪恨心,
因为我怀疑这精力充沛的摩尔人
骑上了我的马鞍;这一个想法
好比是毒药,咬我的心肝脏腑;
而没有东西能够、或将会满足
我灵魂,直等到我同他交一个平手,
妻子对妻子;或者,若是不成功,
我至少要叫这摩尔人妒忌得那么凶,
使冷静的判断也无法医治那创伤。
为了这件事,倘若我从威尼斯
带来的这滥贱的废料听受我指挥,——
我经常盯住他,催他迎上前去猎取,——
我们这位玛格尔·凯昔欧的髋骨
我会要狠狠地把它压住;我要在
摩尔人面前用最好的办法诋毁他,——
因为我恐怕凯昔欧也戴过我的睡帽,
叫这摩尔人感谢我、心爱我、酬报我,
为了我恶极无赖地使他变成了
一只蠢驴,且又施展出计谋
破坏他的安心和宁静,逼得他疯狂。
这事件到现在为止还迷糊不清:
奸恶未实践,真面目决不会分明。　　　　　[下。

SCENE II. *A street.*

[*Enter a* Herald *with a proclamation;*
People *following.*]

HERALD It is Othello's pleasure, our noble and valiant
general, that upon certain tidings now arrived, impor-
ting the mere perdition of the Turkish fleet, every
man put himself into triumph; some to dance, some
to make bonfires, each man to what sport and revels
his addiction leads him: for, besides these beneficial
news, it is the celebration of his nuptial: — so much
was his pleasure should be proclaimed. All offices are
open; and there is full liberty of feasting from this
present hour of five till the bell have told eleven.
Heaven bless the isle of Cyprus and our noble general
Othello!   [*Exeunt.*]

SCENE III. *A Hall in the Castle.*

[*Enter* Othello, Desdemona, Cassio, *and* Attendants.]
Othello Good Michael, look you to the guard to-night:
Let's teach ourselves that honourable stop,
Not to out-sport discretion.
Cassio Iago hath direction what to do;
But, notwithstanding, with my personal eye
Will I look to't.
Othello   Iago is most honest.
Michael, good night: to-morrow with your earliest
Let me have speech with you. — [*To* Desdemona] Come,
    my dear love, —
The purchase made, the fruits are to ensue;
That profit's yet to come 'tween me and you. —
Good-night.
              [*Exeunt* Othello, Desdemona, *and* Attendants.]
                        [*Enter* Iago.]
Cassio Welcome, Iago; we must to the watch.

第 二 景

[一街道]

[奥赛罗之传令官上,手执布告。民众后随。

传 令 官　我们高贵勇武的将军奥赛罗,得到了某些刚到的、关于土耳其舰队全军覆灭的消息,高兴居民们每一个人都兴高采烈去庆贺这际会,有的去跳舞,有的燃祝火,各人随自己意思去娱乐和庆喜;因为除了这些有利的新闻之外,这也是他新婚的祝典。将军喜欢这么样,应当公告。堡垒里所有的厨房、酒窖、伙食间、总管房等都将开放,从此刻五点钟到钟鸣十一下,有充分欢快的许可。上天赐福于塞浦路斯岛和我们高贵的将军奥赛罗!

[俱下。

第 三 景

[堡垒内一厅事]

[奥赛罗、珉思狄莫娜、凯昔欧与随从人等上。

奥 赛 罗　亲爱的玛格尔,你留神今夜夜班:
让我们教自己顾体面适可而止,
休玩过了分寸。

凯 昔 欧　伊耶戈有指示怎样去处置;可是,
虽然如此,我准会亲自去注意。

奥 赛 罗　伊耶戈这人极诚实。玛格尔,晚安;
容我明天一清早和你再谈吧。
[向珉思狄莫娜]来,亲爱的小妹,事情已成功,
后果自会跟着来;那好处将会到
你我之间来。晚安。[与珉思狄莫娜及从人等同下。
[伊耶戈上。

凯 昔 欧　欢迎,伊耶戈,我们得去上夜班。

Iago Not this hour, lieutenant; 'tis not yet ten o' the clock. Our general cast us thus early for the love of his Desdemona; who let us not therefore blame: he hath not yet made wanton the night with her; and she is sport for Jove.

Cassio She's a most exquisite lady.

Iago And, I'll warrant her, full of game.

Cassio Indeed, she is a most fresh and delicate creature.

Iago What an eye she has! methinks it sounds a parley to provocation.

Cassio An inviting eye; and yet methinks right modest.

Iago And when she speaks, is it not an alarm to love?

Cassio She is, indeed, perfection.

Iago Well, happiness to their sheets! Come, lieutenant, I have a stoup of wine; and here without are a brace of Cyprus gallants that would fain have a measure to the health of black Othello.

Cassio Not to-night, good Iago: I have very poor and un-happy brains for drinking: I could well wish courtesy would invent some other custom of entertainment.

Iago O, they are our friends; but one cup: I'll drink for you.

Cassio I have drunk but one cup to-night, and that was craftily qualified too, and behold, what innovation it makes here: I am unfortunate in the infirmity, and dare not task my weakness with any more.

Iago What, man! 'tis a night of revels: the gallants de-sire it.

Cassio Where are they?

Iago Here at the door; I pray you, call them in.

Cassio I'll do't; but it dislikes me.   [*Exit.*]

Iago If I can fasten but one cup upon him,
With that which he hath drunk to-night already,
He'll be as full of quarrel and offense
As my young mistress' dog. Now, my sick fool Roderigo,

伊　耶　戈	这一晌不去,副将军,现在还不到十点钟。我们将军遣走我们得这么早是为了要跟他的玳思狄莫娜去亲昵,可是莫让我们为了这事见怪他;他还没有和她开动手脚哩,而她是堪供天王乔旷去耍乐的。
凯　昔　欧	她是个绝世无双的美婵娟。
伊　耶　戈	而且,我保证她身上功夫来得。
凯　昔　欧	果真,她是个极年轻可爱的人儿。
伊　耶　戈	她那眼波儿多俏! 我看来它逗得人欲火上升。
凯　昔　欧	那目光是动人的;可是我看来却羞答答十分端庄贞静。
伊　耶　戈	而她说起话来,不是在响亮地叫人爱上她吗?
凯　昔　欧	她的确十全十美。
伊　耶　戈	很好,祝他们在床上快乐! 来,副将军,我有一瓿酒在此,而这里有一双塞浦路斯的公子哥儿在外边,他们乐意来喝一点酒为黑将军祝贺。
凯　昔　欧	今夜不喝了,亲爱的伊耶戈:我喝了酒脑筋不行,要出乱子:我老大愿意人们要是殷勤好礼的话,尽可设法想出些什么别的习俗来欢娱。
伊　耶　戈	啊! 他们是我们的朋友;只喝一杯;我替您喝吧。
凯　昔　欧	我今夜只喝了一杯,而且那是大大搀淡了的,可是,你瞧,它在这儿捣出多大的麻烦:我在这缺陷上头是不幸的,再不敢在我的弱点上加重负担了。
伊　耶　戈	什么,仁兄! 这是个欢庆的夜宵;贵家公子们要求这个。
凯　昔　欧	他们在哪里?
伊　耶　戈	这里,在门首;请您叫他们进来。
凯　昔　欧	我来叫;可是我不喜欢这么办。　　　　　〔下。
伊　耶　戈	假使我只要能再骗他喝上一杯, 加上他今晚上已经喝了的那盅, 他将会争吵不休,满肚子恼怒, 像那年轻主母娘的小花儿一般。 现在病恹恹的蠢货那洛窦列谷,

Whom love hath turn'd almost the wrong side out,
To Desdemona hath to-night carous'd
Potations pottle-deep; and he's to watch:
Three lads of Cyprus, — noble swelling spirits,
That hold their honours in a wary distance,
The very elements of this warlike isle, —
Have I to-night fluster'd with flowing cups,
And they watch too. Now, 'mongst this flock of drunk-
ards,
Am I to put our Cassio in some action
That may offend the isle: — but here they come:
If consequence do but approve my dream,
My boat sails freely, both with wind and stream.

> [*Re-enter* Cassio; with him Montano *and* Gentlemen;
> *followed by* Servant *with wine.*]

Cassio   'Fore heaven, they have given me a rouse already.

Montano   Good faith, a little one; not past a pint, as I am
a soldier.

Iago   Some wine, ho!

> [*Sings.*] *And let me the canakin clink* , *clink*;
> *And let me the canakin clink.*
> *A soldier's a man* ;
> *O, man's life's but a span* ;
> *Why then let a soldier drink.*

Some wine, boys!

Cassio   'Fore God, an excellent song.

Iago   I learned it in England, where, indeed, they are
most potent in potting: your Dane, your German, and
your swag-bellied Hollander, — Drink, ho! — are
nothing to your English.

Cassio   Is your Englishman so expert in his drinking?

Iago   Why, he drinks you, with facility, your Dane dead
drunk; he sweats not to overthrow your Almain; he
gives your Hollander a vomit ere the next pottle can
be filled.

Cassio   To the health of our general!

相思闹得几乎中了邪,今晚上
对玳思狄莫娜祝酒已喝干一大觥;
是他来守夜。有三个塞浦路斯人,
是贵家子弟们,气概得不可一世,
把荣誉擎举得奇高,防卫得老远,
乃是这英武的海岛所荟萃的精华,
今夜我也一盅盅灌得火热,
他们也要来守夜。如今,在这群
醉汉中,我要使凯昔欧行动起来,
激怒这整个岛。他们已经来到。
如其后果只要能证实我的梦,
风也顺,水也顺,我的船驶得畅通。
　　　[凯昔欧、蒙塔诺与士子三人上。仆从数人携酒后随。

凯　昔　欧　上帝在上,他们已经给了我一满盅。
蒙　塔　诺　说老实话,一小杯;不到二两,正如我是个军人。
伊　耶　戈　来点酒,喂!
　　　　　[唱]"让我把小罐儿来碰,来碰;
　　　　　　　让我把小罐儿来碰:
　　　　　　　　一个兵是个人;
　　　　　　　　生命啊,短得很;
　　　　　　　　那么,让个兵把酒来饮。"
　　　　　来点酒,小崽子们!
凯　昔　欧　上帝在上,一只出色的歌儿。
伊　耶　戈　这我是在英国学来的,他们那儿实在唱得厉害;你们
　　　　　那丹麦人,你们那日耳曼人,还有你们那大肚子的荷
　　　　　兰人,——喝酒,喂!——比起你们那英吉利人来就
　　　　　算不得什么了。
凯　昔　欧　你们那英吉利人喝酒这样能干在行吗?
伊　耶　戈　哎也,他毫不费力替你把你们那丹麦人赌喝得烂醉
　　　　　如泥;他汗也不出把你们那日耳曼人就摔倒了;他第
　　　　　二觥还没斟已经叫你们那荷兰人呕吐了。
凯　昔　欧　祝我们的将军健康!

Montano I am for it, lieutenant; and I'll do you justice.

Iago O sweet England!

> [*Sings.*] *King Stephen was and a worthy peer,*
> *His breeches cost him but a crown;*
> *He held them sixpence all too dear,*
> *With that he call'd the tailor lown.*
> *He was a wight of high renown,*
> *And thou art but of low degree:*
> *'Tis pride that pulls the country down;*
> *Then take thine auld cloak about thee.*

Some wine, ho!

Cassio Why, this is a more exquisite song than the other.

Iago Will you hear it again?

Cassio No; for I hold him to be unworthy of his place that does those things. — Well, — God's above all, and there be souls must be saved, and there be souls must not be saved.

Iago It's true, good lieutenant.

Cassio For mine own part, — no offence to the general, nor any man of quality, — I hope to be saved.

Iago And so do I too, lieutenant.

Cassio Ay, but, by your leave, not before me; the lieutenant is to be saved before the ancient. Let's have no more of this; let's to our affairs. — Forgive us our sins! —Gentlemen, let's look to our business. Do not think, gentlemen, I am drunk: this is my ancient; this is my right hand, and this is my left: — I am not drunk now; I can stand well enough, and I speak well enough.

All Excellent well.

Cassio Why, very well then: you must not think, then, that I am drunk.   [*Exit.*]

Montano To the platform, masters; come, let's set the watch.

Iago You see this fellow that is gone before; —
He is a soldier fit to stand by Caesar

蒙　塔　诺　　我赞成这个,副将军;我跟您对干一杯。

伊　耶　戈　　啊,亲爱的英伦!

　　　　　　　　[唱]史梯芬是个出色的好君王,

　　　　　　　　　　　他那条裤子只花他五先令;

　　　　　　　　　　　他嫌多花了半先令太冤枉,

　　　　　　　　　　　因此上他叫那裁缝阿木林。

　　　　　　　　　　　他声名响得哪个不知道,

　　　　　　　　　　　你这个小子地位低,又加穷:

　　　　　　　　　　　骄傲能掀翻一个大王朝,

　　　　　　　　　　　所以你还是去披件旧斗篷。

　　　　　　　　来点酒,喂!

凯　昔　欧　　哎也,这一只歌比那一只还要妙。

伊　耶　戈　　您还要听吗?

凯　昔　欧　　不了;因为我认为他做那样的事儿对于他的身份不
　　　　　　　相称。很好,上帝在一切之上;有些灵魂一定得给拯
　　　　　　　救,有些灵魂一定得不给拯救。

伊　耶　戈　　一点不错,亲爱的副将军。

凯　昔　欧　　为我自己起见,——对于将军并无触犯,对于别的高
　　　　　　　品位人物也没有,——我希望能得拯救。

伊　耶　戈　　我也这么希望,副将军。

凯　昔　欧　　是的;但是,你允许的话,不在我之前;副将军要在旗
　　　　　　　手之前得到拯救。让我们莫再谈这个吧;让我们干
　　　　　　　事情去。上帝饶恕我们的罪过! 列位,让我们注意
　　　　　　　到我们的公务。列位,莫以为我醉了:这是我的旗
　　　　　　　手;这是我的右手,这是我的左手。我此刻没有醉;
　　　　　　　我能站得够好的,说话也说得够好的。

众　　　人　　非常好。

凯　昔　欧　　哎也,那么,很好;那么,你们切莫以为我喝醉了。

　　　　　　　　　　　　　　　　　　　　　　　　　[下。

蒙　塔　诺　　禁卫坛上去,列位;来吧,让我们去警卫。

伊　耶　戈　　您见到这个先我们而去的人儿;

　　　　　　　他是个军人,配得上在恺撒身旁

And give direction; and do but see his vice;
'Tis to his virtue a just equinox,
The one as long as the other; 'tis pity of him.
I fear the trust Othello puts him in,
On some odd time of his infirmity,
Will shake this island.

Montano   But is he often thus?

Iago 'Tis evermore the prologue to his sleep;
He'll watch the horologe a double set
If drink rock not his cradle.

Montano   It were well
The general were put in mind of it.
Perhaps he sees it not, or his good nature
Prizes the virtue that appears in Cassio,
And looks not on his evils; is not this true?

                 [*Enter* Roderigo.]

Iago   [*Aside to him.*] How now, Roderigo!
I pray you, after the lieutenant; go.

                         [*Exit* Roderigo.]

Montano   And 'tis great pity that the noble Moor
Should hazard such a place as his own second
With one of an ingraft infirmity;
It were an honest action to say
So to the Moor.

Iago   Not I, for this fair island;
I do love Cassio well; and would do much
To cure him of this evil. —But, hark! What noise?

                 [*Cry within,* — *Help*! *help*!]

             [*Re-enter* Cassio, *driving* in Roderigo.]

Cassio   You rogue! you rascal!

Montano   What's the matter, lieutenant?

站着任指挥；可是，只瞧他的差失；
对于他的品德，这正好如日夜平分，
一般长短各相当；对他说，真可惜。
我生怕奥赛罗对他所寄的信任，
在他精神阉弱的偶然间付与他，
将震惊这个岛。

蒙 塔 诺　　　　　　但是他时常这样吗？

伊 耶 戈　这总是他临睡之前的开场楔子：
他准会望着自鸣钟短针走两圈，
如果没有酒来为他摇摇篮。

蒙 塔 诺　　　　　　　　　将军
若经人提醒这件事，倒是件好事。
也许他没见到；或是他那好性情
重视凯昔欧所显示的美德，而没有
看到他那些坏处。这话对不对？

　　　　　　［洛窦列谷上。

伊 耶 戈　［旁白，对他］有什么事情，洛窦列谷？
我请你，跟着副将军；跟着他去。

　　　　　　　　　　　　［洛窦列谷下。

蒙 塔 诺　这真是十分可惜，那高贵的摩尔人
竟将他自己副手的位置冒险
交给这样个阉弱毛病根深
柢固的人；把这话告诉摩尔人
将会是可敬的行为。

伊 耶 戈　　　　　　我不说，即令是
为了这美好的岛屿：我很爱凯昔欧；
要尽力医好他这毛病。但是听啊！
什么响声？　　　　［幕后呼声："救命！救命！"］
　　　　　　［凯昔欧追赶洛窦列谷上。

凯 昔 欧　你这混混，你这坏蛋！
蒙 塔 诺　　　　　　　什么事，
副将军？

Cassio A knave teach me my duty!

I'll beat the knave into a twiggen bottle.

Roderigo Beat me!

Cassio   Dost thou prate, rogue?

[*Striking* Roderigo.]

Montano   [*Staying him*] Nay, good lieutenant;

I pray you, sir, hold your hand.

Cassio   Let me go, sir,

Or I'll knock you o'er the mazard.

Montano   Come, come, you're drunk.

Cassio Drunk!

[*They fight.*]

Iago [*Aside to* Roderigo.] Away, I say! go out and cry a

   mutiny.   [*Exit* Roderigo.]

Nay, good lieutenant, —alas, gentlemen: —

Help, ho! — Lieutenant, — sir, — Montano, — sir: —

Help, masters! — Here's a goodly watch indeed!

[*Bell rings.*]

Who's that that rings the bell? — Diablo, ho!

The town will rise: God's will, lieutenant, hold;

You will be sham'd forever.

[*Re-enter* Othello *and* Attendants.]

Othello   What is the matter here?

Montano Zounds, I bleed still; I am hurt to the death.

Othello Hold, for your lives!

Iago Hold, ho! lieutenant, — sir, — Montano, —gentle-

   men, —

Have you forgot all sense of place and duty?

Hold! the general speaks to you; hold, hold, for shame!

Othello Why, how now, ho! from whence ariseth this?

Are we turn'd Turks, and to ourselves do that

Which Heaven hath forbid the Ottomites?

For Christian shame, put by this barbarous brawl:

凯 昔 欧	一个流氓教训我尽职！

凯　昔　欧　　　　　　一个流氓教训我尽职！
　　　　　　　　我把这流氓揍成个藤柳框的瓶。
洛 窦 列 谷　揍我！
凯　昔　欧　　　　还乱说，混混？　　　　　　［打洛窦列谷］
蒙　塔　诺　　　　　［拦阻凯］亲爱的副将军，
　　　　　　　　莫那样；我请您，阁下，住手。
凯　昔　欧　　　　　　　　　　　　　　让开，
　　　　　　　　阁下，不然我要来砸你的脑袋。
蒙　塔　诺　算了，算了；你酒喝醉了。
凯　昔　欧　　　　　　　　　　喝醉了！　　［他们打斗］
伊　耶　戈　［旁白，向洛窦列谷］去吧，我说！出去，去叫嚷兵变。
　　　　　　　　　　　　　　　　　　　　　［洛窦列谷下。

　　　　　　　　莫那样，亲爱的副将军！上帝的愿望，
　　　　　　　　大人们！救人，喂哟！副将军！大人！
　　　　　　　　蒙塔诺！大人！救人，诸位袍泽们！
　　　　　　　　这里真是好一个警卫的夜班！

　　　　　　　　　　　　　　　　　　　　　　［钟声鸣响］

　　　　　　　　是谁敲响了这钟声？魔鬼，喂哟！
　　　　　　　　全城要起来了：上帝的愿望！副将军，
　　　　　　　　住手！您将会永远蒙上耻辱。
　　　　　　　　　　　　　　　［奥赛罗与从人等上。

奥　赛　罗　这里有什么事情？
蒙　塔　诺　他奶奶！我还在流着血；我伤重得将死。
奥　赛　罗　停住，为你们的生命！
伊　耶　戈　停住，喂哟，副将军！大人！蒙塔诺！
　　　　　　　　大人们！你们忘怀了一切身份、
　　　　　　　　职务的感觉吗？停住！将军有话
　　　　　　　　要对你们说；停住，你们好意思！
奥　赛　罗　嗳哟，干什么，喂！怎样开的头？
　　　　　　　　我们可成了土耳其人，对我们自己
　　　　　　　　干出了上天不叫土耳其人做的事？
　　　　　　　　若知道什么是基督徒的羞耻，就丢开

He that stirs next to carve for his own rage
Holds his soul light; he dies upon his motion. —
Silence that dreadful bell; it frights the isle
From her propriety. — What is the matter, masters? —
Honest Iago, that look'st dead with grieving,
Speak, who began this? on thy love, I charge thee.

Iago I do not know; — friends all but now, even now,
In quarter, and in terms like bride and groom
Devesting them for bed; and then, but now—
As if some planet had unwitted men, —
Swords out, and tilting one at other's breast
In opposition bloody. I cannot speak
Any beginning to this peevish odds;
And would in action glorious I had lost
Those legs that brought me to a part of it!

Othello How comes it, Michael, you are thus forgot?

Cassio I pray you, pardon me; I cannot speak.

Othello Worthy Montano, you were wont be civil;
The gravity and stillness of your youth
The world hath noted, and your name is great
In mouths of wisest censure; what's the matter,
That you unlace your reputation thus,
And spend your rich opinion for the name
Of a night-brawler? give me answer to it.

Montano Worthy Othello, I am hurt to danger;
Your officer, Iago, can inform you, —
While I spare speech, which something now offends
   me, —
Of all that I do know; nor know I aught
By me that's said or done amiss this night;
Unless self-charity be sometimes a vice,

这野蛮的争闹；谁再动一动去纵任
他自己的暴怒，就把他的灵魂当儿戏；
谁动谁就死。停止那可怕的钟声！
它惊动全岛，使它不得有安宁。
为了什么事，诸君？诚实的伊耶戈，
你看来伤心得要死，你说，谁开始
这般轰闹的？我命令你，凭你的爱顾。

伊 耶 戈　我不知道；只刚才，还没一会儿，
都是好好的朋友；友好相处得
像新郎新妇一般，在宽衣上床；
于是，只刚才，——像什么星宿夺去了
人们的理智，——彼此利剑出鞘来，
你刺我戳，对准着胸腔，来一场
血淋淋的格斗。这番无谓的争吵
怎么样开始，我说不上来；但愿
我在光荣的战阵中失去这两条腿，
因为是它们带我来看到这光景！

奥 赛 罗　怎么会，玛格尔，你这般忘怀了自己？

凯 昔 欧　我请您原谅；我说不上来。

奥 赛 罗　高贵的蒙塔诺，您平素谦谨有礼；
您年青时日的庄严与沉静，世人
都知晓，在极有明智舆论的众人间
您声名藉藉：什么事招致您这般
玷辱您自己的令誉，把宝贵的声华
抛弃掉，换一个夜间闹街者的徽号？
请给我回答。

蒙 塔 诺　高贵的奥赛罗，我受伤得危险；伊耶戈，
您当班的军官，能把经过告诉您，
我所知道的一切我此刻得俭约，
因为现在我说话颇有点伤痛；
我不知我今夜说错、做错了什么事，
除非对自己爱护有时是非行，

And to defend ourselves it be a sin
When violence assails us.

Othello   Now, by heaven,
My blood begins my safer guides to rule;
And passion, having my best judgement collied,
Assays to lead the way. If I once stir,
Or do but lift this arm, the best of you
Shall sink in my rebuke. Give me to know
How this foul rout began, who set it on;
And he that is approv'd in this offense,
Though he had twinn'd with me, both at a birth,
Shall lose me. — What! in a town of war
Yet wild, the people's hearts brimful of fear,
To manage private and domestic quarrel,
In night, and on the court and guard of safety!
'Tis monstrous. — Iago, who began't?

Montano   If partially affin'd, or leagu'd in office,
Thou dost deliver more or less than truth,
Thou art no soldier.

Iago   Touch me not so near:
I had rather have this tongue cut from my mouth
Than it should do offence to Michael Cassio;
Yet, I persuade myself, to speak the truth
Shall nothing wrong him. — Thus it is, general.
Montano and myself being in speech,
There comes a fellow crying out for help;
And Cassio following him with determin'd sword,
To execute upon him. Sir, this gentleman
Steps in to Cassio and entreats his pause:
Myself the crying fellow did pursue,
Lest by his clamour, — as it so fell out, —
The town might fall in fright: he, swift of foot,
Outran my purpose; and I return'd the rather
For that I heard the clink and fall of swords,
And Cassio high in oath; which till to-night

强暴来袭时自卫是一桩罪愆。

奥 赛 罗 如今，青天在上，我的火性开始在
主宰我较安全的指引者，而我的激情
乌黑了我最好的判断，试着要领路。
我只需动一下，或只要举起这胳膊，
你们之中最强的将受罚而丧命。
给我知道这可耻的轰闹是怎样
开的头，是谁先起哄；谁若经证实
犯了这过误，即令跟我是同胞
一母所双生，他也将丧失我。什么！
在一个有战事的城中，还动荡不定，
人民的心里满都是惶恐，来安排
私人间内部的争吵，而且在夜晚，
在保安的主防厅，警卫的岗哨之上！
真骇人听闻。伊耶戈，是谁开的头？

蒙 塔 诺 假使为偏爱所羁縻，或者因职位
关连而友好，你说过了实事或不及，
你就算不得是军人。

伊 耶 戈 　　　　　　莫触及我痛处；
我但愿这舌头从我口中剜出来，
也不肯叫它损及玛格尔·凯昔欧；
可是，我认为说真话并不损害他。
事情是这样，将军。蒙塔诺和我
正在说话，有个人叫喊着呼救，
凯昔欧跟随着，用剑断然邀击他。
将军，这位大人跨几步挨近凯昔欧，
请求他停住，而加以考虑；我自己
当即追赶那叫喊者，怕他的喧嚷，
张扬开去，会使这城厢受惊恐；
那个人，步子快，一溜烟失去了踪影，
而我打回头，更因为听到了剑刃
玎玎砍击声，凯昔欧则高声赌咒，

I ne'er might say before. When I came back, —
For this was brief, — I found them close together,
At blow and thrust; even as again they were
When you yourself did part them.
More of this matter cannot I report; —
But men are men; the best sometimes forget: —
Though Cassio did some little wrong to him, —
As men in rage strike those that wish them best, —
Yet surely Cassio, I believe, receiv'd
From him that fled some strange indignity,
Which patience could not pass.

Othello   I know, Iago,
Thy honesty and love doth mince this matter,
Making it light to Cassio. Cassio, I love thee;
But never more be officer of mine. —
                    [*Re-enter* Desdemona, *attended.*]
Look, if my gentle love be not rais'd up! —
[*To* Cassio] I'll make thee an example.

Desdemona   What's the matter?

Othello   All's well now, sweeting; come away
          to bed.   [*To* Montano, *who is led off.*]
Sir, for your hurts, myself will be your surgeon:
Lead him off.
Iago, look with care about the town,
And silence those whom this vile brawl distracted. —
Come, Desdemona: 'tis the soldiers' life
To have their balmy slumbers wak'd with strife.
                    [*Exeunt all but* Iago *and* Cassio.]

Iago   What, are you hurt, lieutenant?

Cassio   Ay, past all surgery.

Iago   Marry, heaven forbid!

Cassio   Reputation, reputation, reputation! O, I have
          lost my reputation! I have lost the immortal part of
          myself, and what remains is bestial. — My reputa-
          tion, Iago, my reputation!

Iago   As I am an honest man, I thought you had
          received some bodily wound; there is more sense

那在今夜以前我从未见到过。

当我回来时，——这其间经过极短暂，——

我看见他们逼近在一起，相砍相刺，

正如同您自己分开他们时一个样。

比这还多的经过我报告不上来；

但人还是人；最好的有时也忘怀；

虽然凯昔欧对他稍有所不当，

正如盛怒者打那些愿他们好的人，

但我信，必然凯昔欧自那个逃跑者

受到了惊人的侮辱，忍耐所不能容。

奥　赛　罗　我知道，伊耶戈，你的诚实和友爱

减轻了这件事，放松了凯昔欧责任。

凯昔欧，我爱你；但决勿再当我的副将。

〔玳思狄莫娜与随从人等上。

瞧吧，我可爱的小妹可不给闹醒了！

〔向凯昔欧〕我要使你做鉴戒的榜样。

玳思狄莫娜　　　　　　　　　　什么事？

奥　赛　罗　现在一切都好了，亲爱的；去睡吧。

〔向蒙塔诺，蒙塔诺被扶走〕

大人，您的伤，我自己将为您包扎。

扶他走。

伊耶戈，小心看顾着坊厢，安抚

这恶劣的轰闹所惊动起来的百姓。

来吧，玳思狄莫娜；过军人的生涯，

温馨的睡眠难免被争吵所破坏。

〔除伊耶戈、凯昔欧外，俱下。

伊　耶　戈　什么，您受伤了吗，副将军？

凯　昔　欧　是的；什么外科手术都医不好。

伊　耶　戈　圣处女，上天莫叫那样！

凯　昔　欧　名誉，名誉，名誉！啊唷！我的名誉丧失掉了。我丧失了我自己神灵的部分，而留下来的是兽性的。我的名誉，伊耶戈，我的名誉！

伊　耶　戈　正如我是个诚实人，我以为您受到了身体上的创伤；

in that than in reputation. Reputation is an idle and most false imposition; oft got without merit and lost without deserving: you have lost no reputation at all, unless you repute yourself such a loser. What, man! there are ways to recover the general again: you are but now cast in his mood, a punishment more in policy than in malice; even so as one would beat his offenceless dog to affright an imperious lion: sue to him again, and he is yours.

Cassio I will rather sue to be despised than to deceive so good a commander with so slight, so drunken, and so indiscreet an officer. Drunk? and speak parrot? and squabble? swagger? swear? and discourse fustian with one's own shadow? — O thou invisible spirit of wine, if thou hast no name to be known by, let us call thee devil!

Iago What was he that you followed with your sword? What had he done to you?

Cassio I know not.

Iago Is't possible?

Cassio I remember a mass of things, but nothing distinctly; a quarrel, but nothing wherefore. — O God, that men should put an enemy in their mouths to steal away their brains! that we should, with joy, pleasance, revel, and applause, transform ourselves into beasts!

Iago Why, but you are now well enough: how came you thus recovered?

Cassio It hath pleased the devil drunkenness to give place to the devil wrath: one unperfectness shows me another, to make me frankly despise myself.

Iago Come, you are too severe a moraler: as the time, the place, and the condition of this country stands, I could heartily wish this had not befallen; but since it is as it is, mend it for your own good.

Cassio I will ask him for my place again; — he shall tell

那个要比名誉更加受不了痛苦。名誉是个无聊而且最奸诈不可靠的骗子；得来并不靠功勋道德，失掉它时则不应当遭受到责罚；您并未损失掉什么名誉，除非您把自己当作这样一个损失者。什么，老兄！还有办法使将军对您回心转意；您只是刚才在他恼怒中被免了职，那责罚是出于处置公务的明智，并非他对您有什么恶意；正好比一个人会打他自己那条无辜的狗，去吓唬一头威胁他的狮子似的。只要央求他，他又会跟您和好如初。

凯　昔　欧　我宁愿央求被他所鄙弃，却不愿欺骗这样好一位首长，让他再起用这样个无足轻重、爱酗酒、不检点的部属。醉了！鹦鹉学舌，瞎说一阵子！吵架，吹牛，赌咒，跟自己的影儿高谈阔论些废话！啊，你这看不见的酒精灵！假如你没有可以给称呼的名号，就让我们叫你魔鬼！

伊　耶　戈　您挥着剑跟在他背后追赶的，那是个什么样人？他对您做了什么事？

凯　昔　欧　我不知道。

伊　耶　戈　这可能吗？

凯　昔　欧　我记得一大堆事，但是都不大清楚；记得吵了一回架，但不知为什么。啊，上帝！人们会把一个敌人放在自己嘴里，去偷走他们的头脑；我们居然会用欢快、作乐、庆祝和赞颂去把我们自己变成畜生。

伊　耶　戈　哎，可是您此刻是够正常的了；您怎么会这般清醒的？

凯　昔　欧　那酒醉魔君高兴让位给恼怒暴君；一个缺陷指给我看另一个缺陷，使我毫不隐讳地鄙薄我自己。

伊　耶　戈　算了，您是个过于严厉的道学说教者。就这时间，这地点，这地方的情势而言，我诚心愿意这件事没有发生，但既然已经如此，为您自己的利益起见，还是补救为妙。

凯　昔　欧　我准定请求他还给我这个位置；他准定会告诉我

me I am a drunkard! Had I as many mouths as Hy-
dra, such an answer would stop them all. To be now
a sensible man, by and by a fool, and presently a
beast! O strange! — Every inordinate cup is unbless'd,
and the ingredient is a devil.

Iago Come, come, good wine is a good familiar creature,
if it be well used: exclaim no more against it. And,
good lieutenant, I think you think I love you.

Cassio I have well approved it, sir. — I drunk!

Iago You, or any man living, may be drunk at a time,
man. I'll tell you what you shall do. Our general's
wife is now the general; — I may say so in this respect, for that he hath devoted and given up himself
to the contemplation, mark, and denotement of her
parts and graces: — confess yourself freely to her; importune her help to put you in your place again: she is
of so free, so kind, so apt, so blessed a disposition,
she holds it a vice in her goodness not to do more than
she is requested: this broken joint between you and
her husband entreat her to splinter; and, my fortunes
against any lay worth naming, this crack of your love
shall grow stronger than it was before.

Cassio You advise me well.

Iago I protest, in the sincerity of love and honest kind-
ness.

Cassio I think it freely; and betimes in the morning I will
beseech the virtuous Desdemona to undertake for me; I
am desperate of my fortunes if they check me here.

Iago You are in the right. Good-night, lieutenant; I
must to the watch.

Cassio Good night, honest Iago.   [*Exit.*]

Iago And what's he, then, that says I play the villain?
When this advice is free I give and honest,
Probal to thinking, and, indeed, the course
To win the Moor again? For 'tis most easy

我是个醉鬼！假使我的嘴巴同九头妖怪一般多，
他这句话会把它们全堵住。此刻是个有头脑的人，
等一下变成个傻瓜，再不久变成头畜生！啊，怪事！
每一杯过量的酒是被诅咒过的，里边的成分是一个
魔鬼。

伊　耶　戈　算了，算了；好酒是个家常的宠儿，有益于人，如果是
好好地饮用；别再叫骂它了。而且，亲爱的副将军，
我想您认为我是爱护您的。

凯　昔　欧　我已经好好体验到这个，足下。我醉了！

伊　耶　戈　您或是不论哪一个活着的人在某个时候可能会喝
醉，老兄。我告诉您您该怎么办。我们将军的娇妻
如今是将军：关于这一层我可以这么说，因为他专心
而且竭诚于沉思、目注与供奉她的窈窕与美慧：您去
对她尽情地忏悔；对她恳求；她会设法将您安置在原
来的位置上。她赋性如此柔和，如此温蔼，如此慈
祥，如此圣洁，她会以为不把您恳求她的做过了头，
便是她美德里一个罪过。央求她将您和她丈夫之间
断了的关节缚扎起来；我把我的好运跟任何值得一
提的赌注相抵，你们感情上的破裂将长得比以前更
加坚固。

凯　昔　欧　你替我设想得周到。

伊　耶　戈　我断言，这是出于恳切或友情以及诚实的善意。

凯　昔　欧　我诚心考虑一下；明晨一早我要恳请贤德的玳思狄
莫娜替我设法。我将对我自己的命运绝望，若是它
在这件事上抑制我使不得成功。

伊　耶　戈　您说得对。晚安，副将军；我一定得去警卫了。

凯　昔　欧　晚安，诚实的伊耶戈！　　　　　　　　　　〔下。

伊　耶　戈　我这番献计既天真无邪，又老实
诚恳，想来合情而合理，果真是
重新取宠于摩尔人的行径，那么，
说我行为如恶棍的任何人，他自己
将成为怎样的人？在正当的恳求上

The inclining Desdemona to subdue
In any honest suit: she's fram'd as fruitful
As the free elements. And then for her
To win the Moor, —were't to renounce his baptism,
All seals and symbols of redeemed sin, —
His soul is so enfetter'd to her love
That she may make, unmake, do what she list,
Even as her appetite shall play the god
With his weak function. How am I, then, a villain
To counsel Cassio to this parallel course,
Directly to his good? Divinity of hell!
When devils will the blackest sins put on,
They do suggest at first with heavenly shows,
As I do now: for whiles this honest fool
Plies Desdemona to repair his fortune,
And she for him pleads strongly to the Moor,
I'll pour this pestilence into his ear, —
That she repeals him for her body's lust;
And by how much she strives to do him good,
She shall undo her credit with the Moor.
So will I turn her virtue into pitch;
And out of her own goodness make the net
That shall enmesh them all.
                    [*Enter* Roderigo.]
                    How now, Roderigo!

Roderigo   I do follow here in the chase, not like a hound
that hunts, but one that fills up the cry. My money is
almost spent; I have been to-night exceedingly well
cudgelled; and I think the issue will be—I shall have
so much experience for my pains: and so, with no
money at all and a little more wit, return again to
Venice.

Iago   How poor are they that have not patience!

要劝说有好意的玳思狄莫娜首肯，
那是非常容易的；她生来就宽怀
大度，如阳光天风雨露。然后，
由她去劝服摩尔人，即令要他
去否认曾受洗入教，——那我们罪孽
得救赎的一切证明和象征，——他灵魂
是这般束缚在对她的情爱上，她能
叫它长，叫它短，要它怎样就怎样，
正如她的心血来潮能任意奴役
他薄弱的心神运用。那么，献计于
凯昔欧，同他的意向相契合，为他好，
我怎么会成个奸人？地狱的神学！
魔鬼们在投射出罪孽之前，一定得
先用圣洁的假象来勾引，正如我
现在一个样；因为这诚实的傻瓜
殷求玳思狄莫娜恢复他时运、
而她为着他极力对摩尔人恳请时，
我将把这害毒注入他耳朵里头去，
说她要将他复职，为肉体的淫欲；
那么，她越是出力想对他行好，
她将越使摩尔人对她丧好感。
我便将这般叫她的美德变漆黑，
用她的好处做成一口网，把他们
一网打尽。

　　　　　[洛窦列谷上。
　　　　做什么，洛窦列谷？

洛窦列谷　我跟着在这儿打猎，不像头真是在狩猎的猎狗，倒像头咙咙吠着、专为凑热闹而来的叫狗。我的钱差不多用光了；我今晚上棍子已吃得够了；我想结果将是，我付出如许麻烦，将得到这么多经验；而于是，囊空如洗，但长了点智慧，我要重新回到威尼斯去。

伊　耶　戈　那些没有忍耐的人儿多可怜！

What wound did ever heal but by degrees?
Thou know'st we work by wit, and not by witchcraft;
And wit depends on dilatory time.
Does't not go well? Cassio hath beaten thee,
And thou, by that small hurt, hast cashier'd Cassio;
Though other things grow fair against the sun,
Yet fruits that blossom first will first be ripe:
Content thyself awhile. — By the mass, 'tis morning;
Pleasure and action make the hours seem short. —
Retire thee; go where thou art billeted:
Away, I say; thou shalt know more hereafter;
Nay, get thee gone.

[*Exit* Roderigo.]

Two things are to be done, —
My wife must move for Cassio to her mistress;
I'll set her on;
Myself the while to draw the Moor apart,
And bring him jump when he may Cassio find
Soliciting his wife. Ay, that's the way;
Dull not device by coldness and delay.

[*Exit.*]

什么创伤会痊愈,除非逐渐好?
你知道我们做事用机巧,不使用
魔法,而机巧要靠迁延的时间。
事情不进展得很好吗? 凯昔欧打了你,
而你,因那点小伤,黜掉他的职。
虽然别的东西在阳光里长得好,
但是先开花的果子总会先成熟:
暂时把心情放宽敞。凭弥撒,早晨了;
愉快与行动使时间显得短。休息去;
去到你给分配的宿舍里。去吧,我说;
今后你将知道更多的后事:
别耽着,去你的。　　　　　　　[洛窦列谷下。
　　　　　两件事需得要去做,
我老婆一定得替凯昔欧向她
主妇去说情;我准要激得她去;
同时,我自己要将摩尔人引开,
要领他正在那时节眼见凯昔欧
在求他老婆;对呀,那正是方法:
莫让冷漠与迁延迟钝我的计划。　　　[下。

ACT III.

SCENE I. *Before the Castle.*

[*Enter* Cassio *and some* Musicians.]

Cassio Masters, play here, — I will content your pains,
Something that's brief; and bid *Good-morrow*, *general.*

[*Music.*]

[*Enter* Clown.]

Clown Why, masters, have your instruments been in Na-
ples, that they speak i' the nose thus?

First Musician How, sir, how!

Clown Are these, I pray you, wind instruments?

First Musician Ay, marry, are they, sir.

Clown O, thereby hangs a tale.

First Musician Whereby hangs a tale, sir?

Clown Marry, sir, by many a wind instrument that I
know. But, masters, here's money for you: and the
general so likes your music, that he desires you, for
love's sake, to make no more noise with it.

First Musician Well, sir, we will not.

Clown If you have any music that may not be heard, to't
again: but, as they say, to hear music the general
does not greatly care.

第 三 幕

第 一 景

[堡垒前]

[凯昔欧与乐人数人上。

凯 昔 欧 诸位乐师,在这里演奏吧,我自会
酬谢你们的辛劳;奏一支短曲;
然后说,"早安,将军。"

[彼等进行演奏,小丑上。

小　丑 哎,乐师们,你们的乐器可是从那坡利来的吗,
它们的鼻音这么重?

乐 人 甲 怎么,先生,怎么?

小　丑 我请问,这些可是吹奏乐器吗?

乐 人 甲 不错,凭圣处女,它们是的,先生。

小　丑 啊!那上头挂一条尾巴。

乐 人 甲 什么上头挂一条尾巴,先生?

小　丑 凭圣处女,先生,我所知道的好些支吹奏乐器上挂得
有。但是,乐师们,这里有点喜封给你们;将军那么
样爱听你们的乐曲,他愿意你们,为爱他起见,莫再
闹响了吧。

乐 人 甲 很好,先生,我们不吹奏就是了。

小　丑 假如你们有什么听不见的音乐,再来一点倒不要紧;
可是,他们说,将军不大高兴听音乐。

First Musician　We have none such, sir.

Clown　Then put up your pipes in your bag, for I'll away:
go, vanish into air, away!

　　　　　　　　　　　　　　　[*Exeunt* Musicians.]

Cassio　Dost thou hear, mine honest friend?

Clown　No, I hear not your honest friend; I hear you.

Cassio　Pr'ythee, keep up thy quillets. There's a poor
piece of gold for thee: if the gentlewoman that attends
the general's wife be stirring, tell her there's one Cassio entreats her a little favour of speech: wilt thou do
this?

Clown　She is stirring, sir; if she will stir hither I shall
seem to notify unto her.

Cassio　Do, good my friend.　　　　　[*Exit* Clown.]

　　　　　　　　　[*Enter* Iago.]

　　　　　　　　　　　　In happy time, Iago.

Iago　You have not been a-bed, then?

Cassio　Why, no; the day had broke
Before we parted. I have made bold, Iago,
To send in to your wife: my suit to her
Is, that she will to virtuous Desdemona
Procure me some access.

Iago　　　　　I'll send her to you presently;
And I'll devise a mean to draw the Moor
Out of the way, that your converse and business
May be more free.

Cassio　I humbly thank you for't. [*Exit* Iago.] I
never knew
A Florentine more kind and honest.

　　　　　　　　[*Enter* Emilia.]

Emilia　Good-morrow, good lieutenant; I am sorry
For your displeasure; but all will sure be well.
The general and his wife are talking of it;
And she speaks for you stoutly: the Moor replies
That he you hurt is of great fame in Cyprus

乐 人 甲　我们没有那样的音乐,先生。

小 　 丑　那就把你们的喇叭装进荷包里去吧,因为我要走了。
　　　　　去;往空气里消失掉;走吧!

　　　　　　　　　　　　　　　　　　　　　　［众乐人下。

凯 昔 欧　你听到吗,我的诚实的朋友?

小 　 丑　不,我没有听到您的诚实朋友;我听到您在说话。

凯 昔 欧　请不妨继续辩驳打趣下去。这儿有一小块赏金给
　　　　　你。假使那个侍候将军娘娘的陪娘已经起身了的
　　　　　话,告诉她有个名叫凯昔欧的请她借光讲一句话:你
　　　　　可能这么办吗?

小 　 丑　她起身了,先生:假如她起到这儿来,我会要好像是
　　　　　告诉她的。

凯 昔 欧　告诉她,我的好朋友。　　　　　　　　［小丑下。

　　　　　　［伊耶戈上。

　　　　　　　　　　碰得巧,伊耶戈。

伊 耶 戈　您没有去睡觉吗,那么?

凯 昔 欧　哎,没有;我们分手前天已经
　　　　　发亮。我冒昧,伊耶戈,叫人传口信
　　　　　给你的太太;我请求她替我设法
　　　　　引见贤淑的玳思狄莫娜。

伊 耶 戈　　　　　　　　　　我马上
　　　　　叫她来见您;我想法使那摩尔人
　　　　　不在跟前,使你们谈话和做事
　　　　　较自由。

凯 昔 欧　　　　　　我对你十分感谢。［伊耶戈下］我从未
　　　　　见过个萧洛伦斯人更好心、更诚实。

　　　　　　　　　　　　　　　　　［爱米丽亚上。

爱 米 丽 亚　早安,亲爱的副将军;我为您遭不快
　　　　　愧惜;可是,一切会重新好转。
　　　　　将军同他的夫人正在谈这件事,
　　　　　她极力替您讲话:摩尔人回说,
　　　　　您刺伤的那人在塞浦路斯名声大,

And great affinity, and that, in wholesome wisdom,
He might not but refuse you; but he protests he loves you
And needs no other suitor but his likings
To take the safest occasion by the front
To bring you in again.

Cassio   Yet, I beseech you, —
If you think fit, or that it may be done, —
Give me advantage of some brief discourse
With Desdemona alone.

Emilia   Pray you, come in:
I will bestow you where you shall have time
To speak your bosom freely.

Cassio   I am much bound to you.

[*Exeunt.*]

SCENE II. *A Room in the Castle.*

[*Enter* Othello, Iago, *and* Gentlemen.]

Othello These letters give, Iago, to the pilot;
And by him do my duties to the senate:
That done, I will be walking on the works;
Repair there to me.

Iago   Well, my good lord, I'll do't.

Othello This fortification, gentlemen, — shall we see't?

Gentlemen We'll wait upon your lordship.

[*Exeunt.*]

SCENE III. *The Garden of the Castle.*

[*Enter* Desdemona, Cassio, *and* Emilia.]

Desdemona Be thou assured, good Cassio, I will do
All my abilities in thy behalf.

Emilia Good madam, do: I warrant it grieves my husband

关系好，以合理的明智来计较，他不能
不对您拒绝；但是他矢言他爱您，
除了他自己的爱赏，不需要任何人
来恳请他抓住最可靠的机会再用您。

凯　昔　欧　可是我请您，若是您以为可以，
或是可以办的话，让我有方便
跟玳思狄莫娜独自简略谈几句。

爱米丽亚　请您进来：我来领您到那里去，
您能有时间去倾吐胸怀。

凯　昔　欧　　　　　　　　我非常感激。

〔同下。

第　二　景

〔堡垒内之一室〕
〔奥赛罗、伊耶戈与士子等上。〕

奥　赛　罗　把这封书束，伊耶戈，交给舵工，
托他替我向知政事公署致敬；
那事办完时，我将在炮台上散步；
去那里找我。

伊　耶　戈　　　　　　是的，主公，当遵命。

奥　赛　罗　这炮台，诸位，我们可能去看看？

士　子　等　我们准要陪侍您钧座。　　　　〔同下。

第　三　景

〔堡垒内之花园〕
〔玳思狄莫娜、凯昔欧与爱米丽亚上。〕

玳思狄莫娜　你可以相信，善良的凯昔欧，我准会
尽力帮你的忙。

爱米丽亚　　　　　　亲爱的娘娘，
请务必：我保证，我丈夫也为此伤心，

As if the cause were his.

Desdemona O, that's an honest fellow. — Do not doubt, Cassio,
But I will have my lord and you again
As friendly as you were.

Cassio   Bounteous madam,
Whatever shall become of Michael Cassio,
He's never anything but your true servant.

Desdemona I know't, — I thank you. You do love my lord;
You have known him long; and be you well assur'd
He shall in strangeness stand no farther off
Than in a politic distance.

Cassio   Ay, but, lady,
That policy may either last so long,
Or feed upon such nice and waterish diet,
Or breed itself so out of circumstance,
That, I being absent, and my place supplied,
My general will forget my love and service.

Desdemona Do not doubt that; before Emilia here
I give thee warrant of thy place; assure thee,
If I do vow a friendship, I'll perform it
To the last article; my lord shall never rest;
I'll watch him tame, and talk him out of patience;
His bed shall seem a school, his board a shrift;
I'll intermingle everything he does
With Cassio's suit; therefore be merry, Cassio;
For thy solicitor shall rather die
Than give thy cause away.

[*Enter* Othello *and* Iago.]

Emilia Madam, here comes my lord.

Cassio   Madam, I'll take my leave.

仿佛这事情就是他的一般。

玳思狄莫娜 啊！那是个诚实人。别怀疑，凯昔欧，
我准使我官人跟您友好如初。

凯 昔 欧 大度的夫人，不论我玛格尔·凯昔欧
将成为怎样的人，他决非别的，
总是您真诚的仆人。

玳思狄莫娜 我知道；多谢您。
您爱我的官人；您认识了他已长久；
您可以确信，他将不再会对您
萧疏冷淡，只除了暂时保一阵
拘谨的距离。

凯 昔 欧 不错，但是，夫人，
那为政的机巧也许会拉得那么久，
或则因未得喂养而滋长无从，
或者那么多事故会发生，经一延
再延，而同时我又不在他跟前，
且位置已为人所占，那时节将军
将会忘怀我对他的爱戴和忠勤。

玳思狄莫娜 莫疑虑会那样；在爱米丽亚面前，
我保证你的职位。你可以相信，
我如果郑重允承了友善相调处，
我定将履行到最后的字句；我官人
将不得安休；我将练鹞子一般
使他定性，讲得他没有个安宁；
他的床将像个学堂，他的餐桌
像个忏悔所；他所做的任何事情里
我将混合你的请求。所以，凯昔欧，
心情愉快吧；你的代言人宁死
也不会将你的利益放弃。
〔奥赛罗与伊耶戈在远处上。

爱 米 丽 亚 娘娘，将爷来了。

凯 昔 欧 夫人，我要告辞了。

Desdemona Why, stay, and hear me speak.

Cassio Madam, not now. I am very ill at ease,
Unfit for mine own purposes.

Desdemona Well, do your discretion.

[*Exit* Cassio.]

Iago Ha! I like not that.

Othello   What dost thou say?

Iago Nothing, my lord: or if—I know not what.

Othello Was not that Cassio parted from my wife?

Iago Cassio, my lord! No, sure, I cannot think it,
That he would steal away so guilty-like,
Seeing you coming.

Othello   I do believe 'twas he.

Desdemona How now, my lord!
I have been talking with a suitor here,
A man that languishes in your displeasure.

Othello Who is't you mean?

Desdemona   Why, your lieutenant, Cassio. Good my
        lord,
If I have any grace or power to move you,
His present reconciliation take;
For if he be not one that truly loves you,
That errs in ignorance and not in cunning,
I have no judgement in an honest face:
I pr'ythee, call him back.

Othello   Went he hence now?

Desdemona Ay, sooth; so humbled
That he hath left part of his grief with me
To suffer with him. Good love, call him back.

Othello Not now, sweet Desdemon; some other time.

Desdemona But shall't be shortly?

Othello   The sooner, sweet, for you.

玳思狄莫娜	哎,待着,听我说。
凯 昔 欧	夫人,此刻不了;我很不舒服,
	不便替自己说话。
玳思狄莫娜	那么,您觉得怎样合式随便吧。 [凯昔欧下。
伊 耶 戈	嘻! 我不高兴那个。
奥 赛 罗	你说什么?
伊 耶 戈	没有事,主公:或许——我不知道什么。
奥 赛 罗	莫非凯昔欧从我妻那里离开?
伊 耶 戈	凯昔欧,主公? 当然不会,我不能
	设想他会看见您到来而偷偷
	溜走,像犯了罪似的。
奥 赛 罗	我相信是他。
玳思狄莫娜	怎么说,官人?
	我在此跟你的一个恳请人在说话,
	他为你的不快而在烦恼。
奥 赛 罗	你意下指谁?
玳思狄莫娜	哎,你副将凯昔欧。亲爱的官人,
	我若有什么好处或能力来打动
	于你,请接受他这下子来求情请罪;
	因为他如果不是真心爱戴你,——
	那疏误是出于无知,并非故意,——
	那我就识不得一个诚实的面孔。
	请叫他回来吧。
奥 赛 罗	他刚从这里走吗?
玳思狄莫娜	不错,果真是;这么样低首下心,
	他将一部分苦恼留下来给我,
	和他一同受罪。亲爱的哥哥,
	叫他回来吧。
奥 赛 罗	现在不,亲爱的小妹;
	等别的时候。
玳思狄莫娜	但准定最近吗?
奥 赛 罗	不会久,

Desdemona Shall't be to-night at supper?

Othello   No, not to-night.

Desdemona To-morrow dinner then?

Othello   I shall not dine at home;
I meet the captains at the citadel.

Desdemona   Why then to-morrow night; or Tuesday
    morn;
On Tuesday noon, or night; on Wednesday morn: —
I pr'ythee, name the time; but let it not
Exceed three days: in faith, he's penitent;
And yet his trespass, in our common reason, —
Save that, they say, the wars must make examples
Out of their best, — is not almost a fault
To incur a private check. When shall he come?
Tell me, Othello: I wonder in my soul,
What you would ask me, that I should deny,
Or stand so mammering on. What! Michael Cassio,
That came awooing with you; and so many a time,
When I have spoke of you dispraisingly,
Hath ta'en your part; — to have so much to do
To bring him in! Trust me, I could do much, —

Othello Pr'ythee, no more; let him come when he will;
I will deny thee nothing.

Desdemona   Why, this is not a boon;
'Tis as I should entreat you wear your gloves,
Or feed on nourishing dishes, or keep you warm,
Or sue to you to do a peculiar profit
To your own person: nay, when I have a suit
Wherein I mean to touch your love indeed,
It shall be full of poise and difficult weight,

亲爱的,为了你。

玳思狄莫娜 好不好今夜晚饭时?

奥 赛 罗 不,不在今夜。

玳思狄莫娜 那就在明天午饭时?

奥 赛 罗 我将不在家吃午饭;要跟联长们
在城防堡垒里碰头。

玳思狄莫娜 那么,就定在
明天晚上;或者在礼拜二早上;
礼拜二中午,或晚上;礼拜三早上:
请你定时间,但是别超过三天:
他的确悔悟前非;但他那错失,
按常理来说,——除非照他们的说法,
战争一定得把最好的人作鉴戒,——
几乎不是个该受私下里责备、
更莫说公开撤职的过误。让他
什么时候来? 告诉我,奥赛罗:我心里
在奇怪,什么事你要我去做,我会
拒绝,或这么犹豫不决。什么!
玛格尔·凯昔欧,他跟着你来,帮同
来求婚,好多次,当我谈起你来
责怪时,替你作辩解;叫他来见你,
得这么麻烦! 信任我,我能做好多——

奥 赛 罗 请你莫说了;他什么时候要来,
就让他来吧;我准定不会拒绝你。

玳思狄莫娜 哎也,这不该是一个恩赐;应当
如同我恳求你戴上手套,或是吃
营养的菜肴,或是把衣裳穿暖,
或者央求你做一件对你自己
特别有利的事情那样子;不光
这么说,当我有一桩恳求,为了它
我果真存心要试验你对我的爱时,
它应当富于分量与困难的重要性,

And fearful to be granted.

Othello   I will deny thee nothing:
Whereon, I do beseech thee, grant me this,
To leave me but a little to myself.

Desdemona Shall I deny you? no: farewell, my lord.

Othello   Farewell, my Desdemona: I'll come to thee
  straight.

Desdemona   Emilia, come. — Be as your fancies teach
  you;
Whate'er you be, I am obedient.

                              [*Exit with* Emilia.]

Othello Excellent wretch! Perdition catch my soul,
But I do love thee! and when I love thee not,
Chaos is come again.

Iago My noble lord, —

Othello   What dost thou say, Iago?

Iago Did Michael Cassio, when you woo'd my lady,
Know of your love?

Othello He did, from first to last: why dost thou ask?

Iago But for a satisfaction of my thought;
No further harm.

Othello   Why of thy thought, Iago?

Iago I did not think he had been acquainted with her.

Othello O, yes; and went between us very oft.

Iago Indeed!

Othello *Indeed*! ay, indeed: — discern'st thou aught in
  that?
Is he not honest?

Iago   Honest, my lord!

Othello   *Honest*! ay, *honest*.

Iago My lord, for aught I know.

Othello What dost thou think?

而且给与时，会引得你牵肠挂肚。

奥　赛　罗　我准定不会拒绝你；然后，要请你
答应我这一点，让我一个人独自
空着一会儿。

玳思狄莫娜　　　　　我可要拒绝你？不会：
再会，官人。

奥　赛　罗　　　　再会，我的玳思狄莫娜：
我马上来跟你在一起。

玳思狄莫娜　　　　　　爱米丽亚，来。
你喜欢怎样就怎样；不论你怎么样，
我总随顺你。　　　　　　〔与爱米丽亚同下。

奥　赛　罗　　　　绝妙的可怜的人儿！
我若不爱你，让毁灭摧折我的灵魂！
我只要片刻不爱你，浑沌又来了。

伊　耶　戈　尊贵的主公，——

奥　赛　罗　　　　　你说什么，伊耶戈？

伊　耶　戈　玛格尔·凯昔欧，当您向夫人求婚时：
他可知道你们之间有爱情吗？

奥　赛　罗　他知道，从头至尾：为什么你要问？

伊　耶　戈　只是为消释我思想里一个疑团；
没有其他的害处。

奥　赛　罗　　　　你想到什么，
伊耶戈？

伊　耶　戈　　　我想他不会跟她认识。

奥　赛　罗　啊！认识的；在我们之间常来往。

伊　耶　戈　当真！

奥　赛　罗　当真！是的，当真；你在那里头
看到了什么？难道他不荣誉不成？

伊　耶　戈　荣誉，主公！

奥　赛　罗　　　　荣誉！是啊，荣誉。

伊　耶　戈　主公，据我所知，——

奥　赛　罗　你怎么想法？

122

Iago   Think, my lord!

Othello   *Think, my lord*! By heaven, he echoes me,
As if there were some monster in his thought
Too hideous to be shown. — Thou dost mean something:
I heard thee say even now, — thou lik'dst not that,
When Cassio left my wife. What didst not like?
And when I told thee he was of my counsel
In my whole course of wooing, thou criedst, *Indeed*!
And didst contract and purse thy brow together,
As if thou then hadst shut up in thy brain
Some horrible conceit: if thou dost love me,
Show me thy thought.

Iago   My lord, you know I love you.

Othello   I think thou dost;
And, — for I know thou'rt full of love and honesty
And weigh'st thy words before thou giv'st them breath, —
Therefore these stops of thine fright me the more:
For such things in a false disloyal knave
Are tricks of custom; but in a man that's just
They're close delations, working from the heart,
That passion cannot rule.

Iago   For Michael Cassio,
I dare be sworn I think that he is honest.

Othello   I think so too.

Iago   Men should be what they seem;
Or those that be not, would they might seem none!

Othello   Certain, *men should be what they seem*.

Iago   Why, then, I think Cassio's an honest man.

Othello   Nay, yet there's more in this:
I pr'ythee, speak to me as to thy thinkings,

| 伊 耶 戈 | 想法，主公！ |

奥 赛 罗 　　　　　　　　"想法，
主公！"老天在上，他回响我的话，
仿佛他思想里有什么妖怪，太骇人，
不堪暴露。你意思该是指什么事：
我听你才说的，你不喜欢那个，
正当凯昔欧离开我妻子的时候；
你对什么不喜欢？而当我告诉你，
在我求婚的全程中他参与隐秘，
你叫道，"当真！"而且还颦眉蹙额，
仿佛那一忽儿在你的心中隐藏着
什么骇怕人的想法。如果你爱我，
告诉我你那个思想。

伊 耶 戈　　主公，您知道我爱您。

奥 赛 罗　　　　　　　　　我想你是
爱我的；因为我知道你很爱，很诚实，
说话之前权衡过字眼的重轻，
所以这些间断吓得我更厉害；
因为这些东西若出于不可靠、
不忠诚的坏人，乃是寻常的诡计，
但出自正直人，便成了秘密的表示，
发自心中，因不能控制住激情。

伊 耶 戈　　至于玛格尔·凯昔欧，我敢起誓，
我想他是诚实的。

奥 赛 罗　　　　　　　　我也这么想。

伊 耶 戈　　做人应当表里如一；而那些
不这样的人，我但愿他们莫那样。

奥 赛 罗　　当然，"做人应当表里如一。"

伊 耶 戈　　哎也，那我想凯昔欧是个诚实人。

奥 赛 罗　　不行，这里头还有别的东西。
我请你对我说话，像对你的思想
一般，怎么样思考便怎么样言宣，

As thou dost ruminate; and give thy worst of thoughts
The worst of words.

Iago   Good my lord, pardon me:
Though I am bound to every act of duty,
I am not bound to that all slaves are free to.
Utter my thoughts? Why, say they are vile and false; —
As where's that palace whereinto foul things
Sometimes intrude not? who has a breast so pure
But some uncleanly apprehensions
Keep leets and law-days, and in session sit
With meditations lawful?

Othello   Thou dost conspire against thy friend, Iago,
If thou but think'st him wrong'd and mak'st his ear
A stranger to thy thoughts.

Iago   I do beseech you, —
Though I perchance am vicious in my guess,
As, I confess, it is my nature's plague
To spy into abuses, and of my jealousy
Shape faults that are not, — that your wisdom yet,
From one that so imperfectly conceits,
Would take no notice; nor build yourself a trouble
Out of his scattering and unsure observance: —
It were not for your quiet nor your good,
Nor for my manhood, honesty, or wisdom,
To let you know my thoughts.

Othello   What dost thou mean?

Iago Good name in man and woman, dear my lord,
Is the immediate jewel of their souls:
Who steals my purse steals trash; 'tis something, noth-
     ing;
'Twas mine, 'tis his, and has been slave to thousands;

想到最坏处就用最坏的言辞。

伊耶戈　　亲爱的主公，原谅我；虽然我对于
　　　　　　每一个本份上的行动担负着义务，
　　　　　　但是我对于一切奴隶们都能够
　　　　　　自由的东西可也不承担责任。
　　　　　　显露我的思想？嗳呀，假定说，它们是
　　　　　　恶劣而假的呢；正好比，那样的宫廷
　　　　　　哪里有，肮脏东西永远不闯入？
　　　　　　谁有这样个纯洁的胸怀，其中
　　　　　　绝没有不洁的思想设立公堂，
　　　　　　跟合法的思想一同开庭审判？

奥赛罗　　你在阴谋反对你的朋友，伊耶戈，
　　　　　　假使明知他遭受到伤害，你却叫
　　　　　　他耳朵对你的思想成陌路。

伊耶戈　　　　　　　　　　　　　　我请您，
　　　　　　既然我在猜测里也许有错误，——
　　　　　　我承认窥探到人家的过误乃是我
　　　　　　心情里一桩烦恼，而我的疑惧
　　　　　　往往把不是错失形成为错失，——
　　　　　　就让您那片明智且莫理会这样个
　　　　　　判断不周全的人，也莫用他那些
　　　　　　随便、没把握的见解，来为您自己
　　　　　　找麻烦。告诉您我想些什么，对于您
　　　　　　心境的安宁和您的利益没好处，
　　　　　　对我的人格、荣誉和明智也不利。

奥赛罗　　你什么意思？

伊耶戈　　　　　　　　　不论对男人，对女人，
　　　　　　好名声，亲爱的主公，是他们灵魂
　　　　　　所直觉的瑰宝：谁偷了我的钱袋，
　　　　　　偷了件废物；那是件东西，却等于
　　　　　　没有；它昨儿是我的，今儿是他的，
　　　　　　曾经是千万人的奴才；但是窃取我

But he that filches from me my good name
Robs me of that which not enriches him
And makes me poor indeed.

Othello By heaven, I'll know thy thoughts.

Iago You cannot, if my heart were in your hand;
Nor shall not, whilst 'tis in my custody.

Othello Ha!

Iago   O, beware, my lord, of jealousy;
It is the green-ey'd monster which doth mock
The meat it feeds on; that cuckold lives in bliss
Who, certain of his fate, loves not his wronger;
But O, what damned minutes tells he o'er
Who dotes, yet doubts, suspects, yet strongly loves!

Othello O misery!

Iago Poor and content is rich, and rich enough;
But riches fineless is as poor as winter
To him that ever fears he shall be poor; —
Good heaven, the souls of all my tribe defend
From jealousy!

Othello   Why, why is this?
Think'st thou I'd make a life of jealousy,
To follow still the changes of the moon
With fresh suspicions? No; to be once in doubt
Is once to be resolv'd; exchange me for a goat
When I shall turn the business of my soul
To such exsufflicate and blown surmises,
Matching thy inference. 'Tis not to make me jealous,
To say my wife is fair, feeds well, loves company,
Is free of speech, sings, plays, and dances well;
Where virtue is, these are more virtuous;

好名声的那人，抢了我不能使他
变富有的东西，却使我真成了穷困。

奥　赛　罗　凭上天，我定要知道你的思想。

伊　耶　戈　您不能，即令我的心在您手掌中，
更何况那不会，当它还为我所保有。

奥　赛　罗　嘻！

伊　耶　戈　　　啊哟！主公呀，请小心妒忌；
那是头绿眼珠的妖怪，好比狸奴
玩耗子，它吃人之前总得把苦主
先将信将疑戏要得恼翻了天；
那偷汉娘子的老公，知道了自己
命运而不爱给他戴绿头巾的害人精，
乃是生活在极乐中；但是，啊哟！
那人儿可熬着多么可恨的恶时分，
他爱极，却心疑；疑心，又心爱得凶！

奥　赛　罗　啊也，惨痛！

伊　耶　戈　贫穷而知足，很富有，富有得足够，
但无边的财富对于总是怕自己
会穷困的那人儿便像是寒冬一个样。
亲爱的上苍，保佑我的族众莫受
妒忌的侵凌。

奥　赛　罗　　　　　为什么？为什么这样？
难道你以为我会以妒忌度生涯，
跟着月亮的盈亏而猜疑不已吗？
不会；怀疑过一次，就会消释掉
犹豫难决。把我当作一只羊，
假使我把我灵魂里的一些事情
变成那么空洞而臃肿的狐疑，
恰好符合你适才所讲的那模样。
说我的妻子长得美，吃得好，爱宾客，
好交谈、歌唱、吹弹、舞蹈得好，
并不会使我生嫉妒；本来有美德，

Nor from mine own weak merits will I draw
The smallest fear or doubt of her revolt;
For she had eyes and chose me. No, Iago;
I'll see before I doubt; when I doubt, prove;
And on the proof, there is no more but this, —
Away at once with love or jealousy!

Iago I am glad of it; for now I shall have reason
To show the love and duty that I bear you
With franker spirit: therefore, as I am bound,
Receive it from me: — I speak not yet of proof.
Look to your wife; observe her well with Cassio;
Wear your eye thus, not jealous nor secure:
I would not have your free and noble nature,
Out of self-bounty, be abus'd; look to't.
I know our country disposition well;
In Venice they do let heaven see the pranks
They dare not show their husbands; their best conscience
Is not to leave undone, but keep unknown.

Othello Dost thou say so?

Iago She did deceive her father, marrying you;
And when she seem'd to shake and fear your looks,
She loved them most.

Othello   And so she did.

Iago   Why, go to then;
She that, so young, could give out such a seeming,
To seal her father's eyes up close as oak, —
He thought 'twas witchcraft, — but I am much to blame;
I humbly do beseech you of your pardon
For too much loving you.

加上了这些,便是锦上添了花。
我也不会在自己微弱的优点上
生些微恐惧,或怀疑她也许会变心;
因为她生得有眼睛,拣中了我。
不会,伊耶戈,我怀疑之前先得看;
而怀疑的时候,就得要证明;等有了
证明,便再无别的,只有这样子,
爱情,或者妒忌,马上就完毕!

伊 耶 戈　我很高兴;因为我现在有理由
以更加坦率的热忱显示给您看
我对您的爱戴和崇敬;我义不容辞,
所以要请您接受;我此刻且不说
什么证据。瞧您的夫人;仔细
去观察她跟凯昔欧在一起;要这般
运用您的目光,莫嫉妒,也不可懈怠:
我不愿您那开诚豪爽的胸怀
为了它天生的慷慨而平白给糟蹋;
注意着:我很知道我乡邦的习性;
在我们威尼斯,她们开的玩笑
能给上天看,可不敢给丈夫们知道;
她们最好的良心不是不去做,
而是不给知道。

奥 赛 罗　　　　　　你这样说吗?
伊 耶 戈　她骗了她父亲,跟您结婚:正当她
似乎在发抖,怕见您相貌的时候,
却最爱它。

奥 赛 罗　　　　　她是这样。
伊 耶 戈　　　　　　　　哎也,那得了;
她这么年轻,能装出这样的外貌,
将她父亲的眼睛缝起来,密不
通风,他以为是魔法——但是我不该:
我恳请您原谅,我对您情意太深。

Othello   I am bound to thee for ever.

Iago   I see this hath a little dash'd your spirits.

Othello   Not a jot, not a jot.

Iago   Trust me, I fear it has.
I hope you will consider what is spoke
Comes from my love; but I do see you're mov'd: —
I am to pray you not to strain my speech
To grosser issues nor to larger reach
Than to suspicion.

Othello   I will not.

Iago   Should you do so, my lord,
My speech should fall into such vile success
Which my thoughts aim'd not. Cassio's my worthy friend: —
My lord, I see you're mov'd.

Othello   No, not much mov'd.
I do not think but Desdemona's honest.

Iago   Long live she so! and long live you to think so!

Othello   And yet, how nature erring from itself, —

Iago   Ay, there's the point: — as, — to be bold with you, —
Not to affect many proposed matches,
Of her own clime, complexion, and degree,
Whereto we see in all things nature tends, —
Foh! one may smell in such a will most rank,
Foul disproportion, thoughts unnatural: —
But pardon me: I do not in position
Distinctly speak of her; though I may fear,
Her will, recoiling to her better judgement,
May fall to match you with her country forms,
And happily repent.

Othello   Farewell, farewell:

奥　赛　罗　我永远对你感激。

伊　耶　戈　　　　　　　　　　我见到，这番话
使您心慌意乱。

奥　赛　罗　　　　　　　一点不，一点不。

伊　耶　戈　说实话，我怕的确是如此。我希望
您会考虑到我讲的都发自我的爱。
可是，我看您激动了；我还得请您
莫把我的话引伸到显见的结论
外面去，也不要扩大得超过了界限，
而仅止于怀疑为止。

奥　赛　罗　　　　　　　　我一定不会。

伊　耶　戈　假使您那样做，主公，我这话就会
堕入可恶的结局中，我绝无意向
它那样。凯昔欧是我上好的朋友——
主公，我看您激动了。

奥　赛　罗　　　　　　　　没有，不很激动：
我深信玳思狄莫娜玉洁冰清。

伊　耶　戈　但愿她长葆如此！长葆您这样想！

奥　赛　罗　可是，天性怎样会迷误失途，——

伊　耶　戈　果真，问题就在那上头：比如说，
跟您随便谈，同她自己在乡邦、
肤色、门第上相称的许多起提亲，
她都不喜欢，对那些，我们知道，
天性在各方面总该容易接近；
唔！这里边就能见到那病态
极严重的意向，邪恶的不正常，思想
乖戾。可是请原谅；我并不断言
这一定就是她，虽然我也许恐怕，
她那阵欲念，由她的天良作判断，
可能会将您同她的乡邦年少们
相比较，而幸而自感惭愧。

奥　赛　罗　　　　　　　　　　再会，

If more thou dost perceive, let me know more;

Set on thy wife to observe: leave me, Iago.

Iago [*Going.*] My lord, I take my leave.

Othello Why did I marry?—This honest creature doubt-
less

Sees and knows more, much more, than he unfolds.

Iago [*Returning.*] My lord, I would I might entreat your
honour

To scan this thing no further; leave it to time:

Though it be fit that Cassio have his place, —

For sure he fills it up with great ability, —

Yet, if you please to hold him off awhile,

You shall by that perceive him and his means:

Note if your lady strain his entertainment

With any strong or vehement importunity;

Much will be seen in that. In the meantime,

Let me be thought too busy in my fears, —

As worthy cause I have to fear I am, —

And hold her free, I do beseech your honour.

Othello Fear not my government.

Iago I once more take my leave.

[*Exit.*]

Othello This fellow's of exceeding honesty,

And knows all qualities, with a learned spirit,

Of human dealings. If I do prove her haggard,

Though that her jesses were my dear heartstrings,

I'd whistle her off, and let her down the wind

To prey at fortune. Haply, for I am black,

And have not those soft parts of conversation

That chamberers have; or for I am declin'd

Into the vale of years, —yet that's not much, —

She's gone; I am abus'd, and my relief

再会:你若是见到更多的事情,
请给我知道;要你的妻子监视着。
离开我,伊耶戈。

伊 耶 戈　　　　　[拟退去]主公,我即此告退。

奥 赛 罗　我为何要结婚? 这诚实的人儿,没疑问,
比他所讲的要见到、知道得多得多。

伊 耶 戈　[回步]主公,我但愿我能恳请钧座
莫再多考虑这件事;耐心等着看。
虽然凯昔欧有他的位置很合式,
因为他尽他的职守极能干,可是,
假使您高兴,且暂时莫给他复职,
您将借此看清他以及他的手段:
请注意您夫人是否坚决相劝
或殷切央求您恢复他的职位;
就在那里边很有些可观。同时,
还得请把我当作无事忙,乱忧疑,——
因为我恐怕有充分原因这么想,——
请钧座,且将她当作天真无辜。

奥 赛 罗　莫担心我的行动。

伊 耶 戈　　　　　　　再一次我告退。　　　　[下。

奥 赛 罗　这人诚实得不得了,且精研深究,
懂得人世间行为的一切情性;
如果我证实她野性难驭难驯,
即令她缚腿的皮带是我的心腱,
我也将顺着风势扔她入风中,
叫她去自找命运。也许,为了我
肤色黝黎,没有浮滑子弟们
那种软绵绵的举止言谈,或者,
为了我已经堕入年齿的幽谷中——
但那还不算深——所以她完蛋,我受骗;
而我要消除烦恼,唯有痛恨她。

Must be to loathe her. O curse of marriage,
That we can call these delicate creatures ours,
And not their appetites! I had rather be a toad,
And live upon the vapor of a dungeon,
Than keep a corner in the thing I love
For others' uses. Yet, 'tis the plague of great ones;
Prerogativ'd are they less than the base;
'Tis destiny unshunnable, like death;
Even then this forked plague is fated to us
When we do quicken. Desdemona comes;
If she be false, O, then heaven mocks itself! —
I'll not believe't.

                  [*Re-enter* Desdemona *and* Emilia.]

Desdemona How now, my dear Othello!
Your dinner, and the generous islanders
By you invited, do attend your presence.

Othello I am to blame.

Desdemona   Why do you speak so faintly?
Are you not well?

Othello I have a pain upon my forehead here.

Desdemona Faith, that's with watching; 'twill away a-
    gain;
Let me but bind it hard, within this hour
It will be well.

Othello   Your napkin is too little;
[*He puts the handkerchief from him, and she drops it.*]
Let it alone. Come, I'll go in with you.

Desdemona I am very sorry that you are not well.

                [*Exeunt* Othello *and* Desdemona.]

Emilia I am glad I have found this napkin;
This was her first remembrance from the Moor.
My wayward husband hath a hundred times
Woo'd me to steal it; but she so loves the token, —

唉哟,结婚的诅咒! 但愿我们
能叫这些可爱的人儿是我们的,
而不属于她们那好恶无常。我宁愿
做一只癞蛤蟆,靠地牢的濛气维生,
也不甘在心爱的人儿胸中局居
一隅,让别人去享用。但这是位重
权高者的苦恼;他们比职小位卑者
更没有保障;这命运无法逃避,
正好比死亡:我们一有了生命,
就命定要遭受绿头巾之劫。瞧吧!
她在那里来了。她如果不真心,啊!
那上苍在嘲弄它自己。我绝对不信。

                   〔玳思狄莫娜与爱米丽亚上。

玳思狄莫娜　　做什么? 亲爱的奥赛罗? 你的午餐,
以及你邀请岛上的贵宾们在等你。

奥　赛　罗　　要怪我不是。

玳思狄莫娜　　　　　　　为什么你说话这般
没精打采? 可是身子不爽快?

奥　赛　罗　　我前额这里边在痛。

玳思狄莫娜　　果真,那是为缺了睡;这就会不疼:
让我来绑紧着,不消一小时就会好。

奥　赛　罗　　你的手绢太小了:
〔将手帕拉去;帕堕地。〕
　　　　　　　　　　让它去。来吧,
我跟你一块儿进去。

玳思狄莫娜　　　　　　　你觉得不舒服,
我很难受。　　　　〔奥赛罗与玳思狄莫娜同下。

爱米丽亚　　　　　我找到这帕子,很高兴;
这是摩尔人赠她的第一件纪念品;
我那任性的丈夫要我偷走它
总不下上百次,可是她这么爱这件

For he conjur'd her she should ever keep it, —
That she reserves it evermore about her
To kiss and talk to. I'll have the work ta'en out,
And give't Iago:
What he will do with it heaven knows, not I;
I nothing but to please his fantasy.

               [*Re-enter* Iago.]

Iago How now! what do you here alone?

Emilia Do not you chide; I have a thing for you.

Iago A thing for me! — it is a common thing.

Emilia Ha!

Iago To have a foolish wife.

Emilia O, is that all? What will you give me now
For that same handkerchief?

Iago   What handkerchief?

Emilia *What handkerchief* !
Why, that the Moor first gave to Desdemona;
That which so often you did bid me steal.

Iago Hast stol'n it from her?

Emilia No, faith; she let it drop by negligence,
And, to the advantage, I being here, took't up.
Look, here it is.

Iago   A good wench; give it me.

Emilia What will you do with't, that you have been so
    earnest
To have me filch it?

Iago [*Snatching it.*] Why, what's that to you?

Emilia If it be not for some purpose of import,
Give't me again: poor lady, she'll run mad
When she shall lack it.

Iago Be not acknown on't; I have use for it.
Go, leave me.

                     [*Exit* Emilia.]

I will in Cassio's lodging lose this napkin,
And let him find it. Trifles light as air

信物,因为他恳请她永远留存着,
所以她经常保持在身边,吻着它,
对它尽说话。我要把花样描出来,
交给伊耶戈:
他将把它怎么样,上天才知道,
我不知;不管它,我只满足他的怪想。
　　　　　　　　[伊耶戈上。

伊　耶　戈　什么事? 你独自在此做什么?
爱米丽亚　休跟我吵嘴;我有件东西给你。
伊　耶　戈　有东西给我? 是件平常东西——
爱米丽亚　吓!
伊　耶　戈　有了个傻老婆。
爱米丽亚　噢! 只是那样吗? 你给我什么,
　　　　　交换我那块手帕?
伊　耶　戈　　　　　　　什么手帕?
爱米丽亚　什么手帕!
　　　　　哎也,摩尔人早先给玳思狄莫娜的:
　　　　　你曾经屡次三番叫我偷的那一方。
伊　耶　戈　你从她那儿偷来了吗?
爱米丽亚　没有,老实说;她大意掉在地下,
　　　　　机会凑巧,我在这里捡到了。
　　　　　你瞧,这就是。
伊　耶　戈　　　　　　亲妹子;把它给了我。
爱米丽亚　你要把它怎么样,这般急切
　　　　　要我把它偷?
伊　耶　戈　　[抢到手]哎也,那关你什么事?
爱米丽亚　若是不为了太重要的正事,还给我;
　　　　　可怜的娘娘! 她发现失掉会急坏。
伊　耶　戈　别承认知道它;我对它自有用处。
　　　　　去吧,离开我。　　　　　[爱米丽亚下。
　　　　　这手帕我要丢在凯昔欧寓所里,
　　　　　让他找到它;轻得像空气的琐屑事,

Are to the jealous confirmations strong
As proofs of holy writ: this may do something.
The Moor already changes with my poison:
Dangerous conceits are in their natures poisons,
Which at the first are scarce found to distaste,
But, with a little act upon the blood,
Burn like the mines of sulphur. —I did say so: —
Look, where he comes!

[*Re-enter* Othello.]

Not poppy, nor mandragora,
Nor all the drowsy syrups of the world,
Shall ever medicine thee to that sweet sleep
Which thou ow'dst yesterday.

Othello   Ha! ha! false to me?

Iago Why, how now, general! no more of that.

Othello Avaunt! be gone! thou hast set me on the
rack: —
I swear 'tis better to be much abus'd
Than but to know't a little.

Iago   How now, my lord!

Othello What sense had I of her stol'n hours of lust?
I saw't not, thought it not, it harm'd not me:
I slept the next night well, was free and merry;
I found not Cassio's kisses on her lips:
He that is robb'd, not wanting what is stol'n,
Let him not know't and he's not robb'd at all.

Iago I am sorry to hear this.

Othello I had been happy if the general camp,
Pioners and all, had tasted her sweet body,
So I had nothing known. O, now, for ever
Farewell the tranquil mind! farewell content!
Farewell the plumed troop and the big wars
That make ambition virtue! O, farewell,

对于嫉妒者是坚定不移的佐证，
赛如圣经里的论据；这也许有用处。
摩尔人中了我的毒，已经在改变：
危险的想法，就它们的性质来说，
是毒药，它们起初并不难上口，
但只须稍稍在血里起了点作用，
便会燃烧得像硫磺矿坑。我说过
这么样：瞧吧！他在那里来了！

    ［奥赛罗上。

罂粟花已不能，曼陀罗也不能，世间
一切催眠的糖浆也不能，使你
再有昨天的安睡。

奥　赛　罗	嘻嘻！跟我 不真诚？
伊　耶　戈	哎也，什么事，将军？别那样。
奥　赛　罗	去你的！走开！你将我架上了拷问台； 我起誓，对我大大过不去也胜如 只给知道一点儿。
伊　耶　戈	你有什么事，主公？
奥　赛　罗	我以前有什么她偷偷淫滥的知觉？ 我不见，不想，那事情不伤我的心； 第二夜我睡得很好，没心事，很快乐； 在她嘴唇上我不见凯昔欧亲的吻； 被盗者不曾缺少他失窃的东西， 不叫他知道，他就不曾被盗窃。
伊　耶　戈	听你说，我感到惋惜。
奥　赛　罗	我本来很愉快，即令是全军上下， 工兵们也在内，都尝到她可爱的肉体， 只要我不知道。嗳哟！但如今，永远 告别了，那安静的心情；告别了，那满足！ 告别了，那羽冠的军兵队伍，使壮志 雄心变美德的那大战！嗳哟，告别了！

Farewell the neighing steed and the shrill trump,

The spirit-stirring drum, the ear-piercing fife,

The royal banner, and all quality,

Pride, pomp, and circumstance of glorious war!

And, O you mortal engines, whose rude throats

The immortal Jove's dread clamors counterfeit,

Farewell! Othello's occupation's gone!

Iago　Is't possible, my lord? —

Othello　Villain, be sure thou prove my love a whore; —

　　　　　　　　　　　　[*Taking him by the throat.*]

Be sure of it. Give me the ocular proof;

Or, by the worth of man's eternal soul,

Thou hadst been better have been born a dog

Than answer my wak'd wrath!

Iago　　　　　　　　　　　　Is't come to this?

Othello　Make me to see't; or at the least so prove it,

That the probation bear no hinge nor loop

To hang a doubt on; or woe upon thy life!

Iago　My noble lord, —

Othello　If thou dost slander her and torture me,

Never pray more; abandon all remorse;

On horror's head horrors accumulate;

Do deeds to make heaven weep, all earth amaz'd;

For nothing canst thou to damnation add

Greater than that.

Iago　　　　　　O grace! O heaven defend me!

Are you a man? have you a soul or sense? —

God be wi' you; take mine office. — O wretched fool,

That liv'st to make thine honesty a vice! —

O monstrous world! Take note, take note, O world,

To be direct and honest is not safe. —

告别了,那鸣嘶的雄骏,那高亢的号角,
那激发勇武的战鼓,那刺耳的军笛,
那庄严的旗纛,那英名赫赫的战阵
所奄有的一切雄奇、鼎盛、辉煌
与威武! 还有你们,啊,大炮们,
你们那粗豪的喉咙,模仿着天王
乔旿那可怕的阗阗雷震,告别了!
奥赛罗的事业就此完结!

伊　耶　戈　　这可能吗,主公?

奥　赛　罗　　坏蛋,你肯定得证明我心爱的人儿
是一个婊子,[掐他的脖子]你肯定;给我看眼证;
否则,凭我这不死的精魂的英气,
你不如生来就是条狗子,可休想
受得了我愤发的暴怒。

伊　耶　戈　　　　　　　到了这地步吗?

奥　赛　罗　　让我眼看到这件事;或者,至少,
证明它,还得使证据不模棱,没漏洞,
无可怀疑;否则,大祸来要你的命!

伊　耶　戈　　尊贵的主公,——

奥　赛　罗　　你如果诽谤了她,又煎熬了我,
便永远莫再去祷告;千万休要想
懊悔;在恐怖的顶巅上堆上了恐怖;
干了使上天哭泣,使人间诧骇的勾当;
因为你加给我永远打入地狱
不超生的苦难,不可能比那么干更其凶。

伊　耶　戈　　嗳哟,主恩! 啊也,上天饶恕我!
您可是个人? 您可有灵魂或理性?
上帝保佑您;收回我的位置。唉也,
可悲的呆子! 你生来把你的诚实
变成了一桩罪孽。咳哪,这世界
好不骇人! 记着,记着,啊唷,
你们大家! 诚恳老实了,不安全。

I thank you for this profit; and from hence
I'll love no friend, sith love breeds such offense.

Othello   Nay, stay; — thou shouldst be honest.

Iago   I should be wise; for honesty's a fool,
And loses that it works for.

Othello   By the world,
I think my wife be honest, and think she is not;
I think that thou art just, and think thou art not:
I'll have some proof: her name, that was as fresh
As Dian's visage, is now begrim'd and black
As mine own face. — If there be cords or knives,
Poison or fire, or suffocating streams,
I'll not endure 't. — Would I were satisfied!

Iago   I see, sir, you are eaten up with passion:
I do repent me that I put it to you.
You would be satisfied?

Othello   *Would* ! nay, I will.

Iago   And may: but how? how satisfied, my lord?
Would you, the supervisor, grossly gape on, —
Behold her tupp'd?

Othello   Death and damnation! O!

Iago   It were a tedious difficulty, I think,
To bring them to that prospect: damn them then,
If ever mortal eyes do see them bolster
More than their own! What then? how then?
What shall I say? Where's satisfaction?
It is impossible you should see this
Were they as prime as goats, as hot as monkeys,
As salt as wolves in pride, and fools as gross
As ignorance made drunk. But yet, I say,

多谢您给我这教训,从今往后,
我不再爱朋友,既然爱了会招致
恼怒。

奥　赛　罗　　　　不对,住口;你应当诚实。

伊　耶　戈　我应当聪明,因为诚实是呆子,
它一心为友情,倒反把友情丢失。

奥　赛　罗　凭这个世界,我想我妻子贞洁,
又想她不贞洁;我想你正直可靠,
又想你不那么。我得要有点证据。
她的这清名,以前跟贞月的清辉
一般皎洁,如今玷污了,已发黑,
如同我自己的脸色。只要有绳子
或短刀,有毒药、火焰或窒息的水流,
我决不能容忍。我但愿弄一个明白!

伊　耶　戈　我见到,钧座,您情绪激动得厉害。
我后悔我把这事情告诉了您。
您愿意弄一个明白?

奥　赛　罗　　　　　　　　愿意! 不是,
我准要。

伊　耶　戈　　　　也可以;但怎样? 怎样弄明白,
主公? 您要站在一旁,呆呆地
张着嘴,眼瞪瞪瞧瞧她给爬在身上?

奥　赛　罗　该死,叫打入阿鼻地狱! 恶!

伊　耶　戈　要使他们干出那样儿,我想
真是件难事;那么,咒他们入地狱,
只要是人的眼睛瞧见了他们
搂抱在一起! 那时节,什么? 怎么样?
我要说什么? 那里去弄得明白?
您要亲眼看到这件事不可能,
即令他们滥淫得像春天的山羊,
火热得像猴子,浪得像性发的狼,
而且还傻得像醉酒的白痴;可是,

If imputation and strong circumstances, —
Which lead directly to the door of truth, —
Will give you satisfaction, you may have't.

Othello   Give me a living reason she's disloyal.

Iago   I do not like the office;
But, sith I am enter'd in this cause so far, —
Prick'd to it by foolish honesty and love, —
I will go on. I lay with Cassio lately;
And, being troubled with a raging tooth,
I could not sleep.
There are a kind of men so loose of soul,
That in their sleeps will mutter their affairs:
One of this kind is Cassio:
In sleep I heard him say, *Sweet Desdemona*,
Let us be wary, *let us hide our loves*;
And then, sir, would he gripe and wring my hand,
Cry, *O sweet creature*! and then kiss me hard,
As if he pluck'd up kisses by the roots,
That grew upon my lips: then laid his leg
Over my thigh, and sigh'd and kiss'd; and then
Cried, *Cursed fate that gave thee to the Moor*!

Othello   O monstrous! monstrous!

Iago   Nay, this was but his dream.

Othello   But this denoted a foregone conclusion:
'Tis a shrewd doubt, though it be but a dream.

Iago   And this may help to thicken other proofs
That do demonstrate thinly.

Othello   I'll tear her all to pieces.

Iago   Nay, but be wise: yet we see nothing done;

我说,假使有一个有坚强的情况
证据的说法,——那会直接引您到
真实的门上,——能使您把这事弄明白,
那您就能够有它。

奥　赛　罗　　　　　　　　　　给我个真切
不虚的理由,为什么她对我不贞。

伊　耶　戈　我不爱这差使;
但是我既已这般深入这事件中,
被愚鲁的诚实与敬爱所刺激前进,
我便得继续进行。我跟凯昔欧
近来同寝榻;为因牙齿痛得凶,
我不能入睡。
这世间有一种相好,心神松懈,
会在睡梦里喃喃谈他们的心事;
凯昔欧就是这类人。
我听他说梦话,"亲爱的玳思狄莫娜,
让我们小心,遮盖住我们的情爱!"
然后,钩上,他抓住我的手使劲挤,
叫道,"啊也,心爱的人儿!"拼命吻,
好像他在把吻儿连根拔起来,
而它们是生在我嘴唇上;还又把腿子
压在我大腿上,叹息着,亲着嘴;又叫道,
"该诅咒的命运,把你给了那摩尔人!"

奥　赛　罗　啊唷,骇人听闻!骇人听闻!

伊　耶　戈　不然,这只是他的梦。

奥　赛　罗　　　　　　　　　　　但这却显示
早先曾有过这样的经过:这是个
不好的猜疑,虽然它只是一个梦。

伊　耶　戈　这又能帮着加重其他的证据,
没有它,它们证明得不够充分。

奥　赛　罗　我准要把她撕得粉碎。

伊　耶　戈　　　　　　　　　　　　不要,

She may be honest yet. Tell me but this, —
Have you not sometimes seen a handkerchief
Spotted with strawberries in your wife's hand?

Othello I gave her such a one; 'twas my first gift.

Iago I know not that: but such a handkerchief, —
I am sure it was your wife's, — did I today
See Cassio wipe his beard with.

Othello   If it be that, —

Iago If it be that, or any that was hers,
It speaks against her with the other proofs.

Othello O, that the slave had forty thousand lives, —
One is too poor, too weak for my revenge!
Now do I see 'tis true. — Look here, Iago;
All my fond love thus do I blow to heaven:
'Tis gone. —
Arise, black vengeance, from thy hollow hell!
Yield up, O love, thy crown and hearted throne
To tyrannous hate! swell, bosom, with thy fraught,
For 'tis of aspics' tongues!

Iago   Yet be content.

Othello O, blood, Iago, blood!

Iago Patience, I say; your mind perhaps may change.

Othello Never, Iago. Like to the Pontic Sea,
Whose icy current and compulsive course
Ne'er feels retiring ebb, but keeps due on
To the Propontic and the Hellespont;
Even so my bloody thoughts, with violent pace,
Shall ne'er look back, ne'er ebb to humble love,
Till that a capable and wide revenge

还得聪明些；我们还未见实事；
她也许还贞洁。只要告诉我这件事：
您可是未曾见到过有一块手帕，
刺绣着草莓，在您的夫人手中？

奥 赛 罗　　那是我给她的；是我的第一件礼物。

伊 耶 戈　　我不知那件事；但这样一块手帕——
我相信那是您夫人的——我今天见到
凯昔欧在抹须髯。

奥 赛 罗　　　　　　　　　如果是那个，——

伊 耶 戈　　如果是那个，或是她别的什么，
那就跟旁的证据总对于她不利。

奥 赛 罗　　啊！但愿那奴才有四万条命；
一条太渺小，太轻微，不够我报复。
如今我见到这件事千真万确。
瞧这里，伊耶戈；我把我全部的痴爱
吹上天：它完了。
恶毒的报复，从深凹的地狱里上升吧！
唉也，爱情呀！放弃掉你那顶冠冕
与我心中的宝座，退让给无情的仇恨。
膨胀吧，胸怀，同你的内蕴一起胀，
因为那是毒蛇舌头上的剧毒！

伊 耶 戈　　莫伤心。

奥 赛 罗　　　　　　唔！血，伊耶戈，血！

伊 耶 戈　　镇静，我说；您心情也许会变动。

奥 赛 罗　　永远不会，伊耶戈。好比邦的海，
它那股寒流与迫进的水程从来
不回流，总是直注进泼罗邦的海
与赫勒斯邦海峡，同样，我满衔
血仇的思想，跨着强劲的步子，
将永不返顾，永不向柔和的情爱
退潮，要直到宽阔广大的报复

Swallow them up. — Now, by yond marble heaven,
In the due reverence of a sacred vow [*Kneels.*]
I here engage my words.

Iago   Do not rise yet. — [*Kneels.*]
Witness, you ever-burning lights above,
You elements that clip us round about, —
Witness that here Iago doth give up
The execution of his wit, hands, heart,
To wrong'd Othello's service! Let him command,
And to obey shall be in me remorse,
What bloody business ever. [*They rise.*]

Othello   I greet thy love,
Not with vain thanks, but with acceptance bounteous,
And will upon the instant put thee to't:
Within these three days let me hear thee say
That Cassio's not alive.

Iago   My friend is dead; 'tis done at your request:
But let her live.

Othello   Damn her, lewd minx! O, damn her!
Come, go with me apart; I will withdraw
To furnish me with some swift means of death
For the fair devil. Now art thou my lieutenant.

Iago   I am your own for ever.

                                   [*Exeunt.*]

SCENE IV. *Before the Castle.*

[*Enter* Desdemona, Emilia, *and* Clown.]

Desdemona   Do you know, sirrah, where Lieutenant Cassio lies?

Clown   I dare not say he lies anywhere.

Desdemona   Why, man?

	把它们吞噬掉。凭那大理石的云天，	[下跪]
	现在，对神圣的誓言尽应有的诚敬，	
	我在此保证我的言辞。	

伊耶戈　　　　　　　　　　　　且莫起身。　　　　　[下跪]
请你们作证，永远燃烧着的日月
星辰！还有你们，围抱在我们
周遭的大气！证明伊耶戈在此
奉献他的智慧、力量、心神的运用，
为受害的奥赛罗效劳！让他发命令，
服从他将是庄严的责任，即令要
流血也不去顾及。　　　　　　　　　　[他们起立]

奥赛罗　　　　　　　　　　我欢迎你的爱，
不用空虚的申谢，而是以友情
满腔来嘉纳，而且立刻要求你
去做这件事：就在这三天之内
让我听你说凯昔欧已不在人世。

伊耶戈　我朋友是死了；那是应您的要求；
但让她活着。

奥赛罗　　　　　　　　叫她进地狱，淫妇！
啊，叫她进地狱！来吧，单跟我
一起去；我要去替我自己张罗个
叫这漂亮的恶魔快死的法子。
你如今是我的副将了。

伊耶戈　我永远是您的忠仆。　　　　　　[同下。

第 四 景

[堡垒前]

[玳思狄莫娜、爱米丽亚与小丑上。]

玳思狄莫娜　你知道吗，小子，副将军凯昔欧呆在哪里？

小　　丑　我不敢说他呆在哪里。

玳思狄莫娜　为什么，人儿？

Clown He's a soldier; and for one to say a soldier lies is stabbing.

Desdemona Go to; where lodges he?

Clown To tell you where he lodges is to tell you where I lie.

Desdemona Can anything be made of this?

Clown I know not where he lodges; and for me to devise a lodging, and say he lies here or he lies there were to lie in mine own throat.

Desdemona Can you inquire him out, and be edified by report?

Clown I will catechize the world for him; that is, make questions and by them answer.

Desdemona Seek him, bid him come hither: tell him I have moved my lord on his behalf, and hope all will be well.

Clown To do this is within the compass of man's wit; and therefore I will attempt the doing it.   [*Exit.*]

Desdemona Where should I lose that handkerchief, Emilia?

Emilia I know not, madam.

Desdemona Believe me, I had rather have lost my purse
Full of crusadoes: and, but my noble Moor
Is true of mind and made of no such baseness
As jealous creatures are, it were enough
To put him to ill thinking.

Emilia   Is he not jealous?

Desdemona Who, he? I think the sun where he was born
Drew all such humours from him.

Emilia   Look, where he comes.

Desdemona I will not leave him now till Cassio
Be call'd to him.

                    [*Enter* Othello.]

                    How is't with you, my lord?

Othello Well, my good lady. — [*Aside.*] O, hardness to dissemble! —

How do you, Desdemona?

Desdemona   Well, my good lord.

小　　丑		他是个军人;说一个军人是个呆子,那是出口伤他。
玳思狄莫娜		得了;他住在哪里?
小　　丑		告诉你他住在哪里是告诉你我呆在哪里。
玳思狄莫娜		还跟你纠缠得清楚吗?
小　　丑		我不知道他住在哪里,若是我想出一个去处来,而说他呆在这里或他呆在哪里,那是我在撒谎胡说。
玳思狄莫娜		你能将他打听出来,从传闻里得到着落吗?
小　　丑		我要对人家使用问答法;那是说,我去问人家,要人家回答。
玳思狄莫娜		找到他,叫他到这儿来;告诉他我替他劝转了我官人,希望没事了。
小　　丑		做这个是在人的机灵范围以内的,所以我会去试着做。　　　　　　　　　　　　　　[小丑下。
玳思狄莫娜		我在哪里丢失这手绢的,爱米丽亚?
爱米丽亚		我不知道,娘娘。
玳思狄莫娜		信我的话,我宁愿失掉那满装着 葡萄牙洋钱的荷包;若不是我官人 心肠真实,不似那拈酸吃醋的, 肚子里卑鄙,这会引起他的坏念头。
爱米丽亚		他不会妒忌吗?
玳思狄莫娜		谁? 他? 我想 他家乡的太阳照得旺,会从他身上 把这样的体液全都吸走。
爱米丽亚		瞧! 他在那里来了。
玳思狄莫娜		凯昔欧给叫来之前, 我将不离他左右。 　　　　　[奥赛罗上。 　　　　　你怎样,官人?
奥赛罗		很好,亲爱的娘子。[旁白]唉,装假 真是件难事! ——你好吗,玳思狄莫娜?
玳思狄莫娜		很好,亲爱的官人。

Othello   Give me your hand; this hand is moist, my lady.

Desdemona   It yet hath felt no age nor known no sorrow.

Othello   This argues fruitfulness and liberal heart: —
Hot, hot, and moist; this hand of yours requires
A sequester from liberty, fasting, and prayer,
Much castigation, exercise devout;
For here's a young and sweating devil here
That commonly rebels. 'Tis a good hand,
A frank one.

Desdemona   You may, indeed, say so;
For 'twas that hand that gave away my heart.

Othello   A liberal hand; the hearts of old gave hands;
But our new heraldry is hands, not hearts.

Desdemona   I cannot speak of this. Come now, your promise.

Othello   What promise, chuck?

Desdemona   I have sent to bid Cassio come speak with you.

Othello   I have a salt and sorry rheum offends me;
Lend me thy handkerchief.

Desdemona   Here, my lord.

Othello   That which I gave you.

Desdemona   I have it not about me.

Othello   Not?

Desdemona   No, faith, my lord.

Othello   That is a fault.
That handkerchief
Did an Egyptian to my mother give;
She was a charmer, and could almost read
The thoughts of people; she told her, while she kept it,
'Twould make her amiable and subdue my father

奥　赛　罗	把手给我。
	你这手是潮的，娘子。
玳思狄莫娜	它还没感到
	岁月，也不知忧愁。
奥　赛　罗	这显示大度
	与心胸放浪；很热，很热，潮的；
	你这只手儿需要跟自由隔离，
	持饿斋与祷告，充分的清修苦戒，
	虔诚的礼拜；因为这是个后生
	而流汗的魔鬼，它老是图谋不轨。
	这是只好手，开诚坦率。
玳思狄莫娜	果真，
	你能这么说，就是它给了你我的心。
奥　赛　罗	一只宽弘的手；旧时候，心与了
	才联手为证，但我们新的纹章学
	只顾联了手，心里却未曾相与得。
玳思狄莫娜	这个我说不上来。来吧，你答应的。
奥　赛　罗	答应什么，小鸡儿？
玳思狄莫娜	我差人去叫了凯昔欧来对你打话。
奥　赛　罗	我伤风眼泪鼻涕感到难受。
	你把手帕借给我。
玳思狄莫娜	这里，官人。
奥　赛　罗	我给你的那条。
玳思狄莫娜	不在我手边。
奥　赛　罗	不在？
玳思狄莫娜	的确不在，官人。
奥　赛　罗	那就不好了。
	那一条手帕
	是个埃及人给我母亲的；她是个
	女巫师，几乎能看透人们的思想；
	她告她，她保有在手里，那能够使她
	显得可爱，完全降服我父亲

Entirely to her love; but if she lost it
Or made a gift of it, my father's eye
Should hold her loathed, and his spirits should hunt
After new fancies: she, dying, gave it me;
And bid me, when my fate would have me wive,
To give it her. I did so: and take heed on't;
Make it a darling like your precious eye;
To lose't or give't away were such perdition
As nothing else could match.

Desdemona   Is't possible?

Othello   'Tis true: there's magic in the web of it:
A sibyl, that had number'd in the world
The sun to course two hundred compasses,
In her prophetic fury sew'd the work;
The worms were hallow'd that did breed the silk;
And it was dy'd in mummy which the skillful
Conserv'd of maiden's hearts.

Desdemona   Indeed! is't true?

Othello   Most veritable; therefore look to't well.

Desdemona   Then would to God that I had never seen't!

Othello   Ha! wherefore?

Desdemona   Why do you speak so startingly and rash?

Othello   Is't lost? is't gone? speak, is it out of the way?

Desdemona   Heaven bless us!

Othello   Say you?

Desdemona   It is not lost; but what an if it were?

Othello   How!

Desdemona   I say, it is not lost.

Othello   Fetch't, let me see't.

Desdemona   Why, so I can, sir, but I will not now.
This is a trick to put me from my suit:

爱着她,但她若失掉或送给了人,
我父亲的眼睛将会厌恶她,他心情
将会去追求新的爱。她临死给了我;
叫我当我的命运要我娶妻时,
就把它送给她。我便这么办:你得要
小心,宝爱它,如同你珍爱的眼睛;
遗失或送人将会是这样的灾祸,
没别的可以比拟。

玳思狄莫娜　　　　　　　　这难道可能吗?

奥　赛　罗　这是确实的;在它丝缕里有法术;
一个女先知,她在这世上计数过
太阳走了两百圈,她缝制这件活
乃在她预言的狂热中;纺制这绢帕,
那抽丝的蚕儿也是供神用的,为把它
染色,巧手灵师把处女的心儿
特制了药浆液。

玳思狄莫娜　　　　　　　当真! 这是真的吗?

奥　赛　罗　千真万确,因此上,你得要当心。

玳思狄莫娜　那但愿上天从未给我见过它!

奥　赛　罗　嘻! 为什么?

玳思狄莫娜　　　　　　　你为何说得这般
突然而急迫?

奥　赛　罗　　　　　　　丢掉了? 没有了? 说呀,
那可是失落了?

玳思狄莫娜　　　　　　上天保佑我们!

奥　赛　罗　你说?

玳思狄莫娜　　　　不曾失掉;但丢了又怎样?

奥　赛　罗　怎么样!

玳思狄莫娜　我说没有失掉。

奥　赛　罗　　　　　　　拿来,给我看。

玳思狄莫娜　哎也,我能那么办,官人,但现在
我可不。这是耍花样,规避我的恳请:

Pray you, let Cassio be receiv'd again.

Othello   Fetch me the handkerchief: my mind misgives.

Desdemona   Come, come;

You'll never meet a more sufficient man.

Othello   The handkerchief!

Desdemona   I pray, talk me of Cassio.

Othello   The handkerchief!

Desdemona   A man that all his time

Hath founded his good fortunes on your love,

Shar'd dangers with you, —

Othello   The handkerchief!

Desdemona   In sooth, you are to blame.

Othello   Away!   [*Exit.*]

Emilia   Is not this man jealous?

Desdemona   I ne'er saw this before.

Sure there's some wonder in this handkerchief;

I am most unhappy in the loss of it.

Emilia   'Tis not a year or two shows us a man:

They are all but stomachs and we all but food:

They eat us hungerly, and when they are full,

They belch us. — Look you, — Cassio and my husband.

                [*Enter* Cassio *and* Iago.]

Iago   There is no other way; 'tis she must do't:

And, lo, the happiness! go and importune her.

Desdemona   How now, good Cassio! what's the news

   with you?

Cassio   Madam, my former suit: I do beseech you

That by your virtuous means I may again

Exist, and be a member of his love,

Whom I, with all the office of my heart,

Entirely honour: I would not be delay'd.

If my offence be of such mortal kind

That nor my service past, nor present sorrows,

请让凯昔欧再来跟你相见吧。

奥 赛 罗 把手帕拿来给我;我心里在害怕。

玳思狄莫娜 来吧,来吧;

你决不会碰到一个更能干的人了。

奥 赛 罗 那手帕!

玳思狄莫娜 我请你,跟我谈起凯昔欧。

奥 赛 罗 那手帕!

玳思狄莫娜 一个人经常把他的好运

寄托在你的厚爱上,和你同艰险,——

奥 赛 罗 那手帕!

玳思狄莫娜 实在要怪你不是了。

奥 赛 罗 走开!

〔奥赛罗下。

爱 米 丽 亚 这人不妒忌吗?

玳思狄莫娜 我在以前从未见过这样子。

定然,这块手帕是有点蹊跷;

我将它丢失了,心里好生难受。

爱 米 丽 亚 不是一两年能显出一个人怎么样;

他们都只是一只只的胃,而我们

都只是食品;他们吃我们狼吞

虎咽,吃饱了就呕吐。你瞧,凯昔欧

和我的丈夫。

〔伊耶戈与凯昔欧上。

伊 耶 戈 没有其他的方法;一定得她去办:

看啊! 运气真好:上前去恳求她。

玳思狄莫娜 什么事,亲爱的凯昔欧? 你们有什么消息?

凯 昔 欧 夫人,还是我以前的恳求:我求您,

经由您贤德的转圜,我可以重新

生活着,做他爱宠下的一员,那爱宠,

我全心全意地尊崇;我不愿再迟延。

倘使我的罪愆有那么不可救药,

以致我过去的劳役,如今的悔恨,

Nor purpos'd merit in futurity,
Can ransom me into his love again,
But to know so must be my benefit;
So shall I clothe me in a forc'd content,
And shut myself up in some other course,
To fortune's alms.
Desdemona   Alas, thrice-gentle Cassio!
My advocation is not now in tune;
My lord is not my lord; nor should I know him
Were he in favour as in humour alter'd.
So help me every spirit sanctified,
As I have spoken for you all my best,
And stood within the blank of his displeasure
For my free speech! You must awhile be patient:
What I can do I will; and more I will
Than for myself I dare: let that suffice you.
Iago Is my lord angry?
Emilia   He went hence but now,
And certainly in strange unquietness.
Iago Can he be angry? I have seen the cannon,
When it hath blown his ranks into the air
And, like the devil, from his very arm
Puff'd his own brother; — and can he be angry?
Something of moment, then: I will go meet him:
There's matter in't indeed if he be angry.
Desdemona I pr'ythee, do so.

[*Exit* Iago.]

Something sure of state, —
Either from Venice or some unhatch'd practice
Made demonstrable here in Cyprus to him, —
Hath puddled his clear spirit, and in such cases
Men's natures wrangle with inferior things,
Though great ones are their object. 'Tis even so;
For let our finger ache, and it indues

将来的一心去求得功绩,都不能
为我赎罪,重复获得他的垂青,
只要知道是这样也对我有益;
那我就可以勉强去自行满足,
限制自己另外走其他的道路,
去营求命运舍慈悲。

玳思狄莫娜　　　　　　　　唉也,十分
善良的凯昔欧! 我如今的恳求不对头;
我官人不是我官人;我不会认识他,
假如他外貌改变得同性情那么样。
让每个神圣的天使帮我忙,我已经
竭尽了我的能力替您说过话,
且为了我替您开怀关说,曾站在
他不快的靶心中。您得暂时耐着些;
我所能做的我会做,且会做更多
我所不敢替自己做的事:我替您
说的话这就够多了。

伊　耶　戈　　　　　　　　主公生气了吧?
爱米丽亚　他刚才离开,确是异样地激动。
伊　耶　戈　他动怒了吧? 我看到那尊大炮,
当它把一排士兵轰入半空中,
好比是魔鬼,把将军自己的弟兄
从他臂腕上轰走;他动怒了吧?
那就有重要事情了;我要去见他;
这里头果真有事情,若是他发怒。
玳思狄莫娜　请你去看他去吧。[伊耶戈下]一定是邦国事,
发自威尼斯,或什么未显露的阴谋,
在这里塞浦路斯呈一点端倪,
混浊了他澄净的心智;在这般情形里,
人们的天性跟次要的情事吵闹,
虽然他们想到的是大事。是这样;
因为只要我们的手指痛,它使得

Our other healthful members even to that sense
Of pain: nay, we must think men are not gods,
Nor of them look for such observancy
As fits the bridal. — Beshrew me much, Emilia,
I was, — unhandsome warrior as I am, —
Arraigning his unkindness with my soul;
But now I find I had suborn'd the witness,
And he's indicted falsely.

Emilia Pray heaven it be state matters, as you think,
And no conception nor no jealous toy
Concerning you.

Desdemona Alas the day, I never gave him cause!

Emilia But jealous souls will not be answer'd so;
They are not ever jealous for the cause,
But jealous for they are jealous: 'tis a monster
Begot upon itself, born on itself.

Desdemona Heaven keep that monster from Othello's
mind!

Emilia Lady, amen.

Desdemona I will go seek him. — Cassio, walk herea-
bout:
If I do find him fit, I'll move your suit,
And seek to effect it to my uttermost.

Cassio I humbly thank your ladyship.

[*Exeunt* Desdemona *and* Emilia.]
[*Enter* Bianca.]

Bianca Save you, friend Cassio!

Cassio What make you from home?
How is it with you, my most fair Bianca?
I'faith, sweet love, I was coming to your house.

Bianca And I was going to your lodging, Cassio.
What, keep a week away? seven days and nights?
Eight score eight hours? and lovers' absent hours,
More tedious than the dial eight score times?

其他的肢体也能感觉到那阵痛。
不光这，我们该想到人不是天神，
也不应对他们要求适于燕尔
新婚时的相敬。我真该死，爱米丽亚，
我是个不公道的战士，我刚才正在
同我的灵魂去传讯他对我的不温存；
但此刻我发现我是串同了伪证，
他却遭到了诬告。

爱米丽亚　求上天，但愿这是邦国事，正如您
所想的，而不是坏念头，或者有关您、
妒忌的妄想。

玳思狄莫娜　可怜见的！我从未给他过原由。

爱米丽亚　但妒忌的灵魂这样去回答它们
可不行，它们从不会为原由而妒忌，
而只是为妒忌而妒忌；这是头妖怪，
它自己生殖，又自己生产。

玳思狄莫娜　　　　　　　　　求上天，
叫那头妖怪莫进奥赛罗的头脑！

爱米丽亚　娘娘，心愿这样。

玳思狄莫娜　我要去找他。凯昔欧，在此散着步；
我若是发现他心情能接受，我将会
提出您的恳请，竭尽能力作成它。

凯　昔　欧　我谨谢您，夫人。〔玳思狄莫娜与爱米丽亚同下。
　　　　　　　　　　　〔碧盎佳上。

碧　盎　佳　保佑你，朋友凯昔欧！

凯　昔　欧　　　　　　　　有什么事出门来？
你身体怎样，我的美人儿碧盎佳？
果真，亲爱的心上人，我要到你家去。

碧　盎　佳　我正要到你住所去看你，凯昔欧。
什么！一星期不来？七天又七夜？
八个二十，又加八小时？意中人
别离的钟点，那要比日晷上八个

O weary reckoning!

Cassio　　　　　　Pardon me, Bianca:

I have this while with leaden thoughts been press'd;

But I shall in a more continuate time

Strike off this score of absence. Sweet Bianca,

　　　　　　[*Giving her* Desdemona's *handkerchief.*]

Take me this work out.

Bianca　　　　　　O Cassio, whence came this?

This is some token from a newer friend.

To the felt absence now I feel a cause:

Is't come to this? Well, well.

Cassio　　　　　　Go to, woman!

Throw your vile guesses in the devil's teeth,

From whence you have them. You are jealous now

That this is from some mistress, some remembrance:

No, in good troth, Bianca.

Bianca　　　　　　Why, whose is it?

Cassio　I know not neither: I found it in my chamber.

I like the work well: ere it be demanded, —

As like enough it will, — I'd have it copied:

Take it, and do't; and leave me for this time.

Bianca　Leave you! wherefore?

Cassio　I do attend here on the general;

And think it no addition, nor my wish,

To have him see me woman'd.

Bianca　　　　　　Why, I pray you?

Cassio　Not that I love you not.

Bianca　　　　　　But that you do not love me.

I pray you, bring me on the way a little;

And say if I shall see you soon at night.

Cassio　'Tis but a little way that I can bring you,

二十圈还难受？嗳也，焦心的计算！

凯 昔 欧　原谅我，碧盎佳，我现在心事如铅，
　　　　　但我将在一个继续不断的时间里
　　　　　还清这别离的旧欠。亲爱的碧盎佳，
　　　　　　　　　［予以玳思狄莫娜之手帕］
　　　　　替我把这花样落下来。

碧 盎 佳　　　　　　　　　　啊唷，凯昔欧！
　　　　　打哪儿来的？这是个新好的信物；
　　　　　如今我感到那别离苦味的原因；
　　　　　到了这地步吗？很好，很好。

凯 昔 欧　　　　　　　　　　　　　得了，
　　　　　姑娘！把你那讨厌的猜想扔进
　　　　　魔鬼嘴里去，你捡来原是从他那里。
　　　　　你此刻在吃醋，以为这是从什么
　　　　　情妇手中来的，是什么纪念品；不对，
　　　　　说真话，碧盎佳。

碧 盎 佳　　　　　　　　哎也，这可是谁的？

凯 昔 欧　不知道，心爱的，我在我房间里捡到。
　　　　　我喜欢这花样；在它给要回去之前，——
　　　　　那个极可能，——我要把花样落下来；
　　　　　收着，替我落；暂且离了我去吧。

碧 盎 佳　离开你！为什么？

凯 昔 欧　我在此侍候着将军；我认为他见我
　　　　　跟一个妇人在一起，既不大体面，
　　　　　也不合我的意。

碧 盎 佳　　　　　　　　为什么，倒要请问你。

凯 昔 欧　不是为了我不爱你。

碧 盎 佳　　　　　　　　为了你爱我不。
　　　　　请你且伴我走一段路儿，跟我说
　　　　　我能否准今晚见到你。

凯 昔 欧　　　　　　　　　　我只能伴你
　　　　　走不远，因为我在此等候着；但不久

For I attend here: but I'll see you soon.

Bianca   'Tis very good; I must be circumstanc'd.

[Exeunt.]

我会来看你。

碧盎佳　　　　　　　　很好，我得将就这情势。

〔同下。

ACT IV.

SCENE I. *Before the Castle.*

[*Enter* Othello *and* Iago.]

Iago Will you think so?

Othello   *Think so*, Iago!

Iago   What,

To kiss in private?

Othello   An unauthoriz'd kiss.

Iago Or to be naked with her friend in bed

An hour or more, not meaning any harm?

Othello Naked in bed, Iago, and not mean harm!

It is hypocrisy against the devil:

They that mean virtuously and yet do so,

The devil their virtue tempts, and they tempt heaven.

Iago So they do nothing, 'tis a venial slip:

But if I give my wife a handkerchief, —

Othello What then?

Iago Why, then, 'tis hers, my lord, and being hers,

She may, I think, bestow't on any man.

第 四 幕

第 一 景

[堡垒前]
[奥赛罗与伊耶戈上。

伊 耶 戈　您会这样想？

奥 赛 罗　　　　　这样想，伊耶戈！

伊 耶 戈　　　　　　　　　什么！
私下里亲嘴？

奥 赛 罗　　　　一个不同意的接吻。

伊 耶 戈　或光着身子跟她的朋友在床上
一点来钟，不想干什么坏事？

奥 赛 罗　光身在床上，伊耶戈，而不想干坏事！
这是对魔鬼装假作歹：他们
用意如果是纯洁的，而那么做了，
魔鬼就试探他们的德性，而他们
则试探了上帝。

伊 耶 戈　　　　　他们若不干什么，
那是个可原谅的疏误；但若是我给
我妻子一块手帕，——

奥 赛 罗　　　　　那便怎么样？

伊 耶 戈　哎也，那就是她的了，主公；而既然
是她的，她可以，我想，把它给任何人。

Othello   She is protectress of her honour too:
May she give that?

Iago   Her honour is an essence that's not seen;
They have it very oft that have it not:
But, for the handkerchief, —

Othello   By heaven, I would most gladly have forgot it: —
Thou said'st, —O, it comes o'er my memory,
As doth the raven o'er the infected house,
Boding to all, —he had my handkerchief.

Iago   Ay, what of that?

Othello   That's not so good now.

Iago   What,
If I had said I had seen him do you wrong?
Or heard him say, —as knaves be such abroad,
Who having, by their own importunate suit,
Or voluntary dotage of some mistress,
Convinced or supplied them, cannot choose
But they must blab, —

Othello   Hath he said anything?

Iago   He hath, my lord; but be you well assur'd,
No more than he'll unswear.

Othello   What hath he said?

Iago   Faith, that he did, —I know not what he did.

Othello   What? what?

Iago   Lie, —

Othello   With her?

Iago   With her, on her, what you will.

Othello   Lie with her! lie on her! —We say lie

奥　赛　罗	她是她荣誉的保护人；她能给掉 那个吗？
伊　耶　戈	她荣誉是个看不见的东西； 他们没名誉的人倒时常有着它： 可是说起那手帕，——
奥　赛　罗	凭上天，我但愿 能把它忘掉：——你说过，——嗳呀！我记起 它来了，好像那染了瘟疫的房子 顶上那乌鸦，兆头总不祥，——他有了 我那块手帕。
伊　耶　戈	不错，那个怎么说？
奥　赛　罗	那事儿如今可不怎么好。
伊　耶　戈	我若说 我见他干了对您不起的勾当，又怎样？ 或是听他说，——外边有这样的坏蛋， 他们凭他们自己那股切的追求， 或者某个娘们自情愿要颠倒， 一旦把她们弄到手，或满足了欲望， 便有口难噤，熬不住要泄漏，——
奥　赛　罗	他说了 什么东西没有？
伊　耶　戈	他说了，主公； 但可以保证您，他会矢口否认。
奥　赛　罗	他说了什么？
伊　耶　戈	当真，他干了那个—— 我不知他干了什么。
奥　赛　罗	什么？什么？
伊　耶　戈	躺在——
奥　赛　罗	和她一起？
伊　耶　戈	她一起，她身上； 您高兴就怎样说吧。
奥　赛　罗	躺在她一起！躺在她身上！我们说，撒她的谎，当他

on her when they belie her. —Lie with her! that's
fulsome. —Handkerchief— confessions— handkerchief!—
To confess, and be hanged for his labour, —first, to
be hanged, and then to confess. —I tremble at it. Nature would not invest herself in such shadowing passion without some instruction. It is not words that
shake me thus: — pish! — noses, ears, and lips. — Is't
possible? — Confess, — handkerchief! — O devil! —

[*Falls in a trance.*]

Iago Work on,
My medicine, work! Thus credulous fools are caught;
And many worthy and chaste dames even thus,
All guiltless, meet reproach. —What, ho! my lord!
My lord, I say! Othello!

[*Enter* Cassio.]

How now, Cassio!

Cassio What's the matter?

Iago My lord is fallen into an epilepsy:
This is his second fit; he had one yesterday.

Cassio Rub him about the temples.

Iago   No, forbear;
The lethargy must have his quiet course:
If not, he foams at mouth, and by and by
Breaks out to savage madness. Look, he stirs:
Do you withdraw yourself a little while,
He will recover straight: when he is gone,
I would on great occasion speak with you.

[*Exit* Cassio.]

How is it, general? have you not hurt your head?

Othello Dost thou mock me?

Iago   I mock you! no, by heaven.
Would you would bear your fortune like a man!

Othello A horned man's a monster and a beast.

Iago There's many a beast, then, in a populous

们捏造她假话的时候。躺在她一起！那叫人作呕。
手帕，——自己招供，——手帕！去自己招供，然后为
他那辛苦而去给绞死。首先，给绞死，然后去自己招
供：我对此要发抖。人的天性不会给这些庞杂的心影
充塞着自己而无动于衷。震动我的不是这几个字眼。
呸！鼻子，耳朵，嘴唇。这可能吗？——自己招认！
—手帕！——啊，魔鬼！

〔昏厥倒地〕

伊　耶　戈　发作吧，
　　　　　我的药，发作！轻信的呆子便这般
　　　　　给逮住；而好多一本清贞的贤淑
　　　　　便如此，无辜受谴责。怎么了，喂！
　　　　　主公！我说呀！奥赛罗，主公！
　　　　　　　　　〔凯昔欧上。
　　　　　　　　　　　　　　你来
　　　　　做什么，凯昔欧？

凯　昔　欧　　　　　　　有什么事情？

伊　耶　戈　我主公昏倒了过去；这是他第二次；
　　　　　他昨天曾有过一回。

凯　昔　欧　　　　　　　　摩擦他太阳穴。

伊　耶　戈　不用，免掉，这昏睡得静静地挺过，
　　　　　否则他口吐白沫，过一会他会
　　　　　有一阵凶暴的疯癫。瞧！他动了；
　　　　　你且走开一会儿，他立刻会醒来；
　　　　　他去后，我有重要的因由跟你谈。〔凯昔欧下。
　　　　　怎样了，将军？脑袋没有摔痛吧？

奥　赛　罗　你嘲笑我吧？

伊　耶　戈　　　　　　嘲笑您！不会，凭上天。
　　　　　但愿您承受命运像个男子汉！

奥　赛　罗　一个人戴了绿头巾便是个妖怪，
　　　　　又是头畜生。

伊　耶　戈　　　　　　在人口稠密的城市中，

city,

And many a civil monster.

Othello   Did he confess it?

Iago   Good sir, be a man;
Think every bearded fellow that's but yok'd
May draw with you: there's millions now alive
That nightly lie in those unproper beds
Which they dare swear peculiar: your case is better.
O, 'tis the spite of hell, the fiend's arch-mock,
To lip a wanton in a secure couch,
And to suppose her chaste! No, let me know;
And knowing what I am, I know what she shall be.

Othello   O, thou art wise; 'tis certain.

Iago   Stand you awhile apart;
Confine yourself but in a patient list.
Whilst you were here o'erwhelmed with your grief, —
A passion most unsuiting such a man, —
Cassio came hither: I shifted him away,
And laid good 'scuse upon your ecstasy;
Bade him anon return, and here speak with me;
The which he promis'd. Do but encave yourself,
And mark the fleers, the gibes, and notable scorns,
That dwell in every region of his face;
For I will make him tell the tale anew, —
Where, how, how oft, how long ago, and when
He hath, and is again to cope your wife:
I say, but mark his gesture. Marry, patience;
Or I shall say you are all in all in spleen,

那就有好多头畜生,好多个温文
尔雅的妖怪。

奥　赛　罗　　　　　　他自己供认吗?

伊　耶　戈　　　　　　　　　　好主公,
要做个汉子;须知每一个须眉
只要成过婚就许会和您同处境;
成百万丈夫每夜躺在那床头,
不光自己睡,滥污不堪,他们却
敢于赌咒那只供他们自己用;
您的处境还算好。唉哪! 这真是
捱地狱的烦恼,当魔鬼的主要大笑柄,
在一只安稳无疑的床上跟一个
淫妇亲着嘴,以为她很清贞。不,
要让我知道;知道了我自己的处境,
我知道该把她怎么样。

奥　赛　罗　　　　　　　　啊! 你想得
周到;这毫无疑问。

伊　耶　戈　　　　　　　　您站开一会儿;
将您自己关闭在能耐心守候处。
您刚才在此因悲伤——一阵不配您
这般身份的激情——而委顿不胜时,
凯昔欧来到了这里;我设法使他走,
对您的这番昏厥则善加以托辞;
我要他立刻回转头,和我来打话;
他答应这么办。您只须将自己藏起来,
观察他满脸到处的轻蔑、讥嘲
与极度的戏谑;因为我要促使他
重讲这故事,在那里,怎样,多久常,
几久前,以及恁时候他已经、且还将
同您的夫人共衾枕;我说,只看他
那表情已经够。凭圣母,务必要耐心;
否则,我要说您整个儿是激情的冲动,

And nothing of a man.

Othello   Dost thou hear, Iago?
I will be found most cunning in my patience;
But, — dost thou hear? — most bloody.

Iago   That's not amiss;
But yet keep time in all. Will you withdraw?

[Othello *withdraws.*]

Now will I question Cassio of Bianca,
A housewife that, by selling her desires,
Buys herself bread and clothes: it is a creature
That dotes on Cassio, — as 'tis the strumpet's plague
To beguile many and be beguil'd by one: —
He, when he hears of her, cannot refrain
From the excess of laughter: — here he comes: —

[*Re-enter* Cassio.]

As he shall smile Othello shall go mad;
And his unbookish jealousy must construe
Poor Cassio's smiles, gestures, and light behavior
Quite in the wrong. How do you now, lieutenant?

Cassio   The worser that you give me the addition
Whose want even kills me.

Iago   Ply Desdemona well, and you are sure on't.
[*Speaking lower.*] Now, if this suit lay in Bianca's pow-
    er,
How quickly should you speed!

Cassio   Alas, poor caitiff!

Othello   [*Aside.*] Look, how he laughs already!

Iago   I never knew a woman love man so.

Cassio   Alas, poor rogue! I think, i'faith, she loves me.

Othello   [*Aside.*] Now he denies it faintly and laughs
    it out.

Iago   Do you hear, Cassio?

Othello   [*Aside.*]   Now he importunes him
To tell it o'er: go to; well said, well said.

Iago   She gives it out that you shall marry her:

　　　　　　　　算不了一个男子汉。

奥　赛　罗　　　　　　　　　　　听见吗,伊耶戈?
　　　　　　　　你将见到我耐心里有异常的机巧;
　　　　　　　　但也有——你听到没有?——异常的杀机。

伊　耶　戈　　那可没有错;但一切进行得要适时。
　　　　　　　您退下如何?　　　　　　　　[奥赛罗退避]
　　　　　　　　　　　现在我要对凯昔欧
　　　　　　　问起碧盎佳,一个靠卖笑来吃饭
　　　　　　　穿衣的花姑娘;那东西爱上了凯昔欧;
　　　　　　　这真是窑姐儿的苦恼,欺骗了众人,
　　　　　　　到头来倒给一个人儿来把她欺。
　　　　　　　他只要听得谈起她,止不住呵呵笑。
　　　　　　　这里他来了:
　　　　　　　　　　[凯昔欧上。
　　　　　　　　　　　他准会咧开口嬉笑,
　　　　　　　奥赛罗准气得发疯;他无知的妒忌
　　　　　　　一定把可怜的凯昔欧的笑乐、姿态、
　　　　　　　轻狂的举动,都缠错。您好,副将军?

凯　昔　欧　　你给我这称呼更加糟,就为了没有它
　　　　　　　才要我的老命。

伊　耶　戈　　　　　　好好求玳思狄莫娜,
　　　　　　　你准会得到手。[声音放低]如今,若是这件事
　　　　　　　碧盎佳力所能及,你多快就成功!

凯　昔　欧　　唉哟! 可怜的阿奴!

奥　赛　罗　　[旁白]瞧! 他已经在笑了!

伊　耶　戈　　我从未听说过女人这么爱男人过。

凯　昔　欧　　唉哟! 可怜的小蹄子,我想她真爱我。

奥　赛　罗　　[旁白]现在他微微地否认,笑一下遮盖过去。

伊　耶　戈　　你听说过吗,凯昔欧?

奥　赛　罗　　[旁白]　　　　　现在他要他
　　　　　　　再把它讲一遍;得了;说得好,说得好。

伊　耶　戈　　她对人声言,你准会跟她结婚;

Do you intend it?

Cassio   Ha, ha, ha!

Othello   [*Aside.*] Do you triumph, Roman? do you triumph?

Cassio   I marry her! — what? A customer! I pr'ythee, bear some charity to my wit; do not think it so unwholesome: — ha, ha, ha!

Othello   [*Aside.*] So, so, so, so: they laugh that win.

Iago   Faith, the cry goes that you shall marry her.

Cassio   Pr'ythee, say true.

Iago   I am a very villain else.

Othello   [*Aside.*] Have you scored me? Well.

Cassio   This is the monkey's own giving out: she is persuaded I will marry her, out of her own love and flattery, not out of my promise.

Othello   [*Aside.*] Iago beckons me; now he begins the story.

Cassio   She was here even now; she haunts me in every place. I was the other day talking on the sea bank with certain Venetians, and thither comes the bauble, and falls thus about my neck, —

Othello   [*Aside.*] Crying, *O dear Cassio*! as it were: his gesture imports it.

Cassio   So hangs, and lolls, and weeps upon me; so hales and pulls me: ha, ha, ha!

Othello   [*Aside.*] Now he tells how she plucked him to my chamber. O, I see that nose of yours, but not that dog I shall throw it to.

Cassio   Well, I must leave her company.

Iago   Before me! look where she comes.

Cassio   'Tis such another fitchew! marry, a perfumed one.

[*Enter* Bianca.]

What do you mean by this haunting of me?

Bianca   Let the devil and his dam haunt you! What did you mean by that same handkerchief you gave me even now? I was a fine fool to take it. I must take

你有意那样吗？

凯　昔　欧　哈,哈,哈!

奥　赛　罗　[旁白]你得胜欢呼吧,罗马人? 你得胜欢呼吧?

凯　昔　欧　我跟她结婚! 什么? 一个妓女? 我请你,对我的常识稍存一点好感吧;莫以为它是这样的一塌糊涂。哈,哈,哈!

奥　赛　罗　[旁白]好,好,好,好。他们赢到了手的,会欢笑。

伊　耶　戈　说实话,传闻说你准会和她结婚。

凯　昔　欧　请你要说真话。

伊　耶　戈　骗了你,我是个坏蛋。

奥　赛　罗　你跟我算清了账吗? 很好。

凯　昔　欧　那是这猴儿自己放出去的空气:她相信我一定会和她结婚,因为她自己眷恋我而自骗自,不是因为我答应了她。

奥　赛　罗　[旁白]伊耶戈在招呼我;现在他要讲这故事了。

凯　昔　欧　刚才她还在这里;她到处缠绕着我。那一天我在海岸边同几个威尼斯人谈话,这玩意儿就去到了那里,凭这只手,她就搂着我的脖子;——

奥　赛　罗　[旁白]叫道,"啊唷,亲爱的凯昔欧!"仿佛是;他的姿态是这样说。

凯　昔　欧　这般挂在我身上,斜倚着我,对我哭闹;这般拖我,拉我;哈,哈,哈!

奥　赛　罗　[旁白]现在他在讲她怎样扯着他到我房间里去。啊! 我瞧见你那个鼻子,待我马上把它揪住了撕下来扔给狗吃。

凯　昔　欧　唔,我一定得离开她。

伊　耶　戈　凭我的灵魂! 瞧,她在那儿来了。

凯　昔　欧　这是这样一只骚猫! 凭圣母,一只骚香的。

　　　　　　　　　　[碧盎佳上。

你是什么意思,这样对我缠绕不清?

碧　盎　佳　让魔鬼和他娘缠绕你! 你刚正给我那条手帕,你是什么意思? 我是个傻瓜蛋,接受了下来。我得把花

out the work?—A likely piece of work that you should find it in your chamber and not know who left it there! This is some minx's token, and I must take out the work? There,—give it your hobby-horse: wheresoever you had it, I'll take out no work on't.

Cassio   How now, my sweet Bianca! how now! how now!

Othello   [*Aside.*] By heaven, that should be my handkerchief!

Bianca   An you'll come to supper to-night, you may; an you will not, come when you are next prepared for.
[*Exit.*]

Iago   After her, after her.

Cassio   Faith, I must; she'll rail in the street else.

Iago   Will you sup there?

Cassio   Faith, I intend so.

Iago   Well, I may chance to see you; for I would very fain speak with you.

Cassio   Pr'ythee, come; will you?

Iago   Go to; say no more.   [*Exit* Cassio.]

Othello   [*Coming forward.*] How shall I murder him, Iago?

Iago   Did you perceive how he laughed at his vice?

Othello   O Iago!

Iago   And did you see the handkerchief?

Othello   Was that mine?

Iago   Yours, by this hand: and to see how he prizes the foolish woman your wife! she gave it him, and he hath given it his whore.

Othello   I would have him nine years a-killing. — A fine woman! a fair woman! a sweet woman!

Iago   Nay, you must forget that.

Othello   Ay, let her rot, and perish, and be damned to-night; for she shall not live: no, my heart is turned to stone; I strike it, and it hurts my hand. — O, the world hath not a sweeter creature: she might lie by an emperor's side, and command him tasks.

Iago   Nay, that's not your way.

Othello   Hang her! I do but say what she is:—so delicate

样落下来！好一片花绣，你在你卧房里找到，而不知道什么人把它留在那里的！这是什么淫妇的信物，而我得落下它的花样！拿去，给还你那匹骑够了的马儿；不管你打哪儿弄来的，我不给落什么花样！

凯　昔　欧　怎么了，亲爱的碧盎佳？怎么了，怎么了？

奥　赛　罗　[旁白]凭上天，那该是我的手帕！

碧　盎　佳　你若是今晚上要来吃饭，可以来；你若是今晚上不来，就下次准备来时来。　　　　　　　　[下。

伊　耶　戈　跟她去，跟她去。

凯　昔　欧　当真，我得去；不然的话，她要在街头骂街了。

伊　耶　戈　你要在那里吃晚饭吗？

凯　昔　欧　当真，我想要那样。

伊　耶　戈　很好，我也许来看你，因为我极愿意跟你去谈谈。

凯　昔　欧　请你来好了；你来吗？

伊　耶　戈　得了；别多说了。　　　　　　　　　[凯昔欧下。

奥　赛　罗　[上前]我将怎样杀掉他，伊耶戈？

伊　耶　戈　您见到没有，他怎样对他的罪孽行为嬉笑？

奥　赛　罗　啊！伊耶戈！

伊　耶　戈　您可见到了那手帕吗？

奥　赛　罗　那是我的吗？

伊　耶　戈　是您的，凭我这只手；您看他怎样瞧得起那傻妇人您的夫人！她把它给了他，他却把它给了他的窑姐儿。

奥　赛　罗　我要杀他九个年头。一个好婆娘！一个标致婆娘！一个可爱的婆娘！

伊　耶　戈　休那样，您一定得忘掉那个。

奥　赛　罗　是哟，让她今晚上就腐烂，死绝，进地狱；因为她不会再活下去了。不光那个，我的心变成了石头；我打它，我的手都打痛了。啊咳！这人间再没有个更可爱的人儿了；她配去躺在一位皇帝身旁而命令他做事情。

伊　耶　戈　不对，您那样讲不对头。

奥　赛　罗　绞死她！我只说她是怎么样的人儿。针线上这么精

with her needle!—an admirable musician! O, she will sing the savageness out of a bear!—Of so high and plenteous wit and invention!—

Iago She's the worse for all this.

Othello O, a thousand, a thousand times:—and then, of so gentle a condition!

Iago Ay, too gentle.

Othello Nay, that's certain:—but yet the pity of it, Iago!

O Iago, the pity of it, Iago!

Iago If you are so fond over her iniquity, give her patent to offend; for, if it touch not you, it comes near nobody.

Othello I will chop her into messes.—Cuckold me!

Iago O, 'tis foul in her.

Othello With mine officer!

Iago That's fouler.

Othello Get me some poison, Iago; this night.—I'll not expostulate with her, lest her body and beauty unprovide my mind again:—this night, Iago.

Iago Do it not with poison; strangle her in her bed, even the bed she hath contaminated.

Othello Good, good: the justice of it pleases: very good.

Iago And for Cassio,—let me be his undertaker:—you shall hear more by midnight.

Othello Excellent good. [*A trumpet within.*] What trumpet is that same?

Iago Something from Venice, sure. 'Tis Lodovico Come from the duke: and, see, your wife is with him.

[*Enter* Lodovico, Desdemona, *and* Attendants.]

Lodovico Save you, worthy general!

Othello   With all my heart, sir.

Lodovico The duke and senators of Venice greet

工！吹弹得好不叫人赞赏！啊也，她能把一头大熊
的凶暴歌唱掉！有这样高超、这样富厚的机灵和
巧慧！

伊　耶　戈　她有了这一切更加坏。

奥　赛　罗　啊！坏一千，一千倍。而且，性情这样温柔！

伊　耶　戈　不错，太温柔了。

奥　赛　罗　不光那样，那还是肯定的；——但是这真叫可怜，伊
耶戈！啊！伊耶戈，这真叫可惜，伊耶戈！

伊　耶　戈　您如果这般爱惜她的罪恶，可以特许她去干坏事；因
为假如这于您无关，对旁人便更无罣碍。

奥　赛　罗　我要把她剁成肉酱。给我做乌龟！

伊　耶　戈　啊！她这下子真恶毒！

奥　赛　罗　跟我的部下！

伊　耶　戈　那更恶毒。

奥　赛　罗　替我弄点毒药来，伊耶戈；今晚上：我将不跟她打话，
否则她那身体和美貌又会要夺掉我的决心。今晚
上，伊耶戈。

伊　耶　戈　不要使毒药，在床上勒死她，就在她弄脏了的那
床上。

奥　赛　罗　好，好，这件事的公平叫人高兴；好得很。

伊　耶　戈　至于凯昔欧，让我去收拾他；您在午夜前准会再听到
消息。

奥　赛　罗　非常好。　　　　　　　　　　　〔幕后作号角声〕
那是什么号角？

伊　耶　戈　一定是威尼斯有什么事情到此。
这是罗铎维哥，公爵派他来；
瞧吧，您夫人和他在一起。
　　〔罗铎维哥、玳思狄莫娜与随从等人上。

罗铎维哥　上帝保佑您，尊贵的将军！

奥　赛　罗　　　　　　　　　　我衷心
祝祷，大人。

罗铎维哥　　　　公爵和威尼斯的知政事

you. [*Gives him a packet.*]

Othello I kiss the instrument of their pleasures.

[*Opens the packet and reads.*]

Desdemona And what's the news, good cousin Lodovico?

Iago I am very glad to see you, signior;
Welcome to Cyprus.

Lodovico I thank you. How does Lieutenant Cassio?

Iago Lives, sir.

Desdemona Cousin, there's fall'n between him and my
lord
An unkind breach: but you shall make all well.

Othello Are you sure of that?

Desdemona My lord?

Othello [*Reads.*] *This fail you not to do, as you
will,* —

Lodovico He did not call; he's busy in the paper.
Is there division 'twixt my lord and Cassio?

Desdemona A most unhappy one: I would do much
To atone them, for the love I bear to Cassio.

Othello Fire and brimstone!

Desdemona   My lord?

Othello   Are you wise?

Desdemona What, is he angry?

Lodovico   May be the letter mov'd him;
For, as I think, they do command him home,
Deputing Cassio in his government.

Desdemona Trust me, I am glad on't.

Othello   Indeed!

Desdemona   My lord?

Othello I am glad to see you mad.

Desdemona   Why, sweet Othello, —

Othello Devil!   [*Striking her.*]

	大夫们向您致意。	［授予彼一缄书帖］
奥　赛　罗	我吻这公文。	［启封阅读］
玳思狄莫娜	有什么消息，好表兄罗铎维哥？	
伊　耶　戈	我很高兴看见您尊驾，大人；	
	欢迎光临到塞浦路斯来。	
罗铎维哥	多谢。副将军凯昔欧怎样了？	
伊　耶　戈	活着，大人。	
玳思狄莫娜	表兄，他跟我官人之间发生了	
	失和的破裂；可是您准会导致	
	和睦。	
奥　赛　罗	你对那可有把握？	
玳思狄莫娜	官人？	
奥　赛　罗	［读书帖］"此事望君毋勿，盖君将"——	
罗铎维哥	他没有招呼；他在忙着看书帖。	
	将军与凯昔欧之间可有不和协？	
玳思狄莫娜	一个非常不幸的不和协；我愿意	
	尽力使他们和解，为了我对于	
	凯昔欧的爱顾。	
奥　赛　罗	天打雷劈	
玳思狄莫娜	官人？	
奥　赛　罗	你懂得羞耻吗？	
玳思狄莫娜	什么！他生气了吗？	
罗铎维哥	也许这书帖激怒了他；因为，我想，	
	他们命令他回去，而叫凯昔欧	
	接任他的指挥。	
玳思狄莫娜	相信我，我很高兴。	
奥　赛　罗	当真！	
玳思狄莫娜	官人？	
奥　赛　罗	我高兴看到你全没有	
	控制。	
玳思狄莫娜	为什么！亲爱的奥赛罗？	
奥　赛　罗	魔鬼！　［击之］	

Desdemona　　　　　I have not deserv'd this.

Lodovico　My lord, this would not be believ'd in Venice,
Though I should swear I saw't: 'tis very much:
Make her amends; she weeps.

Othello　　　　　　　　O devil, devil!
If that the earth could teem with woman's tears,
Each drop she falls would prove a crocodile. —
Out of my sight!

Desdemona　[*Going.*] I will not stay to offend you.

Lodovico　Truly, an obedient lady: —
I do beseech your lordship, call her back.

Othello　Mistress!

Desdemona　　　　My lord?

Othello　　　　　　　　What would you with her, sir?

Lodovico　Who, I, my lord?

Othello　Ay; you did wish that I would make her turn:
Sir, she can turn, and turn, and yet go on,
And turn again; and she can weep, sir, weep;
And she's obedient, as you say, — obedient, —
Very obedient. — Proceed you in your tears. —
Concerning this, sir, — O well-painted passion!
I am commanded home. — Get you away;
I'll send for you anon. — Sir, I obey the mandate,
And will return to Venice. — Hence, avaunt!
　　　　　　　　　　　　[*Exit* Desdemona.]
Cassio shall have my place. And, sir, to-night,
I do entreat that we may sup together:
You are welcome, sir, to Cyprus. — Goats and monkeys!
　　　　　　　　　　　　　　[*Exit.*]

Lodovico　Is this the noble Moor whom our full senate

玳思狄莫娜	我不该遭受这样子。
罗铎维哥	将军,威尼斯 不会有人相信这件事,虽然我 会赌咒曾亲自见到:这真受不了; 对她赔个不是吧,她在哭了。
奥　赛　罗	啊,魔鬼,魔鬼! 假使这地土里 落进了女人的眼泪能怀胎,每一颗 她掉的泪水会变成一条鳄鱼。 莫在我跟前!
玳思狄莫娜	〔拟下〕我不会呆着惹你恼。
罗铎维哥	真是位温顺的贤淑; 我请您将军,叫她回来。
奥　赛　罗	娘子!
玳思狄莫娜	官人?
奥　赛　罗	您要跟她说什么,大人?
罗铎维哥	谁,我,将军?
奥　赛　罗	不错,您要我叫她回来:大人, 她能回来,回来,再走开,又回来; 她能哭泣,大人,哭泣;她温顺, 如您所说的,温顺,温顺之至。 继续淌你的眼泪吧。关于这个, 大人,——啊,装得好像真伤心! —— 我被命令回家去。你跟我走开; 我就会来叫你。大人,我服从命令, 我将回到威尼斯。走开! 去你的!

〔玳思狄莫娜下。

凯昔欧将接我的位置。还有,大人,
今晚上我请您和我一同进晚餐;
您受欢迎,大人,到塞浦路斯来。
山羊和猴子! 〔下。

罗铎维哥	这就是这位高贵 恢弘的摩尔人吗,我们整个知政事

Call all-in-all sufficient? Is this the nature
Whom passion could not shake? whose solid virtue
The shot of accident nor dart of chance
Could neither graze nor pierce?

Iago   He is much chang'd.

Lodovico   Are his wits safe? is he not light of brain?

Iago   He's that he is: I may not breathe my censure
What he might be, — if what he might he is not, —
I would to heaven he were!

Lodovico   What, strike his wife!

Iago   Faith, that was not so well; yet would I knew
That stroke would prove the worst!

Lodovico   Is it his use?
Or did the letters work upon his blood,
And new-create this fault?

Iago   Alas, alas!
It is not honesty in me to speak
What I have seen and known. You shall observe him;
And his own courses will denote him so
That I may save my speech: do but go after,
And mark how he continues.

Lodovico   I am sorry that I am deceiv'd in him.

                              [*Exeunt.*]

SCENE II. *A Room in the Castle.*

[*Enter* Othello *and* Emilia.]

Othello   You have seen nothing, then?

Emilia   Nor ever heard, nor ever did suspect.

Othello   Yes, you have seen Cassio and she together.

公署称之为完全称职而能干？
这般的天性，激情不能动摇吗？
他那坚实的美德，祸患的弹丸
或命运的箭镞，既不能擦伤毫厘，
也不能穿刺透不成？

伊　耶　戈　　　　　　　　他变得厉害。

罗铎维哥　他心神安全吗？他头脑没有毛病？

伊　耶　戈　他就是他这样；我不便说我的意见。
我但愿上天使他该怎样便怎样，
假如他不是像他该怎样的那样！

罗铎维哥　什么！打他的妻子！

伊　耶　戈　当真，那是不怎么好；可是，但愿我
确知那一下已坏到了尽头！

罗铎维哥　　　　　　　　　　　他惯常
这样吗？还是这缄帖激得他暴怒，
新造成这个过错？

伊　耶　戈　　　　　　　唉呀，唉呀！
我所见到的、知道的，由我说出来
不怎么适当。您准会亲自看到他，
他自己的行径会显示他的为人，
所以我可以省掉了言语。您只须
跟他走，注意他怎样继续行动。

罗铎维哥　我很抱憾弄错了他的为人。

　　　　　　　　　　　　　　　　　　　〔同下。

第　二　景

〔堡垒内一室〕
〔奥赛罗与爱米丽亚上。

奥　赛　罗　那么，你没有见到什么吗？

爱米丽亚　也从未听到过，也从未有过怀疑。

奥　赛　罗　不对，你见过凯昔欧跟她在一起。

Emilia But then I saw no harm, and then I heard
Each syllable that breath made up between them.

Othello What, did they never whisper?

Emilia   Never, my lord.

Othello Nor send you out o' the way?

Emilia   Never.

Othello To fetch her fan, her gloves, her mask, nor
nothing?

Emilia Never, my lord.

Othello   That's strange.

Emilia I durst, my lord, to wager she is honest,
Lay down my soul at stake: if you think other,
Remove your thought, — it doth abuse your bosom.
If any wretch have put this in your head,
Let heaven requite it with the serpent's curse!
For if she be not honest, chaste, and true,
There's no man happy; the purest of their wives
Is foul as slander.

Othello   Bid her come hither. — Go.

                              [*Exit* Emilia.]

She says enough; yet she's a simple bawd
That cannot say as much. This is a subtle whore,
A closet-lock-and-key of villainous secrets:
And yet she'll kneel and pray; I have seen her do't.

                    [*Enter* Emilia *with* Desdemona.]

Desdemona My lord, what is your will?

Othello   Pray, chuck, come hither.

Desdemona What is your pleasure?

Othello   Let me see your eyes;
Look in my face.

Desdemona   What horrible fancy's this?

爱 米 丽 亚	可是那时候我不见有什么害处，
	我听到他们之间每一个语音。
奥 赛 罗	什么！他们从不耳语吗？
爱 米 丽 亚	从来不，
	主公。
奥 赛 罗	也不差开你。
爱 米 丽 亚	从来不。
奥 赛 罗	比如，
	去取她的扇子，手套，假面，或别的？
爱 米 丽 亚	从来没有，主公。
奥 赛 罗	那倒奇怪了。
爱 米 丽 亚	我敢于打赌，主公，她是贞洁的，
	敢押下灵魂作注子：您如作别想，
	就丢开那想法；那会玷辱您的心。
	倘有个坏蛋使您相信这件事，
	让上天把加给长虫的诅咒责罚他！
	因为，如果她还不能算老实、贞洁
	与真诚，天下就再无快乐的男人了；
	他们最纯洁的妻子会得同丑闻
	一般腌臜。
奥 赛 罗	叫她到这里来；你去。 〔爱米丽亚下。
	她说够了；不过她是个没脑筋的鸨妈，
	说不出真情来。这是个奸诈的婊子，
	重门深锁，一库房下流的秘密；
	但她会跪下来祷告；我见过她这样。
	〔爱米丽亚与玳思狄莫娜上。
玳思狄莫娜	官人，你要怎么样？
奥 赛 罗	小鸡，这里来。
玳思狄莫娜	你乐意什么事？
奥 赛 罗	让我看你的眼睛；
	对我的脸望。
玳思狄莫娜	是什么可怕的怪想？

Othello [*To* Emilia.]Some of your function, mistress,
Leave procreants alone and shut the door;
Cough, or cry hem, if anybody come.
Your mystery, your mystery; — nay, despatch.

[*Exit* Emilia.]

Desdemona Upon my knees, what doth your speech import?
I understand a fury in your words,
But not the words.

Othello　　　　　Why, what art thou?

Desdemona Your wife, my lord; your true and loyal wife.

Othello Come, swear it, damn thyself;
Lest, being like one of heaven, the devils themselves
Should fear to seize thee: therefore be double-damn'd. —
Swear thou art honest.

Desdemona　　　　　Heaven doth truly know it.

Othello Heaven truly knows that thou art false as hell.

Desdemona To whom, my lord? with whom? how am I false?

Othello O Desdemona! — away! away! away!

Desdemona Alas the heavy day! — Why do you weep?
Am I the motive of these tears, my lord?
If haply you my father do suspect
An instrument of this your calling back,
Lay not your blame on me: if you have lost him,
Why, I have lost him too.

Othello　　　　　Had it pleas'd heaven
To try me with affliction; had they rain'd
All kinds of sores and shames on my bare head;
Steep'd me in poverty to the very lips;
Given to captivity me and my utmost hopes;

奥　赛　罗	[向爱米丽亚]来一点你的老本行,老板娘; 让男女两个在一起,把门关起来; 若是有人来,咳嗽或者哼一声。 你那秘密,那秘密;休那样,赶快。

　　　　　　　　　　　　　　　　　　　　　　[爱米丽亚下。

玳思狄莫娜	我跪在地上,你这话什么意思? 我懂得你话里有暴怒,但不懂你的话。
奥　赛　罗	哎也,你是什么?
玳思狄莫娜	你的妻,官人; 你真心和忠诚的妻子。
奥　赛　罗	来,起个誓, 咒你自己进地狱;否则,像是个 从上界下来的,魔鬼们不敢抓你去; 所以,要双重入地狱;发誓你贞洁。
玳思狄莫娜	上天真知道我如此。
奥　赛　罗	上天真知你 无信义跟地狱一般。
玳思狄莫娜	对谁,官人? 同谁? 我怎样无信义,不忠贞?
奥　赛　罗	啊! 玳思狄莫娜,走开,走开,走开!
玳思狄莫娜	唉哟,悲痛的日子! ——你为什么哭? 我可是你这眼泪的因由,官人? 假使你也许怀疑我父亲是使你 被召唤回去的主动者,莫对我责难; 你若是失掉了他,哎也,我同样 也失掉了他呀。
奥　赛　罗	如果上苍高兴 用悲怆来把我考验,他若把一应 伤痛和耻辱下降到我光着的头上, 把我沉浸在寒苦中直到嘴唇边, 使我和我最可靠的指望被奴役,

I should have found in some place of my soul
A drop of patience; but, alas, to make me
A fixed figure for the time, for scorn
To point his slow unmoving finger at! —
Yet could I bear that too; well, very well;
But there, where I have garner'd up my heart;
Where either I must live or bear no life, —
The fountain from the which my current runs,
Or else dries up; to be discarded thence!
Or keep it as a cistern for foul toads
To knot and gender in! — turn thy complexion there,
Patience, thou young and rose-lipp'd cherubin, —
Ay, there, look grim as hell!

Desdemona   I hope my noble lord esteems me honest.

Othello   O, ay; as summer flies are in the shambles,
That quicken even with blowing. O thou weed,
Who art so lovely fair, and smell'st so sweet,
That the sense aches at thee, — would thou hadst ne'er
    been born!

Desdemona   Alas, what ignorant sin have I committed?

Othello   Was this fair paper, this most goodly book,
Made to write whore upon? *What committed*!
Committed! — O thou public commoner!
I should make very forges of my cheeks,
That would to cinders burn up modesty,
Did I but speak thy deeds. — What committed!
Heaven stops the nose at it, and the moon winks;
The bawdy wind, that kisses all it meets,
Is hush'd within the hollow mine of earth,
And will not hear it. — *What committed*! —
Impudent strumpet!

我还能在我灵魂的深处找到
些微的宁静，但是，唉哟！叫我做
那固定的中心，给讥嘲的时世把它
那慢得几乎不动的指针指着走！
但那个我也能好好、很好地忍受；
可是那所在，——我精灵寄托的所在，
我生命的肇端或死亡之始初，那源泉
我这水流从其中溢出来或未溢
而先已干涸，——给从那去处驱逐掉！
或者，留得那去处作为脏水坑，
供丑秽的癞蛤蟆去交尾、生育、繁殖！
将花容变过去，你这"宁静"美姣娘；
你俊俏后生、贝齿朱唇的小仙娇，
是哟，暴露你地狱般可怕的真相吧！

玳思狄莫娜 我希望我高贵的官人认为我贞洁。

奥　赛　罗 啊也！不错，像夏天屠场里的苍蝇，
下过卵马上又怀胎。你啊，秽草！
你这般艳丽妖娆，芳香馥郁得
知觉想跟你接触，想念得发痛，
但愿你从未出生到这世上来。

玳思狄莫娜 唉呀！我犯了什么未知的罪辜？

奥　赛　罗 难道这洁白的纸张，这美好的书本，
是用来写上"娼妓"这名儿的吗？
犯了什么！犯了！啊，你这个
公开的窑姐！假如我讲你的行为，
我会把自己这两片脸颊化作
炼铁的熔炉，把羞耻烧成灰烬。
犯了什么！天公对它掩鼻子，
月亮闭着眼睛不要看，跟任何
它碰到的东西都接吻的滥贱的风儿，
也躲进了地穴不做声，不要听这件事。
犯了什么！不知羞耻的婊子！

Desdemona   By heaven, you do me wrong.

Othello   Are not you a strumpet?

Desdemona   No, as I am a Christian:
If to preserve this vessel for my lord
From any other foul unlawful touch
Be not to be a strumpet, I am none.

Othello   What, not a whore?

Desdemona   No, as I shall be sav'd.

Othello   Is't possible?

Desdemona   O, heaven forgive us!

Othello   I cry you mercy then:
I took you for that cunning whore of Venice
That married with Othello. — You, mistress,
That have the office opposite to Saint Peter,
And keep the gate of hell!

                    [*Re-enter* Emilia.]
                  You, you, ay, you!
We have done our course; there's money for your pains:
I pray you, turn the key, and keep our counsel.

                             [*Exit.*]

Emilia   Alas, what does this gentleman conceive? —
How do you, madam? how do you, my good lady?

Desdemona   Faith, half asleep.

Emilia   Good madam, what's the matter with my lord?

Desdemona   With who?

Emilia   Why, with my lord, madam.

Desdemona   Who is thy lord?

Emilia   He that is yours, sweet lady.

Desdemona   I have none: do not talk to me, Emilia;
I cannot weep; nor answer have I none
But what should go by water. Pr'ythee, to-night
Lay on my bed my wedding sheets, — remember; —

玳思狄莫娜	凭上天,你侮辱了我。
奥 赛 罗	你不是个婊子?
玳思狄莫娜	不是,正如我是个基督徒。假使 为我官人保持这身躯不受 旁人非法的肮脏的接触就不是 个婊子,我就不是。
奥 赛 罗	什么! 不是个 娼妓?
玳思狄莫娜	不是,正如我将会得拯救。
奥 赛 罗	这可能吗?
玳思狄莫娜	啊! 上天饶了我们吧。
奥 赛 罗	那么, 我请你原谅;我把你当作跟奥赛罗 结婚的那个狡诈的威尼斯娼妇。 你啊,老板娘,你门庭开设在圣彼得 对过,你守着地狱的大门! 　　　〔爱米丽亚重上。 你呀,你呀,是啊,你呀! 我们 已完了这一遭;这里有点钱给你。 我请你,把房门开锁,保守着秘密。　　　　〔下。
爱 米 丽 亚	唉哟! 这位将爷转什么念头? 怎么了,娘娘? 你怎样,亲爱的夫人?
玳思狄莫娜	当真,昏昏沉沉。
爱 米 丽 亚	亲爱的娘娘,我家将爷怎么了?
玳思狄莫娜	谁?
爱 米 丽 亚	哎也,我家将爷,娘娘。
玳思狄莫娜	你家将爷是谁?
爱 米 丽 亚	是你的官人,好夫人。
玳思狄莫娜	我没有官人;别跟我说话,爱米丽亚; 我不能哭泣,也不能回答你我没有, 只除了用眼泪。请你今晚上把我 结婚时的床单铺在床上;记住了:

And call thy husband hither.

Emilia   Here's a change indeed!

[*Exit.*]

Desdemona 'Tis meet I should be us'd so, very meet.

How have I been behav'd, that he might stick

The small'st opinion on my least misuse?

[*Re-enter* Emilia *with* Iago.]

Iago What is your pleasure, madam? How is't with you?

Desdemona I cannot tell. Those that do teach young babes

Do it with gentle means and easy tasks:

He might have chid me so; for in good faith,

I am a child to chiding.

Iago   What's the matter, lady?

Emilia Alas, Iago, my lord hath so bewhor'd her,

Thrown such despite and heavy terms upon her,

As true hearts cannot bear.

Desdemona Am I that name, Iago?

Iago   What name, fair lady?

Desdemona Such as she says my lord did say I was.

Emilia He call'd her whore: a beggar in his drink

Could not have laid such terms upon his callet.

Iago Why did he so?

Desdemona I do not know; I am sure I am none such.

Iago Do not weep, do not weep: — alas the day!

Emilia Hath she forsook so many noble matches,

Her father, and her country, and her friends,

To be call'd whore? would it not make one weep?

Desdemona It is my wretched fortune.

Iago   Beshrew him for't!

How comes this trick upon him?

Desdemona   Nay, heaven doth know.

还叫你丈夫这里来。

爱米丽亚　　　　　　　　　　这真是个巨变！　　　　　［下。

玳思狄莫娜　我会受这样的对待倒合适，很合适。
　　　　　我做了什么，就把我最坏的事儿
　　　　　来说，他怎么能说我犯什么罪辜？
　　　　　　　［伊耶戈与爱米丽亚上。

伊　耶　戈　您乐意什么事，娘娘？您觉得怎样？

玳思狄莫娜　我说不上来。他们教训小孩子，
　　　　　用温柔的手段，把轻松的事儿要他们
　　　　　去做；他也尽可以这样责骂我；
　　　　　因为，说实话，对责骂，我还是个小孩。

伊　耶　戈　什么事，夫人？

爱米丽亚　　　　　　　　唉哟！伊耶戈，将爷
　　　　　大骂她娼妓，一叠连鄙蔑她，把重话
　　　　　堆在她头上，肉做的心肠受不了。

玳思狄莫娜　我是那称呼吗，伊耶戈？

伊　耶　戈　　　　　　　　　什么称呼，
　　　　　明艳的夫人？

玳思狄莫娜　　　　　　如她所说的我官人
　　　　　叫我的那称呼。

爱米丽亚　他叫她娼妓；一个化子喝了酒
　　　　　也不能用这般丑话骂他的贱穷婆。

伊　耶　戈　为什么他这样？

玳思狄莫娜　我可不知道；我自知不是那种人。

伊　耶　戈　不要哭，不要哭。唉哟，天可怜见的！

爱米丽亚　是否她回绝了那么多贵家子的姻亲，
　　　　　舍弃了父亲，离别了乡邦，告辞了
　　　　　亲友们，为的是给叫作娼妓？那不要
　　　　　叫人伤心吗？

玳思狄莫娜　　　　　　这是我命里该受苦。

伊　耶　戈　要怪他太不该！他怎么想出这花样？

玳思狄莫娜　不懂，上天才知道。

Emilia   I will be hang'd,

if some eternal villain,

Some busy and insinuating rogue,

Some cogging, cozening slave,

to get some office,

Have not devis'd this slander;

I'll be hang'd else.

Iago   Fie,

there is no such man; it is impossible.

Desdemona   If any such there be,

heaven pardon him!

Emilia   A halter pardon him!

and hell gnaw his bones!

Why should he call her whore? who keeps her company?

What place? what time? what form? what likelihood?

The Moor's abused by some most villainous knave,

Some base notorious knave, some scurvy fellow: —

O heaven, that such companions thou'dst unfold,

And put in every honest hand a whip

To lash the rascals naked through the world

Even from the east to the west!

Iago   Speak within door.

Emilia   O, fie upon them!

some such squire he was

That turn'd your wit the seamy side without,

And made you to suspect me with the Moor.

Iago   You are a fool; go to.

Desdemona   Alas, Iago,

What shall I do to win my lord again?

Good friend, go to him;

for by this light of heaven,

爱 米 丽 亚	我宁愿给绞死，

爱 米 丽 亚　　　　　　　　我宁愿给绞死，
若不是什么骇人的坏蛋，什么
狗颠屁股、巴结拍马的恶棍，
什么欺哄诓骗的贼奴才，为谋求
职位，故意编造出这么个诽谤来；
我宁愿给绞死，如果不。

伊　耶　戈　　　　　　　　　　呸！没有
这样的人儿；不可能。

玳思狄莫娜　　　　　　　假使有这样人，
上天饶恕他！

爱 米 丽 亚　　　　　　让一条绞索饶恕他，
让恶痛在他骨头里边慢慢咬！
为什么他叫她娼妓？谁跟她在一起？
在什么地方？在什么时候？什么个
形象？有什么朕兆？这个摩尔人
上了那最混帐不过的恶贼的当，
那一准是个卑鄙龌龊得极荒唐、
十恶不赦的大王八。啊，天哟！
但愿你能暴露出这样的坏家伙，
叫每个诚实人手里有一根鞭子，
望那些赤裸裸的混混身上尽力抽，
打这世界的尽东头直抽到尽西头！

伊　耶　戈　轻声些。

爱 米 丽 亚　　　　　　啊！滚他们的蛋。那就是
这样个家伙，他把你理性的里子
翻到了外面来，叫你疑心我跟这
摩尔人有关系。

伊　耶　戈　　　　　　　你是个傻瓜；得了吧。

玳思狄莫娜　啊，好心的伊耶戈，我将怎么办，
才好使我的官人能回心转意？
我把你当朋友，请你去到他那里；
因为，凭这上苍的天光，我不知

I know not how I lost him. Here I kneel: —
If e'er my will did trespass 'gainst his love,
Either in discourse of thought or actual deed;
Or that mine eyes, mine ears, or any sense,
Delighted them in any other form;
Or that I do not yet, and ever did,
And ever will, though he do shake me off
To beggarly divorcement, — love him dearly,
Comfort forswear me! Unkindness may do much;
And his unkindness may defeat my life,
But never taint my love. I cannot say *whore*, —
It does abhor me now I speak the word;
To do the act that might the addition earn
Not the world's mass of vanity could make me.

Iago I pray you, be content; 'tis but his humour:
The business of the state does him offence,
And he does chide with you.

Desdemona If 'twere no other, —

Iago   'Tis but so, I warrant.

                           [*Trumpets* within.]

Hark, how these instruments summon to supper!
The messengers of Venice stay the meat:
Go in, and weep not; all things shall be well.

                   [*Exeunt* Desdemona *and* Emilia.]

                [*Enter* Roderigo.]

How now, Roderigo!

Roderigo I do not find that thou dealest justly with me.

Iago What in the contrary?

Roderigo Every day thou daffest me with some device, Iago; and rather, as it seems to me now,
keepest from me all conveniency than suppliest
me with the least advantage of hope. I will indeed
no longer endure it; nor am I yet persuaded to

我怎样会失掉了他。我在此下跪：
假使我这心志曾经触犯过他的爱，
不论在思想里头或者在行动中；
或是我的眼睛、耳朵、别的知觉
喜爱了除他以外的其他的形象；
或是我如今还没有、以前尚未曾、
将来若不会深深地爱他，即令他
用异常贫贱的离婚将我摒弃掉，
让欢乐永远跟我绝了缘！寡情
能造成绝大的后果；他对我恩断
义绝可能会斩除我这命，但决计
不会分毫损及我对他的爱。
我不能说"娼妓"这名儿：如今说它时，
我满腔恐怖而作呕；要僭得那称号，
就是满天下的虚荣也不能叫我
去干那勾当。

伊耶戈　　　　　　　我请你安心，这只是
他一时的性发；邦国的事务恼了他，
所以他对您会责怪。

玳思狄莫娜　　　　　　若不为别的，——
伊耶戈　只为了这个，我保证。　　　［幕后号角声起］
听吧！这些号子在传唤晚餐了；
威尼斯派来的信使们等着吃饭：
里边去，不要哭；一切事都会好转。

　　　　　　　　　［玳思狄莫娜与爱米丽亚下。
　　　　　　　　［洛窦列谷上。
你好，洛窦列谷？
洛窦列谷　我不见你在老实对待我。
伊耶戈　你怪我不好，根据的是什么？
洛窦列谷　你每天要耍点花样把我搪塞过去，伊耶戈；显得你，据我现在看来，宁愿不给我一切机会，也不肯给我些些哪怕是希望中的有利条件。我当真再也不能忍受

put up in peace what already I have foolishly suffered.

Iago   Will you hear me, Roderigo?

Roderigo   Faith, I have heard too much; for your words and performances are no kin together.

Iago   You charge me most unjustly.

Roderigo   With naught but truth. I have wasted myself out of my means. The jewels you have had from me to deliver to Desdemona would half have corrupted a votarist: you have told me she hath received them, and returned me expectations and comforts of sudden respect and acquaintance; but I find none.

Iago   Well; go to; very well.

Roderigo   *Very well! go to!* I cannot go to, man; nor 'tis not very well: nay, I say 'tis very scurvy, and begin to find myself fobbed in it.

Iago   Very well.

Roderigo   I tell you 'tis not *very well*. I will make myself known to Desdemona: if she will return me my jewels, I will give over my suit and repent my unlawful solicitation; if not, assure yourself I will seek satisfaction of you.

Iago   You have said now.

Roderigo   Ay, and said nothing but what I protest intendment of doing.

Iago   Why, now I see there's mettle in thee; and even from this instant do build on thee a better opinion than ever before. Give me thy hand, Roderigo. Thou hast taken against me a most just exception; but yet, I protest, I have dealt most directly in thy affair.

Roderigo   It hath not appeared.

Iago   I grant indeed it hath not appeared, and your suspicion is not without wit and judgement. But, Roderigo, if thou hast that in thee indeed, which I have greater reason to believe now than ever, — I mean purpose, courage, and valour, — this night show it: if thou the next night following enjoy not Desdemona, take me from this world with

下去了,你休想再叫我不声不响把我傻子般吃的苦头吞下去。

伊　耶　戈　你听我说好不好,洛窦列谷?

洛窦列谷　说实话,我听得太多了,因为你的话跟实际行动没有关系。

伊　耶　戈　你责备我得非常不公平。

洛窦列谷　完全凭事实。我浪费得超过了我的财力。你打我这里拿去的金珠宝石,交给玳思狄莫娜的,差不离能腐败一个立过誓笃信耶稣的圣处女;你告诉过我,她已经接受了它们,你带回来的是指望和鼓励,说马上能得到她注意和彼此相熟,但是我什么也不曾见到。

伊　耶　戈　好;得了,很好。

洛窦列谷　很好!得了!我不能得了,汉子;也不是很好:凭我这只手,我说,是很糟,我开始发现自己在这里头遭了骗。

伊　耶　戈　很好。

洛窦列谷　我告诉你这不是很好。我要对玳思狄莫娜去露我的真面目;如果她把我的珍宝还给我,我准会停止我对她的追求,改悔我非法的引诱;若是她不还的话,你可以拿稳,我要叫你赔偿损失。

伊　耶　戈　你现在说的。

洛窦列谷　不错,我所说不是别的,只是矢言我用意要去做到。

伊　耶　戈　哎也,如今我见到你有刚勇之气,从此刻开始我对你要比过去更加尊重了。把手伸给我,洛窦列谷;你对我不满极有道理;不过我矢言,我非常诚实地替你出过力。

洛窦列谷　未曾见得。

伊　耶　戈　我承认当真还未曾见得,而你的怀疑心是合乎情理的。但是,洛窦列谷,如其你胸中当真有那个在里头,我现在要比以往有更多的理由相信如此,我是说决断、勇气和果敢,今晚上须得把它显示出来;假使你明天晚上还享受不到玳思狄莫娜的话,用奸险的

treachery and devise engines for my life.

Roderigo Well, what is it? is it within reason and compass?

Iago Sir, there is especial commission come from Venice to depute Cassio in Othello's place.

Roderigo Is that true? why then Othello and Desdemona return again to Venice.

Iago O, no; he goes into Mauritania, and takes away with him the fair Desdemona, unless his abode be lingered here by some accident: wherein none can be so determinate as the removing of Cassio.

Roderigo How do you mean removing of him?

Iago Why, by making him uncapable of Othello's place; — knocking out his brains.

Roderigo And that you would have me to do?

Iago Ay, if you dare do yourself a profit and a right. He sups to-night with a harlotry, and thither will I go to him: — he knows not yet of his honourable fortune. If you will watch his going thence, — which I will fashion to fall out between twelve and one, — you may take him at your pleasure: I will be near to second your attempt, and he shall fall between us. Come, stand not amazed at it, but go along with me; I will show you such a necessity in his death that you shall think yourself bound to put it on him. It is now high supper-time, and the night grows to waste: about it.

Roderigo I will hear further reason for this.

Iago And you shall be satisfied.   [*Exeunt.*]

SCENE III. *Another Room in the Castle.*

[*Enter* Othello, Lodovico, Desdemona, Emilia, *and* Attendants.]

Lodovico I do beseech you, sir, trouble yourself no further.

Othello O, pardon me; 'twill do me good to walk.

办法弄死我,策划出巧计来斩断我这条命。

洛窦列谷　好,是什么事?那是在理性范围之内的吗?

伊　耶　戈　先生,威尼斯有特别命令到来,委任凯昔欧接替奥赛罗的职位。

洛窦列谷　那是真的吗?哎也,那么奥赛罗和玳思狄莫娜要回威尼斯去了。

伊　耶　戈　啊,不对!他去到毛列台尼亚,要带同了那标致的玳思狄莫娜一起去,除非有意外发生使他逗留下去;在那上头,除了干掉凯昔欧之外,没有事能起这样的决定作用。

洛窦列谷　你这是什么意思,干掉他?

伊　耶　戈　哎也,叫他不能接替奥赛罗的位置;砸烂他的脑子。

洛窦列谷　而那个你要我去干吗?

伊　耶　戈　不错;假如你敢于对自己做一件有利而公道的事。今晚上他跟一个烟花姑娘一起吃饭,我要到那里去看他,他还没有知道他这高贵的命运呢。若是你瞧准了他往那里去时,——我将使它在十二点和一点之间发生,——你可以任意拦截住他;我将在附近帮你忙,他一定会在你我之间给结果掉。来吧,莫在那里犹豫不决,跟我一起走;我要讲给你听他不死不行,然后你将理会到你非对他下手不可。此刻是早该吃晚饭的时候了,这黄昏快完了;上紧吧。

洛窦列谷　我还得再听听这正经的因由。

伊　耶　戈　你定将给说得满意信服。　　　　　〔同下。

第　三　景

〔堡垒内另一室〕

〔奥赛罗、罗铎维哥、玳思狄莫娜、
爱米丽亚与随从等人上。

罗铎维哥　我请您,将军,尊驾就在此留步。

奥　赛　罗　啊!原谅我;走走对我有好处。

Lodovico Madam, good night; I humbly thank your ladyship.

Desdemona Your honour is most welcome.

Othello   Will you walk, sir? —
O, — Desdemona, —

Desdemona   My lord?

Othello Get you to bed on the instant; I will be returned
forthwith: dismiss your attendant there: look't be
done.

Desdemona I will, my lord.

     [*Exeunt* Othello, Lodovico, *and* Attendants.]

Emilia How goes it now? he looks gentler than he did.

Desdemona He says he will return incontinent:
He hath commanded me to go to bed,
And bade me to dismiss you.

Emilia   Dismiss me!

Desdemona It was his bidding; therefore, good Emilia,
Give me my nightly wearing, and adieu:
We must not now displease him.

Emilia I would you had never seen him!

Desdemona So would not I: my love doth so approve
him,
That even his stubbornness, his checks, his frowns, —
Pr'ythee, unpin me, — have grace and favour in them.

Emilia I have laid those sheets you bade me on the bed.

Desdemona All's one. — Good faith, how foolish are our
minds! —
If I do die before thee, pr'ythee, shroud me
In one of those same sheets.

Emilia   Come, come, you talk.

Desdemona My mother had a maid call'd Barbara;
She was in love; and he she lov'd prov'd mad
And did forsake her: she had a song of *willow*;
An old thing 'twas, but it express'd her fortune,
And she died singing it: that song to-night

罗铎维哥	夫人,晚安了;多谢您盛情款待。
玳思狄莫娜	阁下能光临,欢迎得很。
奥 赛 罗	请先走一步好吗,大人? 噢! 玳思狄莫娜,——
玳思狄莫娜	官人?
奥 赛 罗	你立刻上床睡觉去;我顷刻就会回来;遣走你那个伴娘;仔细着做到这点。
玳思狄莫娜	我自会,官人。

[奥赛罗与罗铎维哥及随从等下。

爱米丽亚	现在怎么样? 他看来比过去要温和些。
玳思狄莫娜	他说他马上就回来;他对我吩咐 就去睡,又要我遣你走。
爱 米 丽 亚	遣我走!
玳思狄莫娜	这是他关照的;所以,好爱米丽亚, 把我的寝衣裤给我,就明儿再见: 我们如今再不能叫他不高兴。
爱 米 丽 亚	我但愿你从未见过他来。
玳思狄莫娜	我不愿如此;我把他喜欢到这样, 就是他的粗暴、责难和颦眉蹙额,—— 请你,将别针解开,——也显得气概, 对我很可爱。
爱 米 丽 亚	你要我铺下的床单 我已经铺在床上了。
玳思狄莫娜	没有关系。说真话! 我们的心思 多笨! 若是我比你先死,要请你 在这两条床单里一条来包扎我。
爱 米 丽 亚	算了,算了,你在胡说。
玳思狄莫娜	我母亲有一个青衣名叫巴白莉; 她爱上了个人,她爱的那个发了疯, 将她抛弃掉,她有只歌儿叫《柳条》; 那是支老山歌,但正好表白她命运, 她临死时节就唱它;今晚上那山歌

Will not go from my mind; I have much to do
But to go hang my head all at one side,
And sing it like poor Barbara.
Pr'ythee, despatch.

Emilia Shall I go fetch your night-gown?

Desdemona   No, unpin me here. —
This Lodovico is a proper man.

Emilia A very handsome man.

Desdemona He speaks well.

Emilia I know a lady in Venice would have walked bare-
foot to Palestine for a touch of his nether lip.

Desdemona [*Sings.*]

   The poor soul sat sighing by a sycamore tree,
      Sing all a green willow;
   Her hand on her bosom, her head on her knee,
      Sing willow, willow, willow:
   The fresh streams ran by her, and murmur'd her
   moans;
      Sing willow, willow, willow;
   Her salt tears fell from her, and soften'd the stones; —
Lay by these: —

[*Sings.*] *Sing willow, willow, willow;* —

Pr'ythee, hie thee; he'll come anon: —

[*Sings.*] *Sing all a green willow must be my garland.*
   Let nobody blame him; his scorn I approve, —

Nay, that's not next. — Hark! who is't that knocks?

Emilia It's the wind.

老在我头脑里打来回；我得极力
控制着自己，不把头偻得很低，
像可怜的巴白莉那样唱着那山歌。
请你快一些。

爱米丽亚   我要去取你的梳妆
长褂吗？

玳思狄莫娜   不用，这里把别针放开。
这罗铎维哥是一个体面人物。

爱米丽亚 出脱得极俊俏风流。

玳思狄莫娜   他很会说话。

爱米丽亚 我知道威尼斯有这么一位娘子，情愿打着赤脚走到
巴勒斯坦去，只要能碰一下他的下嘴唇。

玳思狄莫娜 ［唱］
"这可怜的人儿悲叹着，坐在棵无花果树旁，
    唱着一枝绿柳条；
她手捧着胸膛，头儿低到在膝盖上，
    唱柳条，柳条，柳条：
清清的河水应和着，流过她跟前；
    唱柳条，柳条，柳条：
她咸咸的眼泪落下来，石头都软绵；"——

把这些留起来：——

［唱］"唱柳条，柳条，柳条"：

请你快一些，他就要来了。——

［唱］"唱一枝绿柳条得要做我的花环。
休让人责备他，他对我的侮慢我喜欢，"——

不对，下面不是那么样。听啊！谁在敲门？

爱米丽亚 这是风。

Desdemona [*Sings.*] *I call'd my love false love; but what said he then?*
Sing willow, willow, willow:
If I court mo women, you'll couch with mo men.
So get thee gone; good night. Mine eyes do itch;
Doth that bode weeping?

Emilia   'Tis neither here nor there.

Desdemona I have heard it said so. — O, these men, these men! —
Dost thou in conscience think, — tell me, Emilia, —
That there be women do abuse their husbands
In such gross kind?

Emilia   There be some such, no question.

Desdemona Wouldst thou do such a deed for all the world?

Emilia Why, would not you?

Desdemona   No, by this heavenly light!

Emilia Nor I neither by this heavenly light; I might do't as well i' the dark.

Desdemona Wouldst thou do such a deed for all the world?

Emilia The world's a huge thing; it is a great price
For a small vice.

Desdemona   In troth, I think thou wouldst not.

Emilia In troth, I think I should; and undo't when I had done. Marry, I would not do such a thing for a joint-ring, nor for measures of lawn, nor for gowns, petticoats, nor caps, nor any petty exhibition; but, for the whole world — why, who would not make her husband a cuckold to make him a monarch? I should venture purgatory for't.

Desdemona Beshrew me, if I would do such a wrong

苔思狄莫娜　　〔唱〕"我说我情郎太负心；他便怎么讲？
　　　　　　　　　唱柳条，柳条，柳条；
　　　　　　　　我若向女娘们求爱，你会跟汉子们要好。"

　　　　　　　　就这样，你去吧，晚安。我眼睛在发痒；
　　　　　　　　那预示要哭吗？

爱 米 丽 亚　　　　　　　　　这没有什么相干。

苔思狄莫娜　　我听人这样说。啊！这些男人，
　　　　　　　这些男人！告诉我，爱米丽亚，
　　　　　　　你果真认为世界上有这样的女人，
　　　　　　　欺骗她们的丈夫有这么荒唐吗？

爱 米 丽 亚　　没疑问，有这样的女人。

苔思狄莫娜　　　　　　　　　　你肯做这事吗，
　　　　　　　即令为天大地大的好处？

爱 米 丽 亚　　　　　　　　　　哎也，
　　　　　　　你不肯做吗？

苔思狄莫娜　　　　　　　　不肯，凭着这天光！

爱 米 丽 亚　　在天光下面我也不肯做这种事；
　　　　　　　但在黑暗里我也许会做。

苔思狄莫娜　　　　　　　　　　你肯做
　　　　　　　这事吗，即令为天大地大的好处？

爱 米 丽 亚　　天大地大的好处是件大好处；
　　　　　　　这是做一件小坏事，博一桩大好处。

苔思狄莫娜　　说真话，我想你不会肯去做。

爱 米 丽 亚　　说真话，我想我应当去做，做过后再设法消除弥补。
　　　　　　　凭圣处女，我不会为了一只和合戒指，或者多少码细
　　　　　　　布，或者多少件长外褂、小衬衣，或者多少顶便帽，或
　　　　　　　者不论什么些的津贴，去做这样件件事儿；但是为整整
　　　　　　　天大地大一桩好处，谁不愿叫她丈夫戴上绿头巾，如
　　　　　　　果能使他变成一位帝王？为这个我甚至愿意冒险跑
　　　　　　　进净土界去经受火炼。

苔思狄莫娜　　天罚我，假使我干得这样的坏事，

for the whole world.

Emilia Why, the wrong is but a wrong i' the world; and having the world for your labour, 'tis a wrong in your own world, and you might quickly make it right.

Desdemona I do not think there is any such woman.

Emilia Yes, a dozen; and as many to the vantage as would store the world they play'd for.

But I do think it is their husbands' faults

If wives do fall: say that they slack their duties

And pour our treasures into foreign laps;

Or else break out in peevish jealousies,

Throwing restraint upon us; or say they strike us,

Or scant our former having in despite;

Why, we have galls; and though we have some grace,

Yet have we some revenge. Let husbands know

Their wives have sense like them: they see and smell

And have their palates both for sweet and sour,

As husbands have. What is it that they do

When they change us for others? Is it sport?

I think it is: and doth affection breed it?

I think it doth: is't frailty that thus errs?

It is so too. And have not we affections,

Desires for sport, and frailty, as men have?

Then let them use us well: else let them know

The ills we do their ills instruct us so.

Desdemona Good-night, good-night: heaven me such usage send,

Not to pick bad from bad, but by bad mend!

[*Exeunt.*]

　　　　　　　即令为天大地大的好处。

爱 米 丽 亚　哎也,那坏事只是天地之间的一桩坏事;而有了天地
　　　　　　　作为你辛苦的报酬,那坏事便成了你自己天地里的
　　　　　　　坏事了,那么,你很快就能把坏事弄好。

玳思狄莫娜　我想这世上不会有这样的女人。

爱 米 丽 亚　有的,有一打;而且再加上那么多,
　　　　　　　她们为赢得这天地间,能叫它生满了人。
　　　　　　　可是我以为这是丈夫们的过错,
　　　　　　　如果妻子们失足。比如说,他们
　　　　　　　忽略了应尽的责任,将我们份内
　　　　　　　该享的财富注入野女人的怀抱,
　　　　　　　或者闹脾气,因为发了呆而嫉妒,
　　　　　　　束缚住我们;或者,比如说,打我们,
　　　　　　　或减少原先的支应,出于恶意;
　　　　　　　哎也,我们会忿怒,虽然我们
　　　　　　　有美德,可也能报复。丈夫们要知道,
　　　　　　　他们的妻子跟他们一般有性欲;
　　　　　　　她们眼能见,鼻能嗅,有味官能知
　　　　　　　酸甜,如同丈夫们一个样。他们
　　　　　　　把我们换上别人时,做的是什么?
　　　　　　　为好玩? 我想那是的;情感冲动
　　　　　　　所造成? 我想那是的;这样的差失
　　　　　　　可是个弱点? 一点都不错;那么,
　　　　　　　我们可没有热情、好玩的欲望、
　　　　　　　弱点吗,跟男子们一样? 所以,让他们
　　　　　　　好好待我们;否则,让他们知道,
　　　　　　　我们的坏事,是他们的坏事所致。

玳思狄莫娜　晚安,晚安;求上帝给我些行止,
　　　　　　　不向坏榜样去学坏,要反自策励。

　　　　　　　　　　　　　　　　　　　　　　　　〔同下。

ACT V.

SCENE I. *A Street.*

[*Enter* Iago *and* Roderigo.]

Iago   Here, stand behind this bulk; straight will he
    come:
Wear thy good rapier bare, and put it home:
Quick, quick; fear nothing; I'll be at thy elbow:
It makes us, or it mars us; think on that,
And fix most firm thy resolution.

Roderigo   Be near at hand; I may miscarry in't.

Iago   Here, at thy hand: be bold, and take thy stand.

                  [*Retires to a little distance.*]

Roderigo   I have no great devotion to the deed;
And yet he hath given me satisfying reasons: —
'Tis but a man gone. — Forth, my sword; he dies.

                      [*Goes to his stand.*]

Iago   I have rubb'd this young quat almost to the sense,
And he grows angry. Now, whether he kill Cassio,
Or Cassio him, or each do kill the other,

第 五 幕

第 一 景

[近碧盎佳住处一街道]
[伊耶戈与洛窦列谷上。

伊 耶 戈 这里,站在这店架子后面;他立刻
就会来:握着你出鞘的匕首在手上,
要刺中。得赶快,赶快;休要害怕;
我将在你近旁。我们成功或失败,
都在这上头;要想到那上头,下定你
最坚强的决心。

洛 窦 列 谷 待在近边;我也许
失着。

伊 耶 戈 在这里,就在你附近:要大胆,
守候在这里。 [退避

洛 窦 列 谷 我对这件事没多大
热忱;可是他给了我满意的理由:
这不过干掉个把人:出盒来,剑儿;
叫他死。 [走到他站立处

伊 耶 戈 我把这小脓疱擦得差点儿
很痛,使他动了火。现在,不拘是
他杀了凯昔欧,或者凯昔欧杀了他,
或彼此互相格杀,都对我有利:

Every way makes my gain: live Roderigo,

He calls me to a restitution large

Of gold and jewels that I bobb'd from him,

As gifts to Desdemona;

It must not be: if Cassio do remain,

He hath a daily beauty in his life

That makes me ugly; and besides, the Moor

May unfold me to him; there stand I in much peril;

No, he must die. —But, so, I hear him coming.

[Enter Cassio. *]*

Roderigo I know his gait; 'tis he. —Villain, thou diest!

[Rushes out , and makes a pass at Cassio. *]*

Cassio That thrust had been mine enemy indeed,

But that my coat is better than thou know'st:

I will make proof of thine.

[Draws, and wounds Roderigo. *]*

Roderigo   O, I am slain!

*[*Iago *rushes from his post , cuts* Cassio *behind*

in the leg , and exit.]

Cassio I am maim'd forever. —Help, ho! murder! mur-

der!

[Falls.]

[Enter Othello *at a distance.]*

Othello The voice of Cassio: Iago keeps his word.

Roderigo O, villain that I am!

Othello   It is even so.

Cassio O, help, ho! light! a surgeon!

Othello 'Tis he: —O brave Iago, honest and just,

That hast such noble sense of thy friend's wrong!

Thou teachest me, —minion, your dear lies dead,

And your unbless'd fate hies. Strumpet, I come!

Forth of my heart those charms, thine eyes, are blotted;

　　　　　若洛窦列谷还活着,他要我取回
　　　　　一大堆金珠宝石,我向他骗来
　　　　　作礼品,说送给了玳思狄莫娜;
　　　　　这决计使不得:假使凯昔欧留下,
　　　　　他活在人间每天便是桩美事,
　　　　　使我相形便见丑;而且这摩尔人
　　　　　可能会告诉他我对他的行径;那样,
　　　　　我地位太危险。不行,他非死不可。
　　　　　就让它这样——我听到他在来了。
　　　　　　　　　　　　　　　　　〔凯昔欧上。

洛窦列谷　我听见他脚步;这是他。坏蛋,叫你死!
　　　　　　　　　　　　　　〔对凯昔欧投一冲刺〕

凯　昔　欧　那一下戳击本该夺掉我的命,
　　　　　　但我这外褂比你所料想的要好;
　　　　　　我试试你的却如何。
　　　　　　　　　　　　　　〔拔剑穿刺,击伤洛窦列谷〕

洛窦列谷　　　　　　　啊! 我死了。
　　　〔伊耶戈自后刺伤凯昔欧之腿,随即下场。

凯　昔　欧　我永远残废了。救人,喂呀! 凶杀!
　　　　　　凶杀!　　　　　　　　　　〔踣地〕
　　　　　　　　〔奥赛罗在远处上。

奥　赛　罗　　　凯昔欧的声音:伊耶戈有信义。

洛窦列谷　啊! 坏蛋,我真是!

奥　赛　罗　　　　　　　　　一点不错,

凯　昔　欧　啊,救人! 喂呀! 火把! 医生!

奥　赛　罗　这是他:啊,好个了不起的伊耶戈,
　　　　　　诚实又可靠,你教我知道你对
　　　　　　你朋友受害,有何等豪侠之感。
　　　　　　刁顽的婢子,你那情郎躺着
　　　　　　已经死,你那可耻的命运来得快;
　　　　　　娼妇,我来了! 那一阵妖媚,你那双
　　　　　　秋波,已永远打我心头上消灭;

Thy bed, lust-stain'd, shall with lust's blood be spotted.

[*Exit.*]

[*Enter* Lodovico *and* Gratiano *at a distance.*]

Cassio   What, ho! no watch? no passage? murder! murder!

Gratiano   'Tis some mischance; the cry is very direful.

Cassio   O, help!

Lodovico   Hark!

Roderigo   O wretched villain!

Lodovico   Two or three groan: — it is a heavy night:

These may be counterfeits: let's think't unsafe

To come in to the cry without more help.

Roderigo   Nobody come? then shall I bleed to death.

Lodovico   Hark!

[*Re-enter* Iago, *with a light.*]

Gratiano   Here's one comes in his shirt, with light and weapons.

Iago   Who's there? whose noise is this that cries on murder?

Lodovico   We do not know.

Iago   Did not you hear a cry?

Cassio   Here, here! for heaven's sake, help me!

Iago   What's the matter?

Gratiano   This is Othello's ancient, as I take it.

Lodovico   The same indeed; a very valiant fellow.

Iago   What are you here that cry so grievously?

Cassio   Iago? O, I am spoil'd, undone by villains!

Give me some help.

Iago   O me, lieutenant! what villains have done this?

Cassio   I think that one of them is hereabout,

你那淫污了的床褥将玷上血迹。

[奥赛罗下。

[罗铎维哥与格拉休阿诺于远处上。

凯　昔　欧	喂呀！没有守夜人？没有人来往吗？ 凶杀！凶杀！
格拉休阿诺	这是什么不幸事，这叫声很可怕。
凯　昔　欧	啊，救人！
罗　铎　维　哥	听呀！
洛　窦　列　谷	啊！可鄙的坏蛋。
罗　铎　维　哥	两三个在呻吟叫苦：这夜晚好阴沉； 这些也许在装假；我们要晓得， 来到呼救处没更多人手不安全。
洛　窦　列　谷	没人来？那我要血流尽而死。
罗　铎　维　哥	听呀！

[伊耶戈持火炬上。

格拉休阿诺	这里有人身穿着衬衫，手拿着 火把同武器在来了。
伊　耶　戈	谁在那里？ 是谁的声音在叫喊凶杀？
罗　铎　维　哥	我们不知道。
伊　耶　戈	你们不听到一声 叫喊吗？
凯　昔　欧	这里，这里！为天公，救我吧。
伊　耶　戈	什么事？
格拉休阿诺	我看这是奥赛罗的旗手。
罗　铎　维　哥	果真就是他；一个很勇敢的汉子。
伊　耶　戈	你们叫得这样惨，是什么样人？
凯　昔　欧	伊耶戈？啊唷！我完了，给坏蛋送了命！ 救我一下。
伊　耶　戈	啊哟，我的天，副将军！ 是什么坏蛋干的事？
凯　昔　欧	我想他们

And cannot make away.

Iago   O treacherous villains! —

[*To* Lodovico *and* Gratiano.] What are you there?

Come in and give some help.

Roderigo   O, help me here!

Cassio   That's one of them.

Iago   O murderous slave! O villain!

                                [*Stabs* Roderigo.]

Roderigo   O damn'd Iago! O inhuman dog!

Iago   Kill men i' the dark! — Where be these bloody
thieves? —

How silent is this town! — Ho! murder! murder! —

What may you be? are you of good or evil?

Lodovico   As you shall prove us, praise us.

Iago   Signior Lodovico?

Lodovico   He, sir.

Iago   I cry you mercy. Here's Cassio hurt by villains.

Gratiano   Cassio!

Iago   How is't, brother?

Cassio   My leg is cut in two.

Iago   Marry, heaven forbid! —

Light, gentlemen: — I'll bind it with my shirt.

                 [*Enter* Bianca.]

Bianca   What is the matter, ho? who is't that cried?

Iago   *Who is't that cried*!

Bianca   O my dear Cassio, my sweet Cassio! O Cassio,
Cassio, Cassio!

Iago   O notable strumpet! — Cassio, may you suspect

Who they should be that have thus mangled you?

Cassio   No.

中间有一个还在这里呢,跑不掉。

伊　耶　戈	啊,一些个奸险的坏蛋! —— [对罗与格]你们是什么样人? 过来,帮帮忙。
洛窦列谷	啊哼! 帮我一下,这儿。
凯　昔　欧	那是他们里头的一个。
伊　耶　戈	啊也, 凶杀人的奴才! 啊,坏蛋! 　[刺击洛窦列谷]
洛窦列谷	啊,打入 地狱的伊耶戈! 啊,没人性的恶狗!
伊　耶　戈	黑暗里杀人! 这些血腥的强盗 往哪里去了? 这坊厢多么静悄! —— 喂哟! 凶杀! 凶杀! ——你们是什么人? 是好人还是坏人?
罗铎维哥	说我们是好人; 你认识我们。
伊　耶　戈	是罗铎维哥大人?
罗铎维哥	正是,足下。
伊　耶　戈	我请您原谅。凯昔欧在这里,有坏蛋 杀伤了他。
格拉休阿诺	凯昔欧!
伊　耶　戈	怎样了,兄长?
凯　昔　欧	我的腿斫成了两橛。
伊　耶　戈	凭圣母,天不许! —— 请照亮,贵人们;我把这衬衫来包扎。 　　　　　　[碧盏佳上。
碧　盏　佳	什么事,喂呀? 谁在这里叫嚷?
伊　耶　戈	谁在这里叫嚷!
碧　盏　佳	啊,亲爱的凯昔欧! 我心头的凯昔欧! 啊也,凯昔欧,凯昔欧,凯昔欧!
伊　耶　戈	啊,出色的婊子! ——凯昔欧,您可能 疑心谁把您剁得血肉横飞的?
凯　昔　欧	不知道。

Gratiano I am sorry to find you thus: I have been to seek you.

Iago Lend me a garter: — so. — O, for a chair,
To bear him easily hence!

Bianca Alas, he faints! — O Cassio, Cassio, Cassio!

Iago Gentlemen all, I do suspect this trash
To be a party in this injury. —
Patience awhile, good Cassio. — Come, come;
Lend me a light. — Know we this face or no?
Alas, my friend and my dear countryman
Roderigo? no: — yes, sure; O heaven! Roderigo.

Gratiano What, of Venice?

Iago Even he, sir: did you know him?

Gratiano   Know him! ay.

Iago Signior Gratiano? I cry you gentle pardon;
These bloody accidents must excuse my manners,
That so neglected you.

Gratiano   I am glad to see you.

Iago How do you, Cassio? — O, a chair, a chair!

Gratiano Roderigo!

Iago He, he, 'tis he. — [*A chair brought in.*] O, that's
well said; — the chair: —
Some good man bear him carefully from hence;
I'll fetch the general's surgeon. [*To* Bianca.] For you,
mistress,
Save you your labour. — He that lies slain here, Cassio,
Was my dear friend: what malice was between you?

Cassio None in the world; nor do I know the man.

Iago [*To* Bianca.] What, look you pale? — O,

格拉休阿诺	我见您这般真伤心;我正来找您。
伊 耶 戈	借给我一条袜带。对了。——啊! 要一架滑竿把他轻手轻脚 打这里抬走!
碧 盎 佳	唉哟!他昏厥了过去!啊唷,凯昔欧, 凯昔欧,凯昔欧!
伊 耶 戈	列位贵人,我怀疑 这垃圾也是凶手中的一个。——且耐着 一会儿,亲爱的凯昔欧。——拿来,拿来。 给我那柱火。——我们认识这脸庞不? 唉呀!是我的朋友和亲爱的同乡, 洛窦列谷?不对:是的,确乎是, 啊也,天呀!洛窦列谷。
格拉休阿诺	什么!是那威尼斯人?
伊 耶 戈	就是他,大人:您认识他吗?
格拉休阿诺	认识他! 当然。
伊 耶 戈	格拉休阿诺大人?我请您 宽和地恕宥;为这些流血的事故, 请原谅我失礼,这般忽略了您大人。
格拉休阿诺	我见到足下很高兴。
伊 耶 戈	您怎样,凯昔欧?—— 啊!要一架滑竿,要一架滑竿!
格拉休阿诺	洛窦列谷!
伊 耶 戈	他,他,这是他。[一肩舆被舁入]——啊!说得对;滑竿: 让什么好心的人儿留神抬走他; 我去请将军的外科医师。——[向碧盎佳]说起你, 嫂子,你不用麻烦。他这里躺着, 遭凶杀,凯昔欧,乃是我亲爱的朋友。—— 你们之间可有什么样的仇恨?
凯 昔 欧	一点都没有;我连这人都不认识。
伊 耶 戈	[向碧盎佳]什么!你脸都急白了?——啊!抬

bear him out o' the air.

[Cassio *and* Roderigo *are borne off.*]

Stay you, good gentlemen. — Look you pale, mistress? —
Do you perceive the gastness of her eye? —
Nay, if you stare, we shall hear more anon. —
Behold her well; I pray you, look upon her:
Do you see, gentlemen? nay, guiltiness will speak
Though tongues were out of use.

[*Enter* Emilia.]

Emilia 'Las, what's the matter? what's the matter, husband?

Iago Cassio hath here been set on in the dark
By Roderigo, and fellows that are 'scap'd:
He's almost slain, and Roderigo dead.

Emilia Alas, good gentleman! alas, good Cassio!

Iago This is the fruit of whoring. — Pr'ythee, Emilia,
Go know of Cassio where he supp'd to-night. —
[*To* Bianca] What, do you shake at that?

Bianca He supp'd at my house;
but I therefore shake not.

Iago O, did he so? I charge you, go with me.

Emilia Fie, fie upon thee, strumpet!

Bianca I am no strumpet, but of life as honest
As you that thus abuse me.

Emilia   As I! foh! fie upon thee!

Iago Kind gentlemen, let's go see poor Cassio dress'd. —
Come, mistress, you must tell's another tale. —
Emilia, run you to the citadel,
And tell my lord and lady what hath happ'd. —

走他，
休在这露天下面。——

        〔凯昔欧与洛窦列谷被异去〕
      且慢走，大人们。——
你脸都急白了，嫂子？——你们可瞧见
她眼神那鬼样。——莫那样，你若呆瞪着，
我们就会有后闻可以听到。——
好好瞧着她；请你们，注意着她：
你们见到吗，大人们？不行，罪恶
会自我暴露，虽然舌头不做声。

      〔爱米丽亚上。

爱米丽亚 唉哟！有什么事情？什么事，丈夫？

伊耶戈 凯昔欧在这里黑暗中，被洛窦列谷
和一些逃走的家伙行凶袭击：
他伤重得快死，洛窦列谷已死了。

爱米丽亚 唉哟！好人君子；唉哟，好凯昔欧！

伊耶戈 这是逛窑姐儿的结果。爱米丽亚，
你去问凯昔欧他今夜在哪里吃晚饭。——
〔对碧盎佳〕什么！你对那发抖吗？

碧盎佳   他在我屋里
吃晚饭，但是我不会因那而发抖。

伊耶戈 啊！他是这样吗？我命令你同我走。

爱米丽亚 呸，不要脸，娼妇！

碧盎佳 我不是娼妇；你把我这样糟蹋，
我跟你生活得一般高贵。

爱米丽亚   跟我！
噢！好不知羞耻！

伊耶戈   宽和的大人们，
让我们去看可怜的凯昔欧裹伤。——
来吧，嫂子，你定得告诉我们
另一桩故事。——爱米丽亚，你赶往
城防堡垒去，去告诉主公与主妇

Will you go on afore? [*Aside.*] This is the night
That either makes me or fordoes me quite.

[*Exeunt.*]

SCENE II. *A Bedchamber in the castle:*
Desdemona in bed asleep; a light burning.

[*Enter* Othello.]

Othello It is the cause, it is the cause, my soul, —
Let me not name it to you, you chaste stars! —
It is the cause. — Yet I'll not shed her blood;
Nor scar that whiter skin of hers than snow,
And smooth as monumental alabaster.
[*Takes off his sword.*]
Yet she must die, else she'll betray more men.
Put out the light, and then put out the light:
If I quench thee, thou flaming minister,
I can again thy former light restore,
Should I repent me: — but once put out thy light,
Thou cunning'st pattern of excelling nature,
I know not where is that Promethean heat
That can thy light relume. When I have pluck'd thy rose,
I cannot give it vital growth again,
It must needs wither: — I'll smell it on the tree. —

[*Kissing her.*]

O, balmy breath, that dost almost persuade
Justice to break her sword! — One more, one more; —
Be thus when thou art dead, and I will kill thee,
And love thee after. — One more, and this the last;
So sweet was ne'er so fatal. I must weep,
But they are cruel tears: this sorrow's heavenly;
It strikes where it doth love. — She wakes.

发生了什么事。你能先去吗？［旁白］这夜晚，
不使我功业成，会叫我完全失败。

［同下。

第 二 景

［堡垒内一卧室，玳思狄莫娜睡在床上，烛光亮着。］
［奥赛罗上。

奥 赛 罗　我为的是大义，是大义，我的灵魂；
莫让我对你们道出那罪名，你们
贞洁的星辰！我为的是大义。可是我
不叫她流血，也不使她那比霜雪
还白，同雪花石膏般光滑的皮肤
受到伤残。［摘下佩剑］但是她一定得死，
否则她将会诓骗更多的男人。
灭掉这支光，然后再灭掉这支光：
我若灭了你，融融的仆使，我还能
恢复你原先的光焰，如果我后悔；
但只要熄灭了你的光，你这奇绝
神天、妙趣千般的杰制，我不知
何处有大罗天灵明的真火，能重燃
你已熄的光焰。当我摘下了玫瑰，
我不能再使它活生生欣荣滋长，
它只有萎谢：我将在枝头上嗅它。　　　　［吻伊］
啊，芳香的气息，你几乎劝得
正义女神砸碎了她的剑！再一次，
再一次。你死后能这样，我把你杀死后
还是会爱你。再一次，这是最后的：
这样温馨的，从没有这样恶毒。
我一定要哭泣，但流的是残忍之泪；
这悲伤只应天上有，它惩罚，可也爱。
她醒了。

Desdemona Who's there? Othello?

Othello   Ay, Desdemona.

Desdemona Will you come to bed, my lord?

Othello Have you pray'd to-night, Desdemona?

Desdemona   Ay, my lord.

Othello If you bethink yourself of any crime

Unreconcil'd as yet to heaven and grace,

Solicit for it straight.

Desdemona Alack, my lord, what may you mean by that?

Othello Well, do it, and be brief; I will walk by.

I would not kill thy unprepared spirit;

No, —heaven forfend! —I would not kill thy soul.

Desdemona Talk you of killing?

Othello   Ay, I do.

Desdemona   Then heaven have mercy

on me!

Othello   Amen, with all my heart!

Desdemona If you say so, I hope you will not kill me.

Othello Hum!

Desdemona And yet I fear you; for you are fatal then

When your eyes roll so: why I should fear I know not,

Since guiltiness I know not; but yet I feel I fear.

Othello Think on thy sins.

Desdemona   They are loves I bear to you.

Othello Ay, and for that thou diest.

Desdemona   That death's unnatural that kills for lov-

ing. —

Alas, why gnaw you so your nether lip?

Some bloody passion shakes your very frame:

玳思狄莫娜	谁在那里？是奥赛罗吗？
奥　赛　罗	是的，玳思狄莫娜。
玳思狄莫娜	你上床来吗，官人？
奥　赛　罗	你今夜祷告了没有，玳思狄莫娜？
玳思狄莫娜	祷告了，官人。

奥　赛　罗　　　　假使你记得有罪过
还不曾向上帝求得宽恕，可马上
去祈求。

玳思狄莫娜　　　唉呀！官人，你什么意思？

奥　赛　罗　唔，祈祷吧，简短些；我在旁踱着步：
我不愿杀掉你不曾准备好的神明；
不；上天莫让我！我不杀你灵魂。

玳思狄莫娜　你说要杀我？

奥　赛　罗　　　　　不错，我是这样说。

玳思狄莫娜　那么，上天对我舍仁慈！

奥　赛　罗　　　　　　　阿门！
我心愿如此。

玳思狄莫娜　　　　你若这么说，我希望
你不会杀我。

奥　赛　罗　呃！

玳思狄莫娜　可是我还是怕你；你这样眼瞪瞪，
煞是骇怕人。为什么我要害怕，
我可不知道，因为我不知有罪过；
但是我仍然觉得怕。

奥　赛　罗　　　　　　　想着你的罪孽。

玳思狄莫娜　它们只是我对你的爱情。

奥　赛　罗　　　　　　　是了，
为那个你将死。

玳思狄莫娜　　　　那死得不合天理，
为爱情而要杀死。唉呀！为什么
你那样咬着你的下嘴唇？有什么
血腥的激情震得你全身颤动；

These are portents; but yet I hope, I hope,
They do not point on me.

Othello   Peace, and be still!

Desdemona   I will so. What's the matter?

Othello   That handkerchief which I so loved and gave thee
Thou gav'st to Cassio.

Desdemona   No, by my life and soul!
Send for the man, and ask him.

Othello   Sweet soul, take heed,
Take heed of perjury; thou'rt on thy death-bed.

Desdemona   Ay, but not yet to die.

Othello   Yes, presently:
Therefore confess thee freely of thy sin;
For to deny each article with oath
Cannot remove nor choke the strong conception
That I do groan withal. Thou art to die.

Desdemona   Then, Lord have mercy on me!

Othello   I say, amen.

Desdemona   And have you mercy too! — I never did
Offend you in my life; never lov'd Cassio
But with such general warranty of heaven
As I might love: I never gave him token.

Othello   By heaven, I saw my handkerchief in 's hand.
O perjur'd woman! thou dost stone my heart,
And mak'st me call what I intend to do
A murder, which I thought a sacrifice:
I saw the handkerchief.

Desdemona   He found it then;

这些是凶兆，可是我希望，我希望
它们并不针对我。

奥　赛　罗　　　　　　禁口，莫做声！

苔思狄莫娜　好的。什么事？

奥　赛　罗　　　　　那手绢我这样心爱，
我给了你，你给了凯昔欧。

苔思狄莫娜　　　　　　　　　没有，
凭我这生命和灵魂！把这人叫来，
问他。

奥　赛　罗　　　　亲爱的人儿，当心啊，当心
赌假咒；你正在你毕命去的床上。

苔思狄莫娜　是的，可还不得死。

奥　赛　罗　　　　　　　不然，马上死；
所以，要坦白供认你所犯的罪辜；
因为，你发誓否认我数你的每一桩
坏事，不可能去除或消灭我胸中
为之呻吟的强烈的毒恨。你得死。

苔思狄莫娜　那么，上帝对我舍仁慈！

奥　赛　罗　　　　　　　　　我说，
心愿如此。

苔思狄莫娜　　　　　你也对我舍仁慈！
我这辈子从未得罪你；我从未
爱过凯昔欧，只除了在上天所允许
那范围里边爱过他；我从未给过他
信物。

奥　赛　罗　　　　　凭上天，我看见我那条手帕
捏在他手里。啊，赌假咒的女人！
你把我的心变成了石头，使我
将我正要做的这事叫做凶杀，
我原来只是想要对上帝献礼：
我亲眼见到那手帕。

苔思狄莫娜　　　　　　　　那是他捡到的；

I never gave it him; — send for him hither;
Let him confess a truth.

Othello   He hath confess'd.

Desdemona   What, my lord?

Othello   That he hath us'd thee.

Desdemona   How? unlawfully?

Othello   Ay.

Desdemona   He will not say so.

Othello   No, his mouth is stopp'd;
Honest Iago hath ta'en order for't.

Desdemona   O, my fear interprets! —What, is he dead?

Othello   Had all his hairs been lives, my great revenge
Had stomach for them all.

Desdemona   Alas, he is betray'd, and I undone!

Othello   Out, strumpet! Weep'st thou for him to my
face?

Desdemona   O, banish me, my lord, but kill me not!

Othello   Down, strumpet!

Desdemona   Kill me to-morrow; let me live to-night!

Othello   Nay, if you strive, —

Desdemona   But half an hour!

Othello   Being done,
there is no pause.

Desdemona   But while I say one prayer!

Othello   It is too late.

                            [*Smothers her.*]

Emilia   [*Within.*] My lord, my lord! what, ho! my
lord, my lord!

Othello   What noise is this? — Not dead? not yet quite
dead?
I that am cruel am yet merciful;
I would not have thee linger in thy pain; —
So, so.

Emilia   [*Within.*] What, ho! my lord, my lord!

Othello   Who's there?

我从未给过他手帕。叫他到这里来；
让他来说句真话。

奥　赛　罗　　　　　　　他已经承认。
玳思狄莫娜　什么，官人？
奥　赛　罗　他承认他已经用过你。
玳思狄莫娜　　　　　　怎样？非法地？
奥　赛　罗　是的。
玳思狄莫娜　　　他不会这么说。
奥　赛　罗　　　　　　不，他的嘴
不响了：诚实的伊耶戈已着手做这件事。
玳思狄莫娜　啊！我的恐惧说明了。什么！他死了？
奥　赛　罗　如果他每一根头发有生命，我对他
无比愤怒的报仇准能把它们
全消灭。
玳思狄莫娜　唉哟！他给出卖了，而我就毁了。
奥　赛　罗　滚蛋，娼妓！你当我的面哭他？
玳思狄莫娜　啊！赶我走，官人，但不要杀死我。
奥　赛　罗　下去，娼妓！
玳思狄莫娜　明天杀我；让我今晚上活一夜！
奥　赛　罗　不行，你若要挣扎，——
玳思狄莫娜　只半个钟头！
奥　赛　罗　　　　　　动了手就不能踌躇。
玳思狄莫娜　让我只做一次祷告！
奥　赛　罗　　　　　　　太晚了。[揪住使窒息而死]
　　　　　　　　[爱米丽亚在门首]
爱米丽亚　[在内]主公，主公！喂呀！主公，主公！
奥　赛　罗　是什么声音？没有死？还没有死透？
我虽然残忍，可是还得要仁慈；
我不愿你在痛苦中迁延不去。
这样，这样。
爱米丽亚　　　[在内]喂呀！主公，主公！
奥　赛　罗　谁在那里？

238

Emilia [*Within.*] O, good my lord, I would speak a
word with you!

Othello Yes: — 'tis Emilia: — by and by. — She's dead. —
'Tis like she comes to speak of Cassio's death;
The noise was high. — Ha! no more moving?
Still as the grave. — Shall she come in? — Were't good? —
I think she stirs again: — no. — What's best to do?
If she come in, she'll sure speak to my wife:
My wife! my wife! what wife? I have no wife.
O, insupportable! O heavy hour!
Methinks it should be now a huge eclipse
Of sun and moon, and that the affrighted globe
Should yawn at alteration.

Emilia [*Within.*] I do beseech you
That I may speak with you, O, good my lord!

Othello I had forgot thee: O, come in, Emilia: —
Soft, — by and by: — let me the curtains draw. —
Where art thou?

[*Unlocks the door.*]

[*Enter* Emilia.]

What's the matter with thee now?

Emilia O, my good lord, yonder's foul murders done!

Othello What, now?

Emilia But now, my lord.

Othello It is the very error of the moon;
She comes more nearer earth than she was wont
And makes men mad.

Emilia Cassio, my lord, hath kill'd a young Venetian
Call'd Roderigo.

Othello Roderigo kill'd?
And Cassio kill'd?

Emilia No, Cassio is not kill'd.

爱米丽亚　　　［在内］啊也，亲爱的主公，
　　　　　　我要跟你说句话！

奥　赛　罗　　　　　　好的；这是
　　　　　　爱米丽亚：等一下。她死了。大概是
　　　　　　她来报信凯昔欧已经死；这声音
　　　　　　轰闹得很。嘻！不再动了吗？
　　　　　　坟墓一般静。她可以进来吗？这可好？
　　　　　　我想她又在动：没有。做什么最好？
　　　　　　她若是进来，准会跟我妻子说话：
　　　　　　我妻子！我妻子！什么妻子？我已经
　　　　　　没妻子：啊，受不了！啊，沉重的时刻！
　　　　　　我看来如今应当有一次大日蚀、
　　　　　　大月蚀，吓坏了的地球应当见到了
　　　　　　这巨变而裂开一个大缺口。

爱米丽亚　　　　　　　　［在内］我请你
　　　　　　让我跟你讲句话，亲爱的主公哎。

奥　赛　罗　我把你忘记了：啊！进来吧，爱米丽亚：
　　　　　　等一下，就来：让我把帐帏放下来。
　　　　　　你在哪里？　　　　　　　　［开门锁］
　　　　　　　　　［爱米丽亚上。
　　　　　　　你现在有什么事情？

爱米丽亚　啊哟，亲爱的主公，那里发生了
　　　　　　凶杀。

奥　赛　罗　　　什么？现在？

爱米丽亚　　　　　　　　刚才，主公。

奥　赛　罗　这正是月亮偏离了她那轨道，
　　　　　　她比素常时行得更近了地球，
　　　　　　使人们疯狂。

爱米丽亚　　　　凯昔欧，主公，杀掉了
　　　　　　一个叫洛窦列谷的威尼斯后生。

奥　赛　罗　杀死了洛窦列谷！凯昔欧给杀了？

爱米丽亚　没有，凯昔欧没有给杀死。

Othello Not Cassio kill'd! then murder's out of tune,
And sweet revenge grows harsh.

Desdemona O, falsely, falsely murder'd!

Emilia   Alas, what cry is that?

Othello That! what?

Emilia Out, and alas! That was my lady's voice. —
Help! help, ho! help! — O lady, speak again!
Sweet Desdemona! O sweet mistress, speak!

Desdemona A guiltless death I die.

Emilia O, who hath done this deed?

Desdemona Nobody; I myself. Farewell:
Commend me to my kind lord: O, farewell!

                                    [*Dies.*]

Othello Why, how should she be murder'd?

Emilia   Alas, who knows?

Othello You heard her say herself it was not I.

Emilia She said so: I must needs report the truth.

Othello She's like a liar, gone to burning hell:
'Twas I that kill'd her.

Emilia   O, the more angel she,
And you the blacker devil!

Othello She turn'd to folly, and she was a whore.

Emilia Thou dost belie her, and thou art a devil.

Othello She was false as water.

Emilia   Thou art rash as fire, to say
That she was false: O, she was heavenly true!

Othello Cassio did tup her; ask thy husband else.
O, I were damn'd beneath all depth in hell,
But that I did proceed upon just grounds
To this extremity. Thy husband knew it all.

奥　赛　罗	不是凯昔欧给杀死！那么，凶杀
	走了腔，甜蜜的报仇变成了酸苦。
玳思狄莫娜	啊！凶杀得错透，错透。
爱　米　丽　亚	唉哟！
	那是什么叫声？
奥　赛　罗	那个！什么？
爱　米　丽　亚	说出来，唉哟！那是娘娘的声音：
	救人！救人，喂呀！救人！啊呀，
	娘娘，再说呀！亲爱的玳思狄莫娜！
	啊也！亲爱的娘娘，说话也吧。
玳思狄莫娜	我没有罪而死。
爱　米　丽　亚	啊！谁干的这事？
玳思狄莫娜	没有人；我自己；祝别了：
	劝我仁慈的官人记念我。啊！祝别了！　　　〔死去〕
奥　赛　罗	哎也，她怎样给凶杀的？
爱　米　丽　亚	唉呀！谁知道？
奥　赛　罗	你听她自己说的，那并非是我。
爱　米　丽　亚	她是这么说；我一定得讲真话。
奥　赛　罗	她像个打入烈火地狱的撒谎者；
	是我杀死了她呀。
爱　米　丽　亚	啊！她更显得
	是个天使，而你更是个恶魔。
奥　赛　罗	她变得淫荡起来，成了个娼妓。
爱　米　丽　亚	你撒谎污蔑了她，你是个魔鬼。
奥　赛　罗	她跟流水般无情义。
爱　米　丽　亚	说她无情义，
	你同烈火般莽撞：啊！她深情
	真挚好比是天人。
奥　赛　罗	凯昔欧登上她身子；问你的丈夫。
	啊！我会给打入地狱的最下层，
	若不凭正确可靠的原由来进行，
	到这般酷烈的程度。你丈夫全知道。

Emilia My husband!

Othello Thy husband.

Emilia That she was false to wedlock?

Othello   Ay, with Cassio. Nay, had she been true,
If heaven would make me such another world
Of one entire and perfect chrysolite,
I'd not have sold her for it.

Emilia My husband!

Othello   Ay, 'twas he that told me first:
An honest man he is, and hates the slime
That sticks on filthy deeds.

Emilia   My husband!

Othello What needs this iterance, woman? I say thy husband.

Emilia O mistress, villainy hath made mocks with love! —
My husband say that she was false!

Othello   He, woman;
I say thy husband: dost understand the word?
My friend, thy husband, honest, honest Iago.

Emilia If he say so, may his pernicious soul
Rot half a grain a day! he lies to the heart:
She was too fond of her most filthy bargain.

Othello Ha!

Emilia Do thy worst:
This deed of thine is no more worthy heaven
Than thou wast worthy her.

Othello   Peace, you were best.

Emilia Thou hast not half that power to do me harm

爱 米 丽 亚　　我丈夫!

奥 赛 罗　　你丈夫。

爱 米 丽 亚　　说她不忠于婚姻?

奥 赛 罗　　不错,是跟凯昔欧。而且,如果她
情义真,即令皇天把整整一巨方
琼珍豪贵的橄榄石给我造成了
另一座这样的世界,也休想叫我
去将她交换。

爱 米 丽 亚　　我丈夫!

奥 赛 罗　　　　　是的,这是他首先告诉我:
他是个诚实人,痛恨粘在淫秽
勾当上的污泥。

爱 米 丽 亚　　　　　　　我丈夫!

奥 赛 罗　　　　　　　　何用这重复,
娘们? 我说你丈夫。

爱 米 丽 亚　　　　　　　啊唷,娘娘!
奸恶对爱情来了个嘲讽。我丈夫
说她无情义!

奥 赛 罗　　　　　是他,娘们;我是说,
你丈夫:你懂得我吗? 是我的朋友,
就是你丈夫,诚实的,诚实的伊耶戈。

爱 米 丽 亚　　如果他这样说,叫他那恶毒的灵魂
每天烂掉它半丁点儿! 他撒谎
撒进了心里头:她太爱她那卑鄙得
不值半文钱的宝货。

奥 赛 罗　　嘻!

爱 米 丽 亚　　随你去怎么办:
你做的这件事见不得皇天,正如你
配不上有她。

奥 赛 罗　　　　　禁声! 我叫你。

爱 米 丽 亚　　　　　　　　你没有
伤害得了我的一半力量来损伤我。

As I have to be hurt. O gull! O dolt!
As ignorant as dirt! thou hast done a deed, —
I care not for thy sword; I'll make thee known,
Though I lost twenty lives. —Help! help, ho! help!
The Moor hath kill'd my mistress! murder, murder!

　　　　[*Enter* Montano, Gratiano, *and* Iago.]

Montano　What is the matter? — How now, general!

Emilia　O, are you come, Iago? you have done well,
That men must lay their murders on your neck.

Gratiano　What is the matter?

Emilia　Disprove this villain, if thou be'st a man:
He says thou told'st him that his wife was false:
I know thou didst not, thou'rt not such a villain:
Speak, for my heart is full.

Iago　I told him what I thought; and told no more
Than what he found himself was apt and true.

Emilia　But did you ever tell him she was false?

Iago　I did.

Emilia　You told a lie; an odious, damned lie;
Upon my soul, a lie; a wicked lie: —
She false with Cassio! —Did you say with Cassio?

Iago　With Cassio, mistress. Go to, charm your tongue.

Emilia　I will not charm my tongue; I am bound to speak:
My mistress here lies murder'd in her bed, —

All　O heavens forfend!

Emilia　And your reports have set the murder on.

Othello　Nay, stare not, masters: it is true, indeed.

Gratiano　'Tis a strange truth.

Montano　O monstrous act!

Emilia　　　　　Villany, villany, villany!
I think upon't, —I think, —I smell't; —O villany! —

啊,蠢奴才! 啊,笨鳖蛋! 跟泥巴
一般吃矢地愚骏! 你干得好事,——
我不把你的剑放在我眼里;我准会
叫大家知道你,即令要丢掉二十条
性命。救人! 救人,喂哟! 救人啊!
摩尔人杀死了我娘娘! 凶杀! 凶杀!
　　　〔蒙塔诺、格拉休阿诺、伊耶戈与随从等上。

蒙 塔 诺　　什么事情? 怎么说法,将军?
爱 米 丽 亚　　啊! 你来了,伊耶戈? 你干得好事,
　　　　　　　人家得把凶杀挂在你头上。
格拉休阿诺　　什么事情?
爱 米 丽 亚　　你若是个人,拆穿这坏蛋的谎话,
　　　　　　　他说你告他,他妻子对他不贞洁。
　　　　　　　我知道你没有,你不是这样个坏蛋。
　　　　　　　说呀,我的心胀得要爆破。
伊 耶 戈　　我把我所想的告诉了他,我讲的
　　　　　　　不超过他自己所见的彰明而真实。
爱 米 丽 亚　　但是你是否对他说过她不贞?
伊 耶 戈　　我说过的。
爱 米 丽 亚　　你撒谎,撒了个龌龊、混帐的恶谎;
　　　　　　　凭我的灵魂,一个狠毒的恶谎。
　　　　　　　她跟凯昔欧通奸! 你说跟凯昔欧?
伊 耶 戈　　是跟凯昔欧,娘子。得了吧,莫多话。
爱 米 丽 亚　　我非得多话不可;我一定得讲。
　　　　　　　我娘娘在这里躺在床上遭凶杀。
众 人　　啊,上天莫叫这样!
爱 米 丽 亚　　而你的话造成了这凶杀。
奥 赛 罗　　别那么眼瞪瞪,大人们;确是的,当真。
格拉休阿诺　　这倒是怪事。
蒙 塔 诺　　　　　　　啊,骇怪的行径!
爱 米 丽 亚　　恶辣! 恶辣! 恶辣! 我此刻想到,
　　　　　　　我想我嗅到;啊,奸险恶辣!

I thought so then; — I'll kill myself for grief: —

O villany, villany!

Iago What, are you mad? I charge you, get you home.

Emilia Good gentlemen, let me have leave to speak:

'Tis proper I obey him, but not now. —

Perchance, Iago, I will ne'er go home.

Othello O! O! O!

[*He falls on the bed.*]

Emilia Nay, lay thee down and roar;

For thou hast kill'd the sweetest innocent

That e'er did lift up eye.

Othello [*Rising.*] O, she was foul! —

I scarce did know you, uncle; there lies your niece,

Whose breath, indeed, these hands have newly stopp'd:

I know this act shows horrible and grim.

Gratiano Poor Desdemona! I am glad thy father's dead:

Thy match was mortal to him, and pure grief

Shore his old thread in twain: did he live now,

This sight would make him do a desperate turn,

Yea, curse his better angel from his side,

And fall to reprobance.

Othello 'Tis pitiful; but yet Iago knows

That she with Cassio hath the act of shame

A thousand times committed; Cassio confess'd it:

And she did gratify his amorous works

With that recognizance and pledge of love

Which I first gave her; I saw it in his hand:

It was a handkerchief, an antique token

My father gave my mother.

Emilia O heaven! O heavenly powers!

Iago Come, hold your peace.

Emilia Twill out, twill out: — I peace!

那时候,我想到;我要伤心得死掉。
啊,恶辣,恶辣!

伊　耶　戈　什么! 你疯了? 关照你,回家里去吧。

爱 米 丽 亚　尊敬的大人们,请准许我来说话:
我应当对他服从,但此刻不能。
也许,伊耶戈,我将永远不回家。

奥　赛　罗　啊! 啊! 啊!　　　　　　　　　　[奥赛罗仆倒床上]

爱 米 丽 亚　　　　　　去吧,倒下去
号叫吧,因为你杀死了曾对这世上
举目过的最可爱的天真无邪的人儿。

奥　赛　罗　[起身]啊! 她是罪恶的。我几乎不知你
在这里,叔父。您侄女躺在那边,
她的气,当真,这双手刚使它停止:
我知道这行动显得可怕而吓人。

格拉休阿诺　可怜的玳思狄莫娜! 我高兴你父亲
已经死。你这桩婚事对他致了命,
把他老命的线儿一剪成两段:
他若是现在还活着,这情景会使他
干出丧心病狂的祸事来,是呀,
诅咒保护他的吉神离开他身边,
而堕入地狱去,永远不能得超生。

奥　赛　罗　这煞是可怜;可是伊耶戈知道
她跟凯昔欧干过那丑事一千遍;
凯昔欧自己供认过:而她便报答
他那些色情的功夫,给了他我早先
送她的誓物和寄爱徽。我见那东西
拿在他手里:这是条手帕,我父亲
给我母亲的一件古老的信物。

爱 米 丽 亚　啊唷,天呀! 啊唷,上天的神威!

伊　耶　戈　来吧,莫做声。

爱 米 丽 亚　　　　　　我要讲出来,讲出来;
要我莫做声么,你? 不成,告诉你;

No, I will speak as liberal as the north:
Let heaven and men and devils, let them all,
All, all, cry shame against me, yet I'll speak.

Iago Be wise, and get you home.

Emilia   I will not.

        [Iago *offers to stab his* wife.]

Gratiano   Fie!
Your sword upon a woman?

Emilia O thou dull Moor! that handkerchief thou
    speak'st of
I found by fortune and did give my husband;
For often with a solemn earnestness, —
More than, indeed, belong'd to such a trifle, —
He begg'd of me to steal it.

Iago   Villanous whore!

Emilia She give it Cassio! no, alas, I found it,
And I did give't my husband.

Iago   Filth, thou liest!

Emilia By heaven, I do not, I do not, gentlemen. —
O murderous coxcomb! What should such a fool
Do with so good a wife?

Othello   Are there not stones in heaven
But what serve for thunder? — Precious villain!

    [*He runs at* Iago, Iago *stabs* Emilia, *and then runs out.*]

Gratiano The woman falls; sure, he hath kill'd his wife.

Emilia Ay, ay: — O, lay me by my mistress' side.

Gratiano He's gone, but his wife's kill'd.

Montano 'Tis a notorious villain. Take you this weapon,
Which I have here recover'd from the Moor:
Come, guard the door without; let him not pass,
But kill him rather. I'll after that same villain,

不行,我要跟老北风一样公开;
尽管上天、人们、魔鬼,让他们
全都,全都羞辱我,我还是要讲。

伊 耶 戈 识相点,回家里去吧。

爱 米 丽 亚　　　　　　　我不去。

［伊耶戈威胁欲刺爱米丽亚］

格拉休阿诺　　　　　　　　　　可鄙!

你的剑用来刺女人?

爱 米 丽 亚 啊,你这蠢家伙摩尔人! 那手帕
是我偶然捡到了,给了我丈夫,
因为屡次三番,以严肃的殷切,——
这么件小东西,当真,不值得如此,——
他央我把它偷到手。

伊 耶 戈　　　　　　　　下贱的娼妇!

爱 米 丽 亚 她把它给的凯昔欧! 不是,唉呀!
我把它捡到,我把它给了我丈夫。

伊 耶 戈 滥污,你撒谎!

爱 米 丽 亚　　　　　　凭上天,我没有,没有,
大人们。啊,杀人凶手傻瓜蛋!
这样个蠢蛋,有了这样好的老婆
怎么办?

奥 赛 罗　　　　天上难道再没有霹雳,
只除了供打雷时候用? 宝贝的坏蛋!
［奔向伊耶戈。伊耶戈冲刺爱米丽亚,随即下场。

格拉休阿诺 这女人倒了:他准是杀了他妻子。

爱 米 丽 亚 是的,是的;啊! 葬我在娘娘
身边。

格拉休阿诺　　　　他走了;他老婆已给他杀掉。

蒙 塔 诺 这是个恶毒透顶的坏蛋。你接下
这柄剑,这是我打摩尔人手里
拿来的。来吧,在外边守卫住大门,
休让他通过,格杀勿论。我也来

For 'tis a damned slave.

[Exit Montano and Gratiano.]

Othello   I am not valiant neither,
But every puny whipster gets my sword: —
But why should honour outlive honesty?
Let it go all.

Emilia   What did thy song bode, lady?
Hark, canst thou hear me? I will play the swan,
And die in music: —
[*Sings.*] *Willow, willow, willow.*
Moor, she was chaste; she lov'd thee, cruel Moor;
So come my soul to bliss, as I speak true;
So speaking as I think, I die, — I die.

[*Dies.*]

Othello   I have another weapon in this chamber;
It is a sword of Spain, the ice-brook's temper: —
O, here it is. — Uncle, I must come forth.

Gratiano   [*Within.*] If thou attempt it, it will cost thee
        dear:
Thou hast no weapon, and perforce must suffer.

Othello   Look in upon me then, and speak with me,
Or, naked as I am, I will assault thee.

[*Re-enter* Gratiano.]

Gratiano   What is the matter?

Othello   Behold, I have a weapon;
A better never did itself sustain
Upon a soldier's thigh: I have seen the day
That with this little arm and this good sword
I have made my way through more impediments
Than twenty times your stop: — but, O vain boast!
Who can control his fate? 'tis not so now. —
Be not afraid, though you do see me weapon'd;

擒拿这恶贼,这是个极可恶的奴才。

[与格拉休阿诺同下。

奥　赛　罗　　我勇武都说不上,每个小猴儿崽子
　　　　　　　都能解除我的剑。但是为什么
　　　　　　　基本的正直已消亡,还残留着尊荣?
　　　　　　　让它也同归于尽。

爱 米 丽 亚　　　　　　　　你的歌,娘娘,
　　　　　　　预兆些什么?听啊,你听到我吗?
　　　　　　　我要像临死的白鹄一般,在挽歌
　　　　　　　声中死去:[唱]
　　　　　　　　　　"柳条,柳条,柳条。"——
　　　　　　　摩尔人,她是贞洁的;她爱你得很,
　　　　　　　狠心的摩尔人;我灵魂要超升极乐界,
　　　　　　　因为我说的尽真话;说着心里事,
　　　　　　　我死去,死去。　　　　　　[死去。

奥　赛　罗　　　　　　　这里我还有柄利器;
　　　　　　　这是把西班牙宝剑,打造时用冰水
　　　　　　　淬炼。啊!在这里。——叔父,我得来。

格拉休阿诺　[在内]假使你要试,就要付很高的代价:
　　　　　　　你没有快口,一定得吃点苦头。

奥　赛　罗　　那么,进来瞧瞧我,跟我来打话,
　　　　　　　或许,赤手空拳,我也能把你斗。

[格拉休阿诺上。

格拉休阿诺　有什么事情?

奥　赛　罗　　　　　　　瞧吧!我有柄利器;
　　　　　　　武士的腰间从未佩带过更好的:
　　　　　　　我见过那日子,使着这小小的臂膀,
　　　　　　　这精良的长铗,我所向披靡无阻,
　　　　　　　穿经你所能起的障碍不下二十倍:
　　　　　　　但那是,啊,无聊的夸耀!谁能够
　　　　　　　控制自己的命运?这如今不然了。
　　　　　　　不用害怕,虽然你见我佩着剑;

Here is my journey's end, here is my butt,

And very sea-mark of my utmost sail.

Do you go back dismay'd? 'tis a lost fear;

Man but a rush against Othello's breast,

And he retires: — where should Othello go? —

Now, how dost thou look now? O ill-starr'd wench!

Pale as thy smock! When we shall meet at compt,

This look of thine will hurl my soul from heaven,

And fiends will snatch at it. Cold, cold, my girl!

Even like thy chastity. —

O cursed, cursed slave! — Whip me, ye devils,

From the possession of this heavenly sight!

Blow me about in winds! roast me in sulphur!

Wash me in steep-down gulfs of liquid fire! —

O Desdemon! dead, Desdemon! dead! O! O! O!

> [*Enter* Lodovico, Montano, Cassio *carried in a chair,*
> *and* Officers *with* Iago *prisoner.*]

Lodovico   Where is this rash and most unfortunate man?

Othello   That's he that was Othello; — here I am.

Lodovico   Where is that viper? bring the villain forth.

Othello   I look down towards his feet; — but that's a fa-
ble. —

If that thou be'st a devil, I cannot kill thee.

> [*Wounds Iago.*]

Lodovico   Wrench his sword from him.

Iago   I bleed, sir, but not kill'd.

Othello   I am not sorry neither: I'd have thee live;

For, in my sense, 'tis happiness to die.

Lodovico   O thou Othello, that wert once so good,

这是我行程的尽头,是我的终局,
我航路已到了极限的标志。你是否
害怕而后退? 这是个徒然的恐惧;
把一根灯心草指向奥赛罗的胸膛,
他就会后退。奥赛罗应往哪里去?
却说,现在你看来是怎么个模样?
啊,命苦的小娘! 跟你的衬衣
一般苍白! 当最后审判那一天
我们相见时,你这般模样将会把
我灵魂从天上扔下来,魔鬼们会抢着
把它抓。冰冷,冰冷,我的姑娘!
跟你的贞洁一个样。
啊! 可恨,可恶的奴才。挥鞭梢,
魔鬼们,鞭去我心中这天人般的形象!
把我在风飚中颠顿! 硫磺里燔烤!
把我投入火流的陡峭的旋涡中!
啊,玳思狄莫娜,玳思狄莫娜!
死了啊! 呀! 呀! 呀!
　　[罗铎维哥、蒙塔诺、凯昔欧坐肩舆、伊耶戈(被逮)、
　　军官数人同上。

罗 铎 维 哥　这莽撞而非常不幸的人在哪里?

奥　赛　罗　那是他,曾经是奥赛罗;我在这里。

罗 铎 维 哥　那毒蛇在哪里? 把那坏蛋带过来。

奥　赛　罗　我低着目光看他的脚;但那是
虚幻的传说。你若是个魔鬼,我不能
杀死你。　　　　　　　　　　　　[刺伤伊耶戈]

罗 铎 维 哥　　　　　夺掉他的剑。

伊　耶　戈　　　　　　　　　我流血,大人;
但没有给杀死。

奥　赛　罗　　　　　　　　我并不可惜;要你活;
因为,据我想来,死去了倒快乐。

罗 铎 维 哥　啊,你这奥赛罗! 你曾经这么好,

Fall'n in the practice of a damned slave,
What shall be said to thee?

Othello   Why, anything;
An honourable murderer, if you will;
For naught did I in hate, but all in honour.

Lodovico This wretch hath part confess'd his villany:
Did you and he consent in Cassio's death?

Othello Ay.

Cassio Dear general, I never gave you cause.

Othello I do believe it, and I ask your pardon.
Will you, I pray, demand that demi-devil
Why he hath thus ensnar'd my soul and body?

Iago Demand me nothing: what you know, you know:
From this time forth I never will speak word.

Lodovico What, not to pray?

Gratiano   Torments will ope your lips.

Othello Well, thou dost best.

Lodovico Sir, you shall understand what hath befall'n,
Which, as I think, you know not. Here is a letter
Found in the pocket of the slain Roderigo,
And here another: the one of them imports
The death of Cassio to be undertook
By Roderigo.

Othello O villain!

Cassio   Most heathenish and most gross!

Lodovico Now here's another discontented paper,
Found in his pocket too; and this, it seems,
Roderigo meant to have sent this damned villain;
But that, belike, Iago in the interim
Came in and satisfied him.

Othello   O the pernicious caitiff! —

　　　　　　　却中了那个贼奴才的奸谋，我们
　　　　　　　将对你怎样说法？

奥　赛　罗　　　　　　　　　哎也，听便：
　　　　　　　一个心地光明的凶杀犯，您可以
　　　　　　　这么说；因为，我所作非出于恚恨，
　　　　　　　而都是为荣誉。

罗铎维哥　　　　　　　　　这恶贼已部分供认
　　　　　　　他那恶辣的行径：你和他同意把
　　　　　　　凯昔欧杀死吗？

奥　赛　罗　唔。

凯　昔　欧　亲爱的将军，我从未给过您缘由。

奥　赛　罗　我信你的话，我要请求你原谅。
　　　　　　　您可能，我请求，问那半个儿魔君吗，
　　　　　　　他为何要这般陷害我的灵魂跟身体？

伊　耶　戈　休问我：你所知道的，你已经知道：
　　　　　　　从今往后我将决不再讲话。

罗铎维哥　什么！不祷告？

格拉休阿诺　　　　　　　　刑讯会叫你开口。

奥　赛　罗　很好，您最好这么办。

罗铎维哥　足下，你该当知道发生了什么事，
　　　　　　　不过，我想，你还不知道。这里有封信，
　　　　　　　从被杀的洛窦列谷身上找到，
　　　　　　　这里又有封，第一封是说，杀死
　　　　　　　凯昔欧由洛窦列谷负责进行。

奥　赛　罗　啊，恶毒！

凯　昔　欧　　　　　　真是穷凶极恶！

罗铎维哥　这里还有封语气很不满的柬帖，
　　　　　　　也从他口袋里找到；这一封，看来，
　　　　　　　洛窦列谷打算要送给这贼坏蛋，
　　　　　　　可是，我猜想，在发出之前伊耶戈
　　　　　　　来到了，使他满了意。

奥　赛　罗　　　　　　　　啊，这恶贼！

How came you, Cassio, by that handkerchief
That was my wife's?

Cassio   I found it in my chamber;
And he himself confess'd but even now
That there he dropp'd it for a special purpose
Which wrought to his desire.

Othello   O fool! fool! fool!

Cassio   There is besides in Roderigo's letter, —
How he upbraids Iago, that he made him
Brave me upon the watch; whereon it came
That I was cast: and even but now he spake,
After long seeming dead, — Iago hurt him,
Iago set him on.

Lodovico   You must forsake this room, and go with us:
Your power and your command is taken off,
And Cassio rules in Cyprus. For this slave, —
If there be any cunning cruelty
That can torment him much and hold him long,
It shall be his. You shall close prisoner rest,
Till that the nature of your fault be known
To the Venetian state. — Come, bring away.

Othello   Soft you; a word or two before you go.
I have done the state some service, and they know't. —
No more of that. — I pray you, in your letters,
When you shall these unlucky deeds relate,
Speak of me as I am; nothing extenuate,
Nor set down aught in malice: then must you speak
Of one that loved not wisely, but too well;
Of one not easily jealous, but, being wrought,
Perplex'd in the extreme; of one whose hand,
Like the base Judean, threw a pearl away
Richer than all his tribe; of one whose subdu'd eyes,
Albeit unused to the melting mood,

你怎么会到手,凯昔欧,我妻子那手帕?

凯　昔　欧　我在我房间里捡到;他自己刚供认,
　　　　　他故意扔在那里,且已经如愿
　　　　　以偿。

奥　赛　罗　　　　啊,蠢才! 蠢才! 蠢才!

凯　昔　欧　洛窦列谷在信里还责骂伊耶戈,
　　　　　怪他叫他在岗哨上向我挑衅;
　　　　　就为了那事我遭到黜职:他刚才,
　　　　　似乎已死了好久之后,还说到
　　　　　伊耶戈煽动他对我袭击,又把他
　　　　　刺伤。

罗铎维哥　你须得离开这房间,和我们同走;
　　　　　你那权位与指挥已经被撤掉,
　　　　　而由凯昔欧在塞浦路斯任统帅。
　　　　　这奴才,假使有什么机巧的酷刑
　　　　　能把他凌迟施虐,定要他去生受。
　　　　　你须得成为个严禁的罪犯,要待
　　　　　罪行的性质报知了威尼斯当道,
　　　　　再对你处置。来吧,将他带起走。

奥　赛　罗　且慢;您去前且容我略谈这一二。
　　　　　我曾为公邦效过些微劳,他们
　　　　　也知道;那不用再提。在您书柬中
　　　　　说起我,当申叙这些不幸的事件时,
　　　　　要请你只照直敷陈;既毋庸缩减,
　　　　　也不必心怀了恼恨漫着笔:然后,
　　　　　您定将诉叙有个人钟情太深重,
　　　　　虽说不聪明;此人轻易不忌妒,
　　　　　但一经着了魔,便惶惑得无所措手足,
　　　　　这人好似那鄙贱的印第安族人,
　　　　　丢掉颗明珠比他那整个部落
　　　　　还珍富:这人的两眼,有伤感动于衷,
　　　　　纵令不惯泣涟洏,也尽会泪涔涔,

Drop tears as fast as the Arabian trees
Their medicinal gum. Set you down this;
And say besides, — that in Aleppo once,
Where a malignant and a turban'd Turk
Beat a Venetian and traduc'd the state,
I took by the throat the circumcised dog
And smote him — thus.

                                         [*Stabs himself.*]

Lodovico   O bloody period!

Gratiano   All that's spoke is marr'd.

Othello   I kiss'd thee ere I kill'd thee: — no way but this,
Killing myself, to die upon a kiss. [*Falling upom* Desde-
    mona.]

Cassio   This did I fear, but thought he had no weapon;
For he was great of heart.

Lodovico   [*To* Iago.] O Spartan dog,
More fell than anguish, hunger, or the sea!
Look on the tragic loading of this bed;
This is thy work: — the object poisons sight;
Let it be hid. — Gratiano, keep the house,
And seize upon the fortunes of the Moor,
For they succeed on you. — To you, lord governor,
Remains the censure of this hellish villain;
The time, the place, the torture, — O, enforce it!
Myself will straight aboard; and to the state
This heavy act with heavy heart relate.

                                          [*Exeunt.*]

如同那阿拉伯香树堕注药胶脂。
请君记下这一笔；此外再说道，
有一次阿兰波地方有一个生性
凶恶、头戴巾帕的土耳其枭民
揍一个威尼斯邦人，且将公邦
来诋毁，我抓着那割掉包皮的狗子，
揪住了脖子给他这一下。　　　　　[以匕首自戮]

罗铎维哥　啊，血染的收场！

格拉休阿诺　所有的话儿都只变成了白说。

奥　赛　罗　杀死你之前，我曾接过你的吻；
如今，再没别的路，杀死我自己，
一吻而死。[倒于玳思狄莫娜身上]

凯　昔　欧　我就怕这样，原以为他已没有了
武器；因为他心胸极光明磊落。

罗铎维哥　[对伊耶戈]啊，忿鸷的斯巴达猛狮！
比惨痛、饥饿或是大海还凶残
狼戾，你看床头这灾祸的负荷；
这是你的勋劳；这形景不堪卒睹；
把它盖起来。格拉休阿诺，你守住
这屋子，领受了摩尔人的财产，因为
它们归你去继承。至于您，总督，
审判这魔鬼似的恶棍，由您去决定
时间、地点、刑讯；啊！贯彻它。
我将立即上船去，以沉重的心情，
将这件悲惨的事变向公政院报明。　　　　　[同下。

图书在版编目（CIP）数据

奥赛罗/[英]莎士比亚著；孙大雨译.
一上海：上海三联书店，2018.
ISBN 978 - 7 - 5426 - 6169 - 2

Ⅰ.①奥…　Ⅱ.①莎… ②孙…　Ⅲ.①英语—
汉语—对照读物 ②悲剧—剧本—英国—
中世纪　Ⅳ.①H319.4：Ⅰ

中国版本图书馆 CIP 数据核字（2017）第 320246 号

奥赛罗（中英文双语对照）

著　　者　[英]威廉·莎士比亚
译　　者　孙大雨

责任编辑　钱震华
装帧设计　陈益平

出版发行　上海三联书店
　　　　　（201199）中国上海市都市路 4855 号
印　　刷　上海昌鑫龙印务有限公司

版　　次　2018 年 4 月第 1 版
印　　次　2018 年 4 月第 1 次印刷
开　　本　890×1240　1/32
字　　数　240 千字
印　　张　8.25
书　　号　ISBN 978 - 7 - 5426 - 6169 - 2/Ⅰ·1356
定　　价　30.00 元